A Carnival of Chimeras

A Carnival of Chimeras

Stephen Woodworth

Hippocampus Press

New York

Published by Hippocampus Press
P.O. Box 641, New York, NY 10156.
http://www.hippocampuspress.com

Cover artwork and design by Daniel V. Sauer, dansauerdesign.com
Hippocampus Press logo designed by Anastasia Damianakos.

First Edition
1 3 5 7 9 8 6 4 2
ISBN 978-1-61498-287-6 paperback
ISBN 978-1-61498-290-6 e-book

This book is dedicated to
S. T. JOSHI,
without whom this collection
and several of the stories within it
would not exist,

and to
KELLY DUNN,
without whom
I would long ago have
ceased to exist.

Contents

Her

She was especially anxious that day. I could feel her eyes blinking and rolling in the back of my head, sticky corneas scraping against the inside fabric of my long-haired wig. Sweat dampened her upper lip as her jaws strained against the duct tape I had used to seal her mouth.

She knew where we were. She knew my thoughts, just as I knew her fear.

"Extraordinary," Dr. Vickers murmured, the circular lenses of his glasses shining and opaque as silver dollars. "May I see the . . . ?" He made a euphemistic gesture with his hand.

I looked away and said nothing. Taking that as a yes, he stood and moved from behind his large mahogany desk to where I sat. Without waiting for me to assist him, he ran his long spindly fingers through the hair at my temples, seeking the bobby pins that fastened the false locks to the thatch of real hair that ran across the top of my head. He peeled off the hairpiece as if it were a surgical dressing, and I shut my eyes in sympathy as the sudden light blinded her.

Dr. Vickers drew a sharp breath. "Extraordinary!"

Leaning close, he touched her cheek with one manicured finger, and I fought to keep her still as the sealed scream ballooned in her mouth. Though my back was to him, I could see him through her eyes—a peering, prodding, white-coated gnome.

He pulled a penlight from his coat pocket and flashed it in both of her eyes. Then I felt his fingernail pick at the tape at one corner of her mouth. I grabbed his wrist.

"Don't."

He shook free of my grasp. "Mr. Harris, if I'm going to help you, you'll have to trust my judgment."

I swallowed. "Can you get rid of it?"

His lips parted, then closed again before he answered, and I should have known right then that he'd be no more help than the others. "Your . . . anomaly is, to my knowledge, utterly unique. However, I think with sufficient study—"

"Now. I want it *gone*." I tensed as I felt her writhe inside our skull. "I have money."

He regarded me with the restrained impatience of a schoolmaster. "Mr. Harris, if we attempt such a radical operation without proper analysis, it would almost certainly kill you."

I carefully replaced my hairpiece and pressed it down. "If that's what it takes."

I rose and strode out of his office.

I didn't see Elle that night. We were supposed to have dinner together at Pizza Hut, but I called and told her I didn't feel good. It wasn't really a lie.

When I got off the phone, I went into the bathroom and turned on the tub's hot water tap full bore. As the tub filled, I stripped naked and regarded myself in the mirror. Not a bad body. An angular chest fringed with hair, muscular arms, a little slack in the gut from too much red meat and chocolate. And the face—normal, maybe even handsome.

The face of an ordinary man.

I glanced at the hand mirror I kept face down beside the sink, the way a suicide keeps a loaded gun in the house. I ripped off the wig and snatched up the hand mirror, angling it so as to glare at her reflection in the wall mirror. It's the only way we can see each other.

There were similarities between us, a sort of family resemblance. The shape of the eyes, the curve of the nose. But this face had a finer bone structure, smoother, smaller-pored skin, a delicacy of expression that could only be a woman's. And everyone who'd seen it recognized it for what it was.

She saw the hate in my stare and averted her eyes. I slapped the hand mirror down on the counter but still felt the drip trickle down her cheek. The steam misting the wall mirror blurred my image to a pink smear.

The water in the tub stung my foot as I stepped in. I lay back, the heat pricking my skin with needles of pain, until everything but my face was submerged. Like bottled messages, little, frantic bubbles streamed past my ears to burst on the surface. I shut my eyes and waited for them to stop.

She wouldn't drown, though. I knew that from experience.

i

I finally took Elle out a week later. It went badly. I was late, the restaurant was slow, the movie was a dog. All evening, my head throbbed as if the scalp had shrunk over my cranium, compressing the brain within.

Afterward, I pulled up in front of the house Elle shared with her roommates, but let the engine idle a moment to cover my embarrassed silence.

"You look as if you hated that flick even more than I did," Elle said as I switched off the ignition. She wore a wry smirk, and her gray-blue eyes flickered with either amusement or irritation.

I rubbed my forehead. "Yeah, sorry about that."

"Lee?" She brushed her knuckles along my forearm. "You okay?"

"Sure."

I'd seen Dr. Vickers again, let him take X-rays and run some tests. Too risky, he concluded. Inoperable. Perhaps with more time . . .

Just like all the others.

"You want to come in for a while?" Elle's voice lilted suggestively. The light from the old mercury-vapor street lamp outside frosted her frizzy blond hair, and her baggy flannel shirt had slipped open to reveal the shadowed swell of her right breast.

I sighed, "I'd like to, but . . ."

She leaned closer until I could smell the crushed-petal scent of her perfume, feel her breath on my cheek. "But?"

"Ah . . . work's got me twisted." I figured she'd heard me bitch enough about life at the warehouse that she'd let it go at that.

"Maybe you need to relax." She planted a kiss on my lips. Her hands clasped my cheeks, then slid up to stroke my hair. My twin's nose twitched beneath Elle's fingers, as if trying to suppress a sneeze.

I flinched, bumping my head against the driver's side window, and brushed her hands away. "Elle, I *told* you—"

She groaned. "Shit, is this the toupee thing again? Get over it! In fact—"

She reached, and I had to clutch the wig to keep her from snatching it away. "Stop!"

Elle sighed and relented. "Okay." She collected her purse and opened the passenger door. "It's been real, and it's been fun—"

"—but it hasn't been real fun," I said in chorus. It was her favorite snide exit line. "I know. Sorry."

She smiled one of her equivocal smiles and gently squeezed my arm. "'Night."

I still felt that tender pressure as I sagged against the steering wheel after she'd gone. It was those tiny gestures of warmth that made me see Elle's face on my bedroom ceiling at night.

And I was losing her, one faux pas at a time.

The following morning, I started searching for another surgeon.

***

I was seven years old when I heard her cry for the first time. Until then, she'd been merely another appendage, a deformity that my parents made me keep hidden, like a wart or a boil.

My friends and I were playing football on the front lawn of my house. Sid hiked the ball to me, and I charged forward. A moment later, hands grasped me from behind, and I was falling.

"Holy shit!" Tommy backpedaled from where he'd tackled me, flinging away the tousled wig in his hand as if it were a dead rat.

"Lee wears a wi-ig! Lee wears a wi-ig!" John-John, Sid's little brother, taunted. He hadn't seen what Tommy had.

Pete, Sid, and the others moved to surround me, leaving the forgotten football on the ground. She looked up at them with blinking, fearful eyes, and I could see their silhouettes eclipse the noontime sun.

"Jesus, what is it?" Pete whispered.

"It's a face, stupid, what does it look like?" Sid answered.

"It's a girl's face!" John-John pointed, bouncing on his heels excitedly. "It's a girl's face!"

On his feet again, Tommy had joined the circle. "He's a goddamn freak! A faggy little girl-boy!"

I pushed myself up, and they all backed off a step. With both pairs of eyes open I could see almost a full 360 degrees, and it made me dizzy. A ring of faces tightened around me, leering and chanting, "Girl-boy! Girl-boy! Faggy little girl-boy!"

I spun left and right, shouting, "Shut up! Shut up!"

Then I heard her bawling sobs.

That really set them off. "Oh, look! She's crying! Don't cry, little girl-boy! Little sissy! Little faggot!"

I felt tears stream down burning cheeks and was furious that I couldn't stop them. I wanted to cry myself, but I converted my shame to anger and shoved Tommy as hard as I could. *STOP IT!*"

He tottered but kept his feet. He clamped his left hand on my forearm until it bruised the skin, then thrust his right fist into my gut. I hunched over, gasping for breath, and he pushed me down. With the others cheering around us, Tommy sat astride my stomach and grabbed hold of my head, grinding my girl-face into the ground. Her shrill wail died, and I tasted the grass and dirt on her tongue. Yet I felt glad, because she was getting what she deserved for humiliating us.

Then, all at once, the jeering stopped. Tommy got off me, and I saw my father looking down on me, his face flushed, his pants and shirt still covered with sawdust from his workshop.

Relieved, I stood and started to brush off my jeans, expecting him to cuss out the other boys for teasing me. Instead, he grabbed the collar of my shirt.

"Come on," he muttered and yanked me toward the front door. He didn't spare a glance at the others, but kept his gaze down as if afraid of them. I couldn't see anything behind me and realized she must have shut her eyes.

Once inside the house, Dad seized my shoulders and leaned forward to shout in my face. "What the hell were you doing out there? Didn't I tell you to be careful?"

"Yeah." I wanted to tell him that I only played football because it was *his* favorite sport, and I really hated the game. Instead, I just stared down at my shoes.

"'Yeah?' Is that all you have to say? Do you have any idea—?" His breath caught in his throat, as if a pressure valve had tightened in his chest. He wiped a hand over his face and calmed himself enough to go on. "We're gonna have to move, I hope you know. Daddy's gonna have to quit his job, we're gonna have to sell the house and move to some state where no one knows us and start all over again."

"Don't you think you're overreacting?" Mom asked, her voice barely audible. She'd withdrawn to a far corner of the den, where she stood hugging herself. "I mean, it was just a bunch of kids—"

He turned on her with the suddenness of a cobra. "And no one's gonna believe them, right? The hell they won't! We'll have goddamn TV crews on our doorstep within a week. All wanting to see the local freak!"

Mom's mouth shrank to a tiny oval. "Jim, don't . . ."

"Christ, seven years! Seven years I managed to keep this under wraps so he could have some kind of normal life, and now—" He sliced the air with his arm. "I don't know, Claire, maybe we should just sell him to the circus. Would you like that, Lee? Dress you in a little tutu and sit you on an elephant—"

"Stop it! Just stop it!" Mom shrieked. "He's still our son!"

Dad gave an arid laugh. "Yeah. My *son*." He glowered at me. "Go to your room."

I went and buried myself between the *Star Wars* sheets on my bed. Dad began shouting at Mom again. I heard her start to cry.

I wrapped my pillow around my head and squeezed. "Shut up, shut up, shut up . . ."

As Dad promised, we moved within a month, living in an apartment until escrow closed on our new house. In our new neighborhood, in my new school, with my new friends, I was very, very careful. I did all the normal things the other boys did, and even took up football again. The game felt much better with a shiny, hard helmet on. The locker room could be a problem, but I had a good collar-length wig and lots of bobby pins. By senior year, I was a starting halfback and a letterman.

Dad died of a coronary the year I started college. I didn't cry at his funeral. I think he would have been proud of me.

Of course, I'd dated girls from the time I was fourteen, got laid by the time I was sixteen. It was expected. I warned them about my hairpiece, told them I got burnt in a fire as a kid and that I was ashamed of my bare, scarred scalp. If, after the first month or two, they said they wanted to see anyway, to know me better, I simply left.

Until Elle.

She lay beside me in the downtown park, the crumpled bag containing the remains of our submarine sandwiches between us. It was late February, and we basked in the first real California-style sunshine of a gray and rainy winter. Elle had cut two of her master's history classes for the occasion.

"Isn't this marvelous?" She stretched languidly and ruffled her hair. The hem of her T-shirt came untucked from her jeans, revealing a strip of her tummy. Her belly button was unique—neither an innie nor an outie, but nearly level with the surface of her skin. I fought the temptation to touch it right then. "Days like this, I wish I could just lie here forever." She pointed her bare toes like a ballet dancer, letting the blades of grass tickle up between them.

"Yeah." I sat with my elbows on my knees, twisting the stem of a dandelion in my fingers, and strained to think of something romantic to say, scanning the vacant blue sky for inspiration.

Suddenly restless, Elle sat up and peered at the grass around her as if looking for a lost contact lens. "I remember coming here as a kid. They used to have ducks in the pond over there." She pointed, then resumed her search. "Mom would let me bring bread scraps for 'em—ah!" She plucked a tiny clover flower and held it to her ear, threading the stem through her pierced lobe. The flower stayed as she pulled her hand away and grinned. "Ta-da!"

I chuckled, and it eased the tightness in my chest. Still, I didn't know what to say, and there was a tension in my limbs, as if my body knew what I was supposed to do and wanted to go on without me.

"Wait! let's see if I can still do this." Elle leapt to her feet and bounded off to the left about ten yards. With a running start, she turned cartwheels in front of me, golden hair tumbling, and I longed to be like her, to skip and dance and do handsprings in the sunlight and not care who was watching or what they thought.

The last thing I remember doing that afternoon was taking off my shoes.

I next became aware of a rhythmic clacking sound and the smell of melting butter. My vision faded in, and I found myself standing in the kitchen of my apartment holding a stainless steel bowl in one hand and a fork in the other. I watched as my hand used the fork to beat the eggs in the bowl. Though I willed it to stop, it continued on autopilot. Behind me, a woman's voice hummed a cheerful tune.

"Elle?" I called, my tongue sluggish.

The woman's voice stopped.

At the same time, my hands went slack, as if they forgot what they were doing, and the fork and bowl clattered to the floor, spattering my jeans with raw egg.

"Crap!" I staggered back from the upset bowl, now bleeding yolk onto the linoleum. I gaped around in confusion, saw the frying pan over a low flame on the stove, the bowls of grated cheese and sliced mushrooms on the counter beside it.

"Elle!" I checked the living room and bedroom. I was alone.

A tremor ran through me. I grabbed the back of my head and felt her bare cheeks, her soft lips.

The duct tape was gone.

She'd been in control for hours, I thought, shaking. Seeing with my eyes, speaking with my voice. I snatched up my phone and dialed Elle's number, trying to steady my breathing as I waited for her to answer.

"Hello?"

"Hi. It's me." I didn't know whether to apologize or what, and I feared she'd hang up the moment she heard me.

"Hey." Her voice was warm and inviting, and I could sense the smile that accompanied it.

"Look, about this afternoon . . ."

She giggled. "As I recall, the hide-and-seek was your idea. I hope I wasn't *too* hard to find."

I rubbed my forehead, straining to remember. "Did—did you have a good time?"

"No." She paused. "I had a great time. I just wish I didn't have this midterm tomorrow so I could've stayed for dinner. You left me hungry," she added with a sensual purr.

"Thanks." I forced a laugh, gnawing at my lower lip.

"Lee? Is something wrong?"

"No. No, I just wanted to tell you what a great time I had. We should do it again soon." My mouth twisted. "Love you."

There was a long pause at the other end, and I thought, *Oh, shit. That did it.*

"I love you, too."

My heart clenched. "Call me tomorrow," my mouth said. "Let me know how the test went."

"Okay."

She said goodbye, and I hung up, a queasiness in my stomach.

That feeling remained with me during the following week, the feeling you have in dreams where you find yourself naked out in public. I became acutely self-conscious of all my actions and mannerisms—how I walked, how I sat, how I spoke. Whenever I found myself drifting off into daydreams, I flinched and glanced at my watch to see how much time I'd lost. At night, I slept with my jaws clenched shut, the tension giving my mind some concrete sensation to grasp as my consciousness slipped away. I often woke with a headache, which also helped to anchor me in my skull.

For once, I appreciated the donkey-work of the warehouse. Fetching case after case of ceramic tile for the orders we had to fill, listening to the rest of the crew describe in pornographic detail the women they'd slept with over the weekend, I settled into a comfortable groove of mindless motion.

"So what about you, man?" Scott asked out of the blue. A spindly beanpole of a guy whose arms jutted out of his Lakers jersey like bent soda straws, he'd just finished telling us about his fifth conquest in as many weeks. "Getting anywhere with La Belle Elle?"

I stood on the penultimate rung of a twenty-foot ladder, scanning the shelves for a stock number, so it took me a second to realize he was talking to me. "Huh? Oh, yeah, Elle's fantastic." I slid a thirty-pound box off a shelf, bracing my shins against the ladder's top step as I swayed with the weight. "We had a wild time in the park last Thursday," I said, descending with the box. It might have been true, for all I could remember about that day.

"All right! The kid has hisself some nookie!" Tony, a burly weightlifter with a spiky black crew cut, clapped and whistled.

Grinning, Scott took the box from me as I got off the ladder and set it on the pallet we'd stacked with the latest order. "About time, too. We were beginning to wonder about you, boy."

I glared at him. "What do you mean?"

"Hey, we've all seen you looking at Tony's ass, okay?" He winked at Tony. They both laughed.

"So what are you saying?" I snapped.

Scott saw the expression my face, and his grin disappeared. "Nothing, dude."

"No, come on. Tell me."

He shrugged and smiled nervously. "Take it easy, man, it was only a joke . . ."

"But there must be something about me to make fun of, right?" My voice quavered on the point of cracking. "Tell me what's so goddamn funny."

Scott backed off a step and held up his hands. "Nothing. Only a joke."

I looked over to see Tony and Carlos glance away, hastily shifting their attention to the boxes at their feet.

"Shit," I muttered, and climbed the ladder again. I worked in silence for the rest of the afternoon, sifting my memory to find any lapses I'd had at work during the past week. If she'd taken control . . . if Scott and the others had seen me when she was in control . . . My face burned as I imagined their contemptuous stares and suppressed laughter.

I brooded in silence at the dinner table that night. Elle had come over to my apartment to cook for me in her latest attempt to convert me to vegetarianism—lentil soup and French bread. Though it tasted fine, I stirred the lumpy, brownish soup without an appetite, staring at the swirls I made.

Elle cast a withering look at me from across the table. "That good, eh!"

"Hmm? No, no, it's great." Guilty, I shoveled a spoonful into my mouth and nodded my appreciation.

"Thanks." She stared into her own bowl for a while. "Is it my breath," she asked at last, "or my scintillating conversation?"

"What?"

"You! You're in a funk."

"I am not! I'm just . . . thinking." I took a big bite of bread to chew on as an excuse not to talk.

"About . . . ?" With a sarcastic smile, Elle gestured for me to elaborate. "Let's verbalize here."

Gooseflesh rose on my arms as *her* jaws strained at their duct-tape seal. I shook my head, both to dismiss Elle's question and to reassert my control. "Bad day at work."

Elle's expression softened. "The boss?"

"Nah, it's the other guys. They're all assholes." I rubbed my forehead.

"Have you thought about getting a better job? You have a degree . . ."

"Yeah, and the private sector's clamoring for art history majors."

"That's not the point. It shows what you can do."

"Elle, I'd really rather drop this."

"Okay, okay." She eyed me thoughtfully as she took a couple more mouthfuls of soup, then waggled her empty spoon at me. "You know what *you* need—"

She dropped the spoon in her bowl and rose from her chair. "Stand up."

"What? I—"

She crossed to my chair. "Come on. Elle says, 'Stand up.'"

With a sigh, I abandoned my own soup and did as she commanded.

"Now, Elle says, 'Stand over there.'" She pointed to the center of the living room floor.

I went to the indicated spot and shrugged.

"Elle says, 'Take off your shirt.'"

I groaned. "Elle, I'm not in the mood—"

She gave me a stern glare, arms akimbo, tapping her foot. Laughing in spite of myself, I stripped off my shirt and tossed it aside. "Now what, Mistress?"

She giggled. "On your belly, slave."

I lay face down on the carpet as she crouched beside me. "Is this going to hurt?"

"Just a little." She straddled my butt and began to knead the muscles of my back with her fingers. "Man, you're tight. No wonder you're on edge."

I winced as she rubbed the taut cords of my shoulders. Her hands pulled the tension from my body, and I let out a soft moan. For the first time that evening, I forgot about the warehouse, about Scott and Tony, about *her*, and lost myself in the present, in Elle's firm but tender touch.

"That's it," she murmured. "Let it all go."

My chin resting on my hands, I drifted into a light doze. I only awoke when the gentle rocking motion of the massage abruptly stopped.

"How did you do that?" Elle asked.

Groggy, I scowled and half-opened my eye. "Do what?"

"Your scalp . . . *moved*."

Before my sluggish brain understood what she meant, Elle had worked her fingers up underneath the padding of my wig.

"*No!*" I yelped as the bobby pins were yanked from my real hair. I tried to wriggle out from under Elle, but I knew it was too late.

Though she was still behind me, I could now see her awestruck face, see the loose wig in her hand. Elle's mouth hung open, but the high-pitched, feminine whimper I heard came from the mouth on the back of my head.

Elle stood and recoiled. "What *are* you?"

I flipped over and jumped to my feet. Elle shrank from me as I moved toward her. "Wait! Please—"

"My God . . . what *is* it?" Dropping the wig, Elle staggered backward into the dining room and sank onto a chair.

"It—it's just a birth defect. Like an extra finger or something." I knelt in front of her and took her hands in mine. "I'm sorry. I couldn't tell you. I was so afraid—"

"Turn around." Elle's voice was hoarse, her face stony and pale.

I squeezed her hands before releasing them, then did as she said. Quivering, I shut my own eyes and met Elle's tremulous gaze with those other eyes.

Elle reached to touch my twin's cheek, but her finger hovered just above the skin as if repelled by magnetic force. "Does she talk?"

"No." A shiver rippled up my spine. "Just some noises. Sometimes she laughs. Cries."

Elle stared into my twin's eyes, a look of strange, fearful recognition on her face. *"No."*

She pushed herself to her feet and fumbled for her purse, which sat on an adjacent chair. "I'm—I've got to go."

I sprang up and caught hold of her arm as she headed toward the front door. "No, don't leave! I promise, you'll never have to see it again."

She tensed, and refused to look at me. "I can't—I'm sorry . . ."

I let go of her, and she hurried out the door.

I stood there for almost a minute, my fists like matching hammers pressed to my temples. Then I reached back and ripped the duct tape off her mouth.

This time I wanted to hear her.

I leaned up against the wall and bowed my head. With a sharp cry, I jerked my head upright to crack it against the concrete. When she shrieked, I did it again. And again, until the flesh at the back of my skull stung with bruised tissue. The two of us screamed in harmony.

About twenty minutes later, a heavy-set cop with squarish, wire-framed glasses rang my doorbell. I answered the door in a bathrobe, skin still clammy from the shower, my wig disheveled but in place.

The cop shifted his gaze from my face to peer past me into the living room. "Sorry to bother you, Mister . . ."

"Harris."

"Mister Harris. We received a call about a possible domestic violence incident in this apartment complex, and wanted to know if you'd seen or heard anything."

I shrugged and shook my head. "Sorry. Can't help you."

"Mind if I come in for a sec?"

"Sure." I stepped aside to let him enter.

"Someone apparently heard a woman cry out. Said it sounded like it came from in here." The cop made a cursory inspection of the living room, then meandered toward the open bedroom door.

"Not here. I live alone."

"Have any guests this evening?" He surveyed the dual place-settings of dirty dishes on the dining room table.

"My girlfriend. She left some time ago, though."

"Uh-huh." He casually poked his head into the bedroom and bathroom as if admiring the decor. "Well, it seems pretty quiet now." He moved back toward the front door. "Like I said, sorry to bother you, but we have to check these things out."

"No problem." Beneath the wig, a trickle of blood ran from her broken nose, over her swollen lips and scraped chin to drip down my back. "You can't be too careful."

I called in sick at work the following morning and spent most of the day in bed with the curtains drawn. The telephone didn't ring. About four o'clock, I got up, went to the bathroom in my boxer shorts, and picked up the hand mirror on the counter.

Her face hung slack, as if anaesthetized, her eyes shut, her lips slightly parted. Though I hadn't replaced the duct tape, she hadn't made a sound since last night. Her nose had stopped bleeding but was puffy and crooked. Her cheeks were blotched with purple. I touched one of the tender spots, but she didn't react. I lifted one eyelid, and the iris beneath seemed clouded, vacant.

An unexpected tremor of fear trilled through me—the same sort of panic you feel when you fall asleep on your arm and awake in the middle of the night to find that your hand has become a lump of lifeless meat.

I stayed home the next two days as well, drowning my brain in daytime television. I risked getting fired, but I didn't care. Every evening at eight I called Elle's number. Her voicemail always responded, and each time I remained silent, leaving an eloquent span of silence after the beep.

I didn't expect to see her again. I certainly didn't expect her to pound on my door after eleven o'clock on Saturday night.

As I inched the door open, she looked at me over the taut door chain with the guilty expression of a child who has either done something bad or is about to. "Can I come in?"

I rubbed the beard stubble on my cheeks as if to wipe it off and patted down the cowlicks in my wig. "Uh . . . sure."

I undid the chain and let her in, shifting my feet as she saw the litter of beer cans and potato chip bags surrounding the easy chair in front of my living room TV. "I'm sorry. I wasn't expecting—"

"I know. I should've called, but . . . I wasn't sure." She hugged herself. "I missed you."

"I missed you, too." We fell into an exhausted embrace.

Her lips brushed my ear as I nuzzled her neck. "I want to see her again," she whispered.

It was my turn to recoil in revulsion. "What? Why on earth—"

Elle's hands fluttered, trying to speak for her. "I—I can't explain. There's something I have to see." She drew close again, her eyes imploring. "Something I have to know."

I wilted against her, gripping her to my chest, figuring that I would lose her no matter what I did.

We went into the bedroom and knelt on my futon. Jaw set, I sat with marble stoicism and let her take off the wig once more. I felt a perverse relief when I heard Elle gasp, for the anxiety and uncertainty would finally be gone. They would leave with Elle.

She lightly prodded one of the bruised cheeks, and I winced. "My God, what did you do?"

"We had a little fight."

"Is she . . . ?"

"I don't know."

Elle traced a fingertip over the peach-tender skin, her breath coming in ragged sighs. "She *can't* be."

A fatalistic sorrow drained the tension from my limbs, and my vision clouded. I blinked to clear the mistiness from my sight, and when I looked again, everything had snapped into sharp focus and I found Elle's face hovering directly in front of me. I saw again all those qualities in her I had loved and coveted—her inner strength and outward tenderness, her sensuality and sensitivity—and it made me want to weep. The breeze-soft touch of her fingers served as a balm to the dull soreness of my wounds.

Elle peered into my eyes, and again recognition dawned on her face. "It was you," she breathed. "In the park—you had that same look . . ."

My mouth opened, but I couldn't find my voice. Perhaps I was afraid to hear it.

Then Elle pressed her lips to mine, and I no longer needed to speak.

Our mouths and tongues moved in perfect counterpoise, now giving, now receiving, gently enough so that the sting of my grazed skin became only a tingle. I kissed her neck, and Elle unbuttoned her blouse.

I bent to lick at the breasts she offered to me, but my backward body lost its balance and almost tipped over, my misdirected arms flailing out behind me, groping for something to hold on to. Elle steadied me, laughing. I giggled in return.

Peeling off her clothes, Elle nudged me into a prone position, my body belly down on the mattress, my frontward face smothered in a pillow, inert and immobile as a discarded mask. Elle crawled over me, letting me make love to each part of her in turn. Sitting up, she arched her thighs over my face and dipped her pubic mound onto my waiting mouth, shuddering as I explored inside her with my tongue.

We lay beside each other for a long time after it was over, communicating only with our eyes. Though I wanted to watch her placid sleeping form all night, I eventually drifted off.

I awoke later as if jarred by a sudden sound. The room was still dark. Instinctively, my hand went to my jaw, where I felt my bristly, unshaven skin. I peered out once more from behind my male face and frowned, wondering if I'd only dreamt the last few hours.

"Love me," a soft voice croaked.

I turned toward Elle. "What?"

But I could tell by the measured rise and fall of Elle's chest that she was asleep.

"Love me," the voice pleaded again. A laryngitic rasp, weak with disuse. "Please."

I trembled. She'd never spoken to me before. Or perhaps I just hadn't listened until now.

I stroked her cheek, my fingers running across the damp track of a tear. "Yes," I repeated, "love me."

We didn't speak again that night, for we knew our thoughts were the same.

The Hidden Track

The voice surfaced in Rick's headphones as if rising from oceanic depths, the words liquid and distorted.

"Coooooooome . . . sssssspeeeeeeeeeaaaak . . ."

The slow speed stretched the sound, lowering the pitch until it resembled the basso gurgling of whalesong. Rick turned a knob on his studio control panel, and the coffee can–sized wax cylinder rolled faster on its spindle. The invisible needle of a helium-neon laser shone a tiny green point on the cylinder's surface as it traced the recorded groove in the century-old wax, registering every change in frequency. The laser's light was weak enough that it would not melt the wax, nor would it damage the delicate cylinder the way a crystal stylus would.

"Come, sssssspirits—sssssspeak." The voice became recognizably human. A man, his tone somnolent, as if muttering in his sleep. "Ssssssssshow yoursssselvessssssss."

Rick fine-tuned the RPMs to eliminate the residual slur. Scratches on the cylinder fuzzed the recording with pops and static, giving the impression that the man spoke through some thick barrier of gauze. Below his words wavered another sound—a low, sonorous hum, as of a large bell that had stopped ringing yet continued to vibrate.

The words came in, clearer now. "We beseech you. Communicate with us. Prove you exist—"

"Honestly, Tompkins," a gruffer male voice broke in. "This is absurd."

"Cyril, hush!" a woman chided the second man.

The first man continued to chant, evidently oblivious to the others. "Come, spirits. Grant us knowledge of your world."

Rick tapped his unlit cigarette on the soundboard and stuck it in the corner of his mouth. As a rule, he never smoked in his recording studio, which was as flammable as a candle factory with all the wax cylinders he stored there; but it had been over an hour since his last drag and he was beginning to have a nic-fit. Like all gramophone recordings, this one was in mono, and Rick had channeled the audio into the headphones' left speaker, which was slowly giving him a headache.

As the medium continued to murmur in his ear, Rick grabbed the wooden box that had contained the cylinder and examined the label with idle curiosity. A small metal frame on the front of the case enclosed a yellowing paper card on which "Tompkins—S. 5" had been written in a cramped cursive script.

The "S." must stand for "Séance," Rick decided. The revelation aroused in him neither more nor less interest than the two dozen other cylinders to which he'd listened in the past week. He'd purchased the lot at auction, and the same collection had included a Caruso performance from *Nabucco*, a racist Jim Crow song from the turn-of-the-century South, and a spoken blessing from Pope Leo XIII. Since he did not believe in ghosts, God, or much of anything else, the recorded séance meant nothing more to him than a historical novelty—something he could transfer to digital media and possibly sell on eBay.

A sudden, sharp, high-pitched whine shot into Rick's left ear, so startling and painful that he yanked off his headphones. At first he thought it might be a surge of feedback in his system, but he checked his VU meters and they seemed to be at normal levels. Furthermore, when he put the left speaker to his ear again, he heard the people on the Victorian-era recording apparently reacting to the same noise.

"What the devil was that?" the man named Cyril grumbled.

"It's them!" the woman breathed. "They've come."

Tompkins spoke louder, either from excitement or to drown out the others. "Spirits, show yourselves. Make your presence known."

The metallic hum grew louder as well, accompanied by a rattling and banging, as of furniture shivering in an earthquake. But all this racket was soon submerged by a new sound, one that the limited fidelity of the phonograph had struggled to capture. Deep, discordant bass tones, like the pedal notes of a monstrous pipe organ, punctuated by shrill screeches. Rick wondered if the cylinder's rotational speed had slowed again. It soon became obvious, however, that this was not the whalesong of aural distortion; this was more like some saurian from Loch Ness.

"Good Lord," exclaimed an awestruck voice on the recording—a third man, who had not spoken before.

By now Tompkins was shouting. "Spirits, prove yourselves to us! Take this shell and transform it as only you can! Give us evidence of your power that we may show the world!"

Without any sort of amplifier, the primitive phonograph that had preserved the séance would have possessed limited ability to capture changes in volume, yet Rick swore that the din of the "spirits" grew louder and more intense. The fillings in his teeth resonated with the vibration, a sensation as odd and unnerving as if he'd chewed aluminum foil. In revulsion, he dropped the headset.

Only then did he realize that the sound that had been mono was now in stereo. It bored into both his ears, and he was not wearing his headphones.

Pressing his hands over his ears, Rick checked the soundboard again to see if somehow the audio had been diverted to the large quadraphonic speakers in each corner of the studio. The reverb now seemed to emanate from the walls themselves . . . or from the air around him. It vibrated in his gut like the blast of a foghorn, and the coffeemaker across the room rattled in sympathy.

Rick stood and glanced around, bracing himself against his chair. He wondered if it might be an earthquake after all.

A colored spot appeared in front of him, hovering in the vacant space near the lighting fixture on the ceiling. He briefly mistook it for an insect—a moth, perhaps—but it soon inflated to the size of a baseball . . . a basketball . . . a medicine ball. It unfolded petals of tissue, red and glistening, and veined with pulsing tubes of purple and black, as if it were some carnivorous flower. These appendages curled back in perfect symmetry from the vortex at the thing's center to form an ever-mutating, undulating sphere of flesh—a kaleidoscope of raw meat instead of tinted glass. An acrid electrical scent akin to that of smoldering circuitry choked the studio, and the room throbbed with the cacophony of treble shrieks and bass slurs.

Although he ought to have run from the room in a panic, Rick was too dumbfounded by the sight to be scared. He merely stared at the thing, fascinated by it but unable to believe in it. It couldn't exist; therefore, he must be imagining it, and so there was nothing to fear. Perhaps he had dozed off while listening to the cylinder and was dreaming the whole spectacle, even to the point of dreaming of himself realizing that it was a dream.

This theory gained credibility a moment later, when the apparition abruptly ceased. The bizarre noise fell silent. The thing above Rick's head inhaled its ribbons of tissue, collapsed in on itself, and vanished into the point from which it had come. The room stopped shuddering. The only sound that remained was the whisper of the wax cylinder as it turned on its spindle.

But Rick could not dismiss the entire experience as a fantasy. The coffeemaker no longer shuddered, but the coffee in its glass pot still sloshed from the disturbance. And that smell—the reek of ozone and silicon—still pervaded the air.

He snatched up the headphones and put the left speaker to his ear. Nothing but a crackling silence. The séance—or at least the recording of it—had ended.

He shut off the spindle and laser, and the wax cylinder slowed to a halt. Rick considered replaying the track to hear the minute of audio he'd missed during his hallucination. It would have been easy—he'd digitized the whole recording with his Mac—but the memory of the vision it had inspired made him hesitate.

Maybe there had been a small tremor, he thought. That would account for the coffeemaker. And the smell could indicate a short in his equipment—he'd have to check that later. As for the rest of it ... that thing near the ceiling ... it was probably a flashback from the acid he'd dropped in his twenties, back when he was a musician rather than a recording engineer, back when he still believed in stupid stuff.

Nevertheless, he burned an audio file of the séance onto a CD with the volume turned all the way down. There would be plenty of time to listen to it tomorrow, in the light of day and reason, he told himself.

Afterward, he stepped out of the studio and onto his front porch and chained half a pack of smokes. As it held the cigarettes, his right hand still quivered as if resonating harmonically with the spirits' call.

***

Rick did not listen to the recording the following day. Instead, he did a Web search to see what he could find out about a man named Tompkins who conducted séances back in the late nineteenth century. Not because it mattered to him, of course. The information would help him find a buyer that would pay him top dollar for the wax cylinder—that was all.

After narrowing his criteria and sifting through a couple hundred irrelevant results and cursory references, he came up with a one-paragraph Wikipedia entry devoted to a "Professor Montague Tompkins," a physics lecturer at Amherst College who lost both his credibility with the scientific establishment and his chance at tenure by becoming obsessed with the Victorian era's Spiritualist movement. "Tompkins fostered numerous theories about the response of spirits to 'sympathetic vibrations' and wished to prove them scientifically," the entry read, and Rick could almost hear the sneer of disdain in the writer's phrasing. "To this end, he staged a series of séances as 'experiments' at his Massachusetts home. His research ended abruptly, however, with his disappearance following a disastrous session in which two people died, most likely by Tompkins's own hand. Although his actual fate has never been determined, authorities of the time believed that Tompkins either killed himself or fled the country in disgrace."

The "References" cited below the entry consisted of a few newspaper and magazine articles from the period, which were probably only available on microfiche in university archives, and one book—*In Tune with the Otherworld: The Life and Theories of Professor Montague Tompkins*. The biography had come out in 1982 and had long since gone out of print. None of the online book dealers even offered a used copy for sale.

Figuring the quest was more trouble than it was worth, Rick was about to forget the whole thing when he noted that Dr. Oswald Holcomb, the biography's author, happened to teach science at Bancroft Community College, about an hour's drive from Rick's house. He could justify sacrificing an afternoon of his time if it upped the asking price for the séance recording. Perhaps Holcomb himself would take it off Rick's hands.

He called the college to find out the professor's schedule, but chose not to call Holcomb ahead of time—he didn't want the scientist to dismiss him as either a fraud or a crackpot before they even met. Instead, he took his CD copy of the séance recording to Bancroft College, where he waited outside Holcomb's final class on a Friday afternoon.

Bancroft was a glorified high school campus, its hallways tiled with chipped gray linoleum that dated to the fifties. At precisely ten to three, students spilled out the door of room 101, most of them taking immediate advantage of the corridor's freedom to check their cell phones. Rick watched them file out and disperse as a voice from inside the room continued to shout for their attention.

"Don't forget: quiz on chapters five through seven on Monday! And you all have research reports due in two weeks."

No one paid attention. As the room emptied, Rick saw a man

inside shake his head. He wore an oxford shirt with the sleeves rolled up to his elbows and stood before a long white dry-erase board covered with notes on Kepler's laws of planetary motion. Bald on top with a mullet of scraggly gray-blond hair, he was a gangly baby boomer who had just started to thicken around the middle but remained thin enough to give the sharp bone structure of his face a stark, severe expression.

Rick leaned into the open doorway to get his attention. "Dr. Holcomb?"

The professor scooped a stack of assignments to be graded from the table in front of him and shoved them into a briefcase. "Yeah?"

"You wrote the book about Professor Tompkins?"

Holcomb made a face and snapped the briefcase shut. "Amazing. Someone's actually heard of it." He pushed past Rick into the hallway.

Rick kept pace as the professor stalked toward his office. "I wondered if you were still researching Tompkins. I think I have something—"

Without slowing his stride, Holcomb raised a hand to cut him off. "Listen, Mr.—"

"Ebbers."

"Mr. Ebbers, that book is why I'm teaching godforsaken survey courses here instead of astrophysics at Caltech. I found out the hard way that the old saw is wrong: sometimes it's publish *and* perish."

"Then you wouldn't be interested in any previously unknown material about Tompkins?"

"Not on this plane of existence."

"Not even an original recording of one of his séances?"

Holcomb stopped so quickly that Rick almost ran into him. "Is it genuine?"

Rick took the CD from the pocket of his windbreaker and held it up. "You tell me."

The professor studied Rick's face, then scanned the surrounding hallway, as though he suspected this proposal was part of a sting operation meant to entrap him. "Come on," he said at last.

Holcomb hustled Rick to his office. When the door was shut and locked, the professor crossed the room to a cheap stereo system set among shelves of academic texts in his bookcase. "Let's hear what you got."

He ejected an R.E.M. disc from the machine and left the CD tray empty. Rick took the cue and placed the séance recording in the machine, but remained close to the stereo's controls as Montague Tompkins again summoned the spirits.

Dr. Holcomb crossed his arms and paced back and forth before the speakers, frowning with deliberate skepticism. His show of doubt did not last long. An eagerness akin to hunger lit his face when he heard the droning murmur underpinning Tompkins's trance-like chant. "My God . . . it really *is* him."

"What is that?" Rick asked, referring to the sound.

"Tibetan singing bowl. Like this, see?" Holcomb hurried over to his desk, where he shoved aside the chaos of scattered papers to make room for a small copper-colored bowl that he moved off a nearby filing cabinet. A thick wooden stick rested inside the bowl, leaning against the rim like a pestle inside an apothecary's mortar. Holcomb picked up the stick and dragged its tip around the rim of the bowl, causing it to hum like the sound in the recording but at a higher pitch. Holcomb beamed. "Tompkins thought the overbeings responded to waves of certain frequencies," he explained.

Overbeings? Rick thought. As if in answer, he heard the shrill squeak that had heralded the start of his hallucination on Tuesday night. The image of the pulsing ball of flesh flickered in his mind, and he shot his hand out to shut off the stereo. "That's as much as you get for free," he said and retrieved his CD from the player.

Holcomb wasn't smiling anymore. "How much you want for it?"

Sensing his advantage, Rick shrugged. "What's it worth to you?"

The professor dropped the wooden rod back into the singing bowl, the glimmer of delight gone from his eyes. "You must have mistaken me for a man of means, Mr.—"

"Ebbers."

"Mr. Ebbers. I teach dumbbell physics to two-year business majors, for Christ's sake. I could scrape up a thousand, maybe." He waited for a reaction from Rick. "Maybe two."

The recording engineer feigned disappointment, although he was secretly ecstatic. He bet that Holcomb was good for even more, however.

"I don't know." Rick shoved the CD back into his jacket pocket. "I'll have to see if any other bids materialize. But here . . . in case you want to raise your offer." He took a business card from his wallet and handed it to the professor. "It has my name on it, in case you forget again."

He turned his back on Holcomb and headed for the door.

"Mr. Ebbers!" Desperation edged the plea.

Rick glanced back.

"I can't pay you much up front," Holcomb said, "but what's on that recording could make us both rich."

Rick let go of the doorknob. "How?"

The professor cocked his head, the hint of a grin returning to his expression. "Just how much do you know about Tompkins's work, anyway?"

Rick silently cursed himself. Now *he* was the one who'd been too eager, who'd tipped his hand in the negotiations. He'd betrayed the fact that he lacked Holcomb's knowledge of the séance's real worth. But the recording was still his, and he expected to get full value for it.

"He was a Spiritualist, wasn't he? Talking to the dead and all that?" Rick tried to sound informed, but he felt like a student who hadn't prepared for class.

Holcomb laughed. "Let me show you something, Rick. Mind if I call you 'Rick'?"

"Not at all, *Oswald*."

"Please . . . it's Ozzie. 'Oswald' was my mother's idea—and before Kennedy was shot, by the way." The professor selected a key from a ring he kept fastened to a belt loop on his jeans and unlocked the largest drawer in his desk. From this, he took an antique stereoscope and a bundle of cardboard photographic plates, one of which he inserted into the wire bracket on the device. Holcomb beckoned. "You gotta see this to believe it."

He forced Rick to come to him—more evidence that he now held the upper hand. To disguise his curiosity, Rick sighed and crossed the room with a brusque stride, as if this whole exercise were wasting his time. He took hold of the stereoscope by its wooden handle and sighted through the goggle-like viewer.

As he slid the bracket back along its rod to adjust the focal length, the twin photographs on the plate meshed into a single three-dimensional image, and the intestines of the man in the picture bulged toward Rick's eyes like a knot of writhing nightcrawlers.

Still staring at the sepia-toned atrocity, Rick lowered himself into the chair in front of Holcomb's desk. "What the hell?"

"Told you," Holcomb said. Rick didn't even need to look up to see the smug grin on the man's face—he could hear it in his voice.

"I see it and I still don't believe it. Who is this guy?"

"Edmund Porter. One of the sitters at Tompkins's final séance."

Obese and bearded, the man in the photo wore a Victorian coat and bow tie and sagged in an overstuffed armchair. His vest and white shirt had been unbuttoned and pulled apart to expose his abdomen, where it appeared that his navel had burst and allowed the avalanche of slick viscera to spill out over his lap, including the sac of his stomach and slab of his liver. Worse than this—his eyes were open, their gaze a gaping stupor.

"What killed him?" Rick wanted to know.

"He isn't dead. At least, not in that picture."

Rick lowered the stereoscope. "You've *got* to be kidding."

As he expected, Holcomb had that infuriating grin on his face.

"Nope. Actually, a surgeon was able to slit open his abdomen, insert the viscera, and sew up the incision. Porter lived another fourteen years, but in a state of perpetual catatonia, so he was never able to describe what happened to him. He died in a madhouse."

"So how did he get like that?"

"If you believe the attending physicians at the time, he was an undiagnosed case of omphalocele."

Rick sighed and cupped a hand to his ear. "Come again? In English this time."

Holcomb's smirk widened, and he reminded Rick of his ninth-grade chem teacher Mr. Franks, who gloated every time he stumped the class with a question. "Omphalocele is a congenital defect in which a child is born with its abdominal organs outside the body cavity. How Porter survived to adulthood in such a state the doctors couldn't say, but it was their only explanation for his condition."

Rick peered at the picture again. "But you don't buy it."

"Neither did Porter's wife. She swore that, before the night of the séance, her husband had his guts on the inside like the rest of us."

"Maybe she was lying. Stranger things have happened."

"Yes. Like this." Holcomb swapped the picture of Porter for another cardboard plate.

As before, the picture deepened into space as Rick viewed it through the scope. Two people, a man and a woman, sat in high-backed chairs at a circular table. The dark-suited man had slumped onto the tabletop, his head angled to reveal a slack face with eyes that stared at nothing. Dressed in a high-necked white gown, the woman had thrown her head back, her features blurred as she twisted in the chair faster than the camera's shutter could click. The blurring did not obscure the fact that the woman's eye sockets were vacant black hollows.

"Cyril and Augusta Delacorte," Holcomb said. "Not a mark on either of them. Not a drop of blood shed. The doctors assumed Cyril must have died from a stroke until they cut him open and discovered his skull cavity empty and his brain inside his stomach.

"Augusta lived for almost an hour after the séance. At the autopsy, they finally found her eyes—inside the chambers of her heart."

"And what theory did the doctors have about *that?*"

"They didn't. But Professor Tompkins did."

Rick laughed, but his throat was dry and it came out as a cough. "Ghosts?"

Holcomb chuckled and pulled a pen from a mug on the desk. He sketched something on the back of one of his students' assignments, took a dime from his pocket, and placed it on the doodle. Then he pushed it toward Nick.

The drawing was the outline of a man. The coin lay where his heart would be.

"Go on," Holcomb urged. "Pick it up."

Rick rolled his eyes and grabbed the dime with his right hand, holding it between his thumb and forefinger. "So?"

Holcomb smiled. "Easy, wasn't it? As a three-dimensional being, you have no problem taking an object out of a two-dimensional enclosure."

Rick thought he knew what the professor was suggesting, but it seemed so absurd that he figured he must be wrong. "'Overbeings'?" he asked, remembering the strange term Holcomb had used a few minutes ago.

"*Exactly.* Entities from a higher spatial dimension. Tompkins was part of the Spiritualist movement, but he suspected that the 'spirits' weren't the souls of the dead at all but rather fourth-dimensional beings. Hence their ability to move matter through seemingly solid objects."

Holcomb's manic enthusiasm disturbed Rick almost more than the pictures. The fact that the prof took this stuff seriously meant he was as much of a crackpot as Tompkins himself.

Rick recalled what he'd read about Tompkins online as he passed the stereoscope back to Holcomb. "Some folks say Tompkins himself killed those people, then ran off to South America or someplace."

Holcomb glowered. "Some people are *idiots*. You've seen the photos. You think a person could have done that? And Tompkins didn't go on the lam—he vanished into thin air. His assistant had locked the room in which the final séance was held from the outside, and he didn't see anyone enter or leave."

Rick tapped the stack of photographic plates. "You actually believe all this?"

"Do you?"

"I'm an agnostic. I don't believe anything."

"Neither do I. Not without proof. That's what your recording can give me." Holcomb leaned over the desk, spreading his hands. "Think of it: actual contact with beings from a higher plane of existence. Oh, we'll make more than money, my friend—we'll make *history*."

Rick's gaze flicked to the double image of Edmund Porter with his entrails falling into his lap. "What would one of these . . . *overbeings* look like?"

The question seemed to surprise the professor. "Well . . . there's no way to know, really. One thing you can be sure of, though—you wouldn't be able to see *all* of it. You'd only be able to perceive a three-dimensional cross-section of its form as it passed through our space, in much the same way that a CAT scan shows only a series of two-dimensional slices of your body as it moves over you." Holcomb narrowed his eyes. "Why? Did you see something?"

Rick pictured the mutating sphere of meat, attempting to mash together the sequence of viscous forms into a cohesive whole. He failed.

"No." He stood and stalked toward the door. "You have my card. Call me if you want to raise your offer."

"Ebbers! *What did you see?*"

Rick left Holcomb's office without looking back.

***

Around three A.M. the following morning, he had a nightmare. At least, he comforted himself with the notion that it was a nightmare, just as he had convinced himself that his vision while listening to the wax cylinder was a hallucination.

The dream began with him waking on his futon in the darkness. He had no memory of opening his eyes, however—he simply became conscious that he was lying on his back, staring at the ceiling. An ultrasonic hiss—a sound he sensed rather than heard, like the inaudible keen of a dog-whistle—excited the air, which was redolent with the odor of sparking electricity.

Rick tensed, board-stiff. Directly above him, the ball of alien tissue coruscated in glistening patterns of sinew and fluid. It shimmered with the purplish bioluminescence of deep-sea creatures, the glow transforming the ceiling's stucco into a calcified landscape of coral and barnacle.

Then a low, guttering groan shivered the room, and the sphere seemed to spread and smear as it dived directly at Rick's head. He pressed back into his pillow and gasped. Inches from his face, the thing disappeared, as if sucked down some cosmic drainpipe, and the room went dark.

Rick sprang upright in bed, abdomen heaving as his diaphragm bellowed breath. He looked around, but found himself alone in the room. The fact that the thing was gone—or had never been there—should have reassured him, yet a nauseating uneasiness, a tension without resolution, remained in the pit of his stomach.

The sensation grew rather than subsided, until he felt as if a giant fist were trying to yank his intestines out through his navel. The stereoscopic image of Edmund Porter flashed in his mind, the 3-D innards exploding from the cardboard photo, and Rick grabbed his midsection. There was another burst of atonal noise—another puff of ozone—and Rick watched a glob of living plasma balloon from his solar plexus, pass *through* his hand, and slither into an unseen wormhole a foot in front of him. It left no trace of itself other than a purplish afterimage in Rick's eyes as he stared into the black vacancy of the bedroom.

Only then did he truly wake from his dream. Or so he must have, although he was already sitting up with his hands still gripping his gut. Rick flicked on the lamp beside his bed and examined his stomach. No burns, no bruises, no scars. And why should there be? It was only a nightmare, inspired by Holcomb's freaky pictures and even freakier theories.

But Rick's abdomen still hurt, right beneath his navel. The thing had touched him *inside*.

***

Holcomb was predictably gleeful when Rick arrived at the professor's beige suburban townhouse later that morning. "Mr. Ebbers! It's a pleasure."

"I'm sure." Rick rubbed his unshaven face to stave off sleepiness. After his dream, he'd stayed up smoking until dawn. "You got the check?"

"Sure! Sure!" Holcomb opened his front door wider in invitation. It was Saturday, and he wore an old Pink Floyd *Dark Side of the Moon* concert tee featuring a Newtonian glass prism splitting a ray of white light into a rainbow of its component colors. "You want to come in for coffee?" he asked.

Rick put a hand to his belly as another twinge seized him. "Nah, I really gotta . . . get home."

"Oh. Okay. In that case, wait a sec." The professor left the door ajar as he hurried back to the table in his breakfast nook and ripped a check from his checkbook. "I must admit, I was surprised when you called this morning. Didn't you have any other bidders?"

He brought the payment back to Rick, who barely glanced at the amount before pocketing it.

"You seem like a good guy," Rick said. "Thought I'd give you a break." He took the CD from his jacket and gave it to the professor.

Holcomb cradled the jewel case in his hands, glorying in it. "I don't know how to thank you . . ."

Rick's lips parted, and he almost spoke the warning that hovered in his mind. But all he mumbled was "Good luck."

"Daddy, can you fix my swing now?" a piping child's voice pleaded.

A girl of about five, with long, stringy blond hair, tugged at the leg of Holcomb's jeans. She was barefoot and wore a teddy-bear print dress short enough to show scabs on her knees from the scrapes of play. The child's presence startled Rick; he'd assumed science guys like Holcomb were all perennial virgins with pocket protectors.

"Daddy's going to be busy today, sweetheart. Maybe we can fix the swing tomorrow." Ignoring his daughter, the professor indicated the CD and gave Rick a quizzical look. "You sure you don't want to . . . ?"

"No. I really need to go." Rick couldn't keep his eyes from darting to the child's wistful face as he turned to walk back to his car.

The girl lingered in his mind on the long drive home, along with a vague, nagging discomfiture. The feeling persisted, intensified. Only when he stood on his own front porch that evening, pluming clouds of smoke into the night instead of sleeping, did he identify the emotion as guilt. But why should he feel guilty about selling a CD, aside from the ridiculous profit he was making?

Because you didn't count on Holcomb having a family, did you? a voice inside him accused. *Let him have his overbeings, you thought. At least you'd be rid of them. The prof was asking for whatever he brought upon himself . . . but his kid? Did she deserve that?*

Did she deserve *what?* Rick wanted to know, stamping on his latest cigarette butt. At most, he had deprived Holcomb's daughter of a couple grand that should have gone to her college fund, and perhaps he bore some of the blame for feeding her old man's delusions. But he hadn't sicced any 4-D monsters on a helpless little girl because there were no such things. Holcomb was as much of a nutcase as Tompkins, and if Rick pitied his kid, it should be for that reason alone.

His conscience salved by cynicism, Rick went back inside to bed. Yet he simply lay there until dawn, eyes open, his right hand clutching his stomach where he'd dreamt that the meat-creature had emerged from his abdomen. It still hurt.

***

At some point, he must have dozed off, for it was late Sunday afternoon when the bleat of his cell phone jerked him back to consciousness. He rubbed his stinging eyes, which had had no chance to adjust to the intrusion of daylight, and swiped his thumb across the phone's touchscreen to answer. "Yeah?"

"Rick?" It was Holcomb, of course. "I need help."

"Help?" Rick snapped upright in bed. "Why? What's wrong?"

"Wrong?" Holcomb laughed. "*Nothing's* wrong. I did it! I saw . . . I made contact."

"Contact." Rick absently massaged his belly.

"Yes, but the recording wasn't complete. I need the rest of the séance."

"No." Rick shook his head for emphasis, as if the professor could see him through the phone. "No, I gave you the whole thing. There wasn't any more."

"There *has* to be more," Holcomb insisted. "Why else would Tompkins mention the phonograph?"

"Tompkins said something about the phonograph?" During the one and only time he'd played the wax cylinder, Rick had been so caught up in watching the meat-thing mutate that, by the end of it, he hadn't even listened to what the humans were saying.

"Yes. Just before the sound cuts off, he yells, 'Porter! The phonograph!' The table-turning must have jarred the machine, maybe even knocked it over, and interrupted the recording. But if Porter managed to set it up again—"

Holcomb waited for Rick to respond. He didn't.

"Could you at least check the cylinder again to make sure?"

Now Rick did reply. "No."

"I'll double your fee."

"No."

"Then sell me the cylinder! Five thousand."

"Sorry—"

"Ten!"

"I thought a humble physics prof couldn't afford more than two grand," Rick muttered.

"I'll take out a second on my house. Name your price."

"It's not for sale."

"*Twenty* thousand." Holcomb panted as if salivating on the phone's receiver.

Rick ground the heel of his palm against his forehead, his resolve weakening. Could he really turn down twenty grand because he feared what had most likely been a delusion?

But it wasn't a delusion. Holcomb had *seen* the overbeings.

"You've already made contact with your 4-D buddies," Rick pointed out. "What good is a few more minutes of audio?" He couldn't believe he was actually trying to talk the prof *out* of the deal.

The scientist was undeterred. "In attempting to understand the overbeings' language, any sample of their speech that I can obtain is essential. Your recording could be the Rosetta Stone for our two species." He paused as if debating whether to continue. "The rest of the séance might also reveal any . . . *errors* Professor Tompkins may have made in his methodology."

Rick recalled the consequences of those errors—the ghastly photos of Porter and the Delacortes. He drew a slow breath to steady his speeding pulse. "I'll see what I can do . . . on one condition."

"Anything."

"You have to make them leave me alone."

"Who?" Holcomb asked.

"You know who."

The professor didn't speak for so long that Rick wondered if he'd hung up. "If I succeed, you'll never have to deal with them again," he said at last. "Just bring me the cylinder—"

"No." Rick pictured the meat-things assaulting Holcomb's little girl. "No, I think you'd better come over here."

***

He was still studying the wax cylinder's surface with a magnifying glass when Holcomb showed up that evening.

"Damn if the boy wasn't right," he murmured, peering at a narrow gap of smoothness that interrupted the winding groove. Whether the phonograph had been knocked over or merely bumped during the chaos of the Tompkins séance, the needle apparently lost contact with the cylinder's malleable wax surface. But the doomed Edmund Porter must have managed to reset the device before the overbeings turned his innards into outards, for the tiny, etched squiggle of the groove resumed after the lapse. When Rick's laser reached the cylinder's smooth patch, it registered only silence, which is why he had assumed the recording had reached its end. In reality, there seemed to be another five minutes or so of audio, judging by the width of grooved surface area that remained. A hidden track, Rick thought wryly, like "Train in Vain" on The Clash's *London Calling* album.

A track that might reveal how four people were either maimed or killed in the space of those five minutes.

Before Rick could contemplate the implications of the track's contents, Holcomb rang the doorbell. Rick hadn't even made it to the door before the professor began pounding on it.

"Wait till you see what I've got here!" The professor set down the video camera case and paper bag he was carrying and took a velvet ring box from his pocket.

"You gonna propose?" Rick shut the door. "Why, Ozzie, I didn't think you cared!"

"Go ahead and laugh. But this is going to win me a Nobel Prize."

Holcomb pried open the ring box, took something the size of a large marble from inside, and put the object in Rick's right hand.

It was a snail shell. Not the parti-colored shell of some exotic sea snail—merely the dirt-brown shell of a common garden pest.

"So?" Rick said, underwhelmed.

Holcomb wore that infuriating grin again. "Notice anything *different* about it?"

Rick examined the shell more closely, and a nebulous unease crept over him. There was something *wrong* about the shell, but he couldn't single out what it was.

"I give up," he admitted. "What is it?"

"The shell of every other garden snail in the world spirals clockwise. So did that one ... until last night." Holcomb's eyes blazed with fanatical excitement.

Rick peered at the shell again. Indeed, it spiraled counter-clockwise—a sight that now seemed so unnatural that Rick nearly dropped the thing in revulsion, as if he'd felt the snail's foot ooz-ing over his palm.

A voice from the séance recording replayed itself in his head. *Spirits, prove yourselves to us! Take this shell and transform it as only you can!*

"Tompkins's experiment," he said.

"*Exactly.*" Holcomb took the shell and held it between his thumb and forefinger. "Tangible proof of the overbeings' exist-ence. Something no human could possibly fake."

Rick stared at the snail's backward spiral. All he managed to say was "How?"

The professor chuckled. "Piece of cake. As easily as you can flip a coin from head to tails, an overbeing can rotate a three-dimensional object through higher-dimensional space and turn it into its own mirror-image." He fluttered his hands in the air as if shooing away a flock of distractions. "But why am I standing here?

We've got work to do."

Holcomb replaced the snail shell in its padded ring box, picked up his grocery bag and video camera, and let Rick conduct him to the studio.

The professor believed that, like most creatures, the overbeings responded best to the language of their own kind. Therefore, in order to provide the longest continuous sample of their bizarre vocalizations, Rick had rigged his sound system to play the partial recording of the Tompkins séance he'd already made before it switched to the hidden track on the wax cylinder. As soon as the MPEG finished, the spindle would begin to turn, and the helium-neon laser would trace the cylinder's final groove to its end.

While Rick set up the audio, he kept darting sidelong glances at Holcomb, who set up his video camera on a tripod, then sat cross-legged on the studio floor and fuddled with a few brass singing bowls that he'd taken from his bag. Rick couldn't decide which was crazier: to be obsessed with the overbeings when they had seemed merely creatures of delusion, or to be obsessed with them now that they were most likely real.

Finally, he had to ask the professor: "Why are you doing this?"

Holcomb looked up. "Hmm?"

"You got your snail shell. You got the séance recording. Why don't you just collect your Nobel Prize money and go to Tahiti?"

The scientist regarded him with a kind of pity. "You don't get it. It's not about money or fame." He gestured expansively. "Don't you want to know there's more than . . . *this*?"

The careless toss of his hand made clear what *this* was: a dead-end teaching job at a community college, a beige McMansion in the suburbs, even a Nobel Prize. All the trappings of a godless material world—the mindless, soulless mechanism of the known universe.

Rick nodded slowly. "Okay. You meet your overbeings. What then?"

"We communicate with them, of course." Holcomb's voice

dropped to a reverent hush. "These entities have knowledge and abilities beyond anything we are capable of experiencing. Can you imagine what they could teach us—what they could *do* for us—if we can establish a rapport with them? It'll make *Close Encounters* look like a dime-store magic show by comparison. Here, look at this . . ."

He reached into the paper bag again and pulled out a bizarre glass object that looked as if a laboratory flask had tried to devour itself. The neck of the container curled down, penetrated a hole in the side of the flask's bulb, and snaked inside to fuse with the base. The topsy-turvy mouth of the flask gaped open at the container's bottom like the funnel of a black hole.

Holcomb waggled the thing in front of the sound engineer's face. "Know what this is?"

Rick sniffed. "A mistake?"

The prof glared but let the joke pass. "It's a Klein bottle," he said. "Well, not a *real* Klein bottle—merely a three-dimensional model of a hypothetical topological construct proposed by German mathematician Felix Klein." He pointed to the swan-like bend of the container's neck. "A real Klein bottle wouldn't need a hole in its side, because this loop would curve through the fourth dimension."

Rick waited for further explanation with a blank look. "So . . . you want these hyper-powerful superbeings to make seventies retro for you. Lava lamps and stuff."

The professor put a hand over his eyes and drew a long breath, either to calm himself or to think of a way to simplify the concept for a rather dense student. "You ever hear of a Möbius strip?"

"You mean the paper ring with only one side?" Rick replied, determined to show that he wasn't completely ignorant.

"Right. You take a two-dimensional strip of paper, twist it through the third dimension, and join the two ends. Suddenly, it only has one side and one edge." He indicated the Klein bottle again. "Same principle. You take the neck of a three-dimensional bottle and twist it through the fourth dimension until its mouth melds with the bottle's interior. Suddenly, you have an object with only one surface: you can't tell where its inside leaves off and its outside begins."

He pointed down the gullet of the bottle's mouth. "Suppose you had a liquid that could cling to the glass. If this were a real Klein bottle, any such liquid you poured into the neck would flow inside, then back out again, then back down the neck in an endless cycle."

"Sounds messy," Rick chuckled. But he studied the faux Klein bottle more closely, intrigued in spite of himself. "Think your 4-D buddies can make this into the real deal?"

Holcomb grinned, evidently pleased that Rick was getting with the program. "If they can, I'll have more than a snail shell to show the Nobel committee."

Rick jerked his head toward the spindle where he'd cued up the wax cylinder. "I'm ready to roll when you are."

Holcomb raised a hand. "One moment . . ."

He rummaged through his bag, while Rick fidgeted with an unlit cigarette, debating again whether to go through with the experiment. A familiar twinge gnawed at his gut.

"What's to keep us from ending up like Tompkins and his friends?" he asked, finally voicing the fear he could not even acknowledge before.

"Because we will speak to the overbeings in a language they can understand—the universal language of mathematics." The professor pulled out several computer-printed sheets and spread them on the studio floor. Schematics of the Klein bottle were surrounded by strings of dots and dashes that resembled Morse code. "I have translated the frequencies of some of the primary tones of the overbeings' language into binary code. I shall mimic these tones with notes of alternating duration from the singing bowls to give the overbeings both visual and auditory signals of our intent to initiate a dialogue with them."

He held up a piece of paper whose dots and dashes were accompanied by diagrams of the snail shell and its mirror image. "This method has already enabled me to succeed with the snail experiment where Tompkins failed—catastrophically, I might add."

"Let's hope they get the message this time," Rick commented dryly and reached toward the soundboard. "You want me to roll it?"

"Wait! Wait!" Holcomb fluttered over to his video camera, smoothed his mullet, and pushed "Record." He had angled the lens downward to focus on the bottle and other items he'd spread on the studio floor, and now he leaned into the camera's view to address the Nobel committee.

"Overbeing experiment number two. Conducted by Dr. Oswald Holcomb. Time—" He glanced at his watch. "—eight-twenty-two P.M." He gave Rick a commanding nod. "Mr. Ebbers."

Rick restrained the urge to roll his eyes in case this video did become a document for posterity. Instead, with exaggerated solemnity, he started the CD of the séance, this time channeling the sound through the studio speakers instead of the headphones. Once more, Professor Tompkins invoked the spirits.

"Come . . . speak . . ."

Holcomb complemented the sonorous tones from Tompkins's singing bowl with those of his own bowls, deftly timing the duration of each note to create the binary sequence he'd described.

"Show yourselves."

Rick tensed as the uncanny bleats and groans commenced. He hadn't listened to this part of the séance since that first night, and he had never heard as it was now, blaring from speakers in all four corners of the studio. Perhaps it was this startling increase in the depth and volume of the inhuman vocalizations that kept him from recognizing precisely when other voices joined the chorus . . . at least until he smelled a pungent stink like that of blown fuses and singed wiring.

"It's them!" Augusta Delacorte gushed on the recording as the studio walls began to resonate with the swelling dissonance.

"They've come!"

The coffeemaker clattered and Holcomb's video camera wobbled on its tripod. The prof still bent over his bowls, drawing a wooden pestle around the rim of one after another to make them hum, although their vibrations seemed drowned in the deluge of noise. A smile of manic delight lit his face as he stared at the bottle set before him on the floor.

"Do you see them?" he shouted. "Ebbers! Do you *see* them?"

"Yeah," Rick said tonelessly, "I see them."

He doubted whether Holcomb heard him or cared if he had. The scientist was too enamored of the flesh globules that had oozed into the studio as if squeezed from an unseen tube in space-time. Half a dozen of them now undulated in midair, elongating and contracting like soap bubbles. Then an ovoid curl of pulsating tissue larger than all the rest licked around the faux Klein bottle like a monstrous tongue. The glass hissed and glowed orange as if fresh from a forge. As the prehensile tongue withdrew, it pulled at the odd curl in the bottle's neck, which lengthened and thinned with molten elasticity. The liquid glass of the bottleneck followed the overbeing into some hidden burrow between dimensions until it disappeared completely. The hole in the container's side sealed over, yet Rick could still make out the funnel-shaped spout inside the bottle where it joined the base. And he was willing to bet that any liquid poured into the funnel would flow back out over the container's surface, since its interior and exterior were now one and the same. It had become a *true* Klein bottle.

"You see! You see!" Holcomb exulted. "They *understand.*"

At that moment, the disembodied voice of Professor Tompkins broke from its measured chant to cry in alarm. *"Porter! The phonograph!"*

Rick shot a glance at the soundboard. His MP3 of the séance had reached its end, and the large wax cylinder started to spin, the green needle of the laser's beam cued up to the hidden track—the final minutes in the lives of Tompkins and the Delacortes.

Since the experiment already appeared to be a success, Rick saw no reason to listen to what happened to them. In fact, he was suddenly desperate *not* to hear it. He put his finger on the Stop button and looked to the professor for approval. "Should I . . . ?"

Holcomb scowled. "For God's sake, no! Let it run."

Rick reluctantly let the cylinder play. There was a gap in continuity, during which time Porter had presumably reset the phonograph, and the recording resumed with a shriek so shrill that Rick assumed it must have been Augusta Delacorte. Before the shriek ended, however, Mrs. Delacorte proved him wrong by crying, *"My God, what is it doing to him?"*

The thought of what "it" was doing to "him"—something that could make a grown man scream like that—made Rick pant for a soothing cigarette. He tapped his finger on the Stop button. "Yo, Ozzie!" he shouted. "Let's wrap it up."

The prof either ignored him or couldn't hear him over the alien coda's final crescendo. In rapture, he smiled at the profusion of flesh-ribbons that had swarmed from the center of the studio to stream and ripple around him in ever-smaller circles. As he continued to play his singing bowls with one hand, he reached out to stroke the slime of a fluttering strip of sinew with the naive delight of a Hawaiian tourist swimming with dolphins.

The sitters at the Tompkins séance babbled incomprehensible things as if their pitiful ghosts had come to the studio to warn Holcomb, but their dying words were buried by an abrupt, multi-octave surge in the pitch of the overbeings' song to a skull-splintering ultrasonic screech. The coffeemaker's glass pot shattered, spraying the studio walls with brown droplets. The tripod with the video camera tipped and toppled.

Rick pressed his palms to his ears to shut out the noise, but it thrummed in his bones. He slapped the Stop button. It made no difference, for the laser had already reached the end of the wax cylinder. All the sound in the studio now emanated from the creatures that swirled in a vortex around Holcomb.

"Wonderful!" The scientist stood and raised his arms, reveling in them as if in an aviary of angels. *"Wonder—"*

Thick eels of flying flesh seized Holcomb like the fingers of a gargantuan hand. As they lifted him into the air, the wooden pestle slid from his grasp and landed in one of the singing bowls with a clang.

Perhaps the overbeings misunderstood the professor's instructions. Perhaps they perceived some threat in his attempt to communicate with them, as they evidently had with Tompkins. Or maybe, like other gods, they simply resented faithless humans pestering them to prove their existence. Whatever the case, they made certain that Oswald Holcomb would need no further proof.

Rick jumped to his feet, yet couldn't bring himself to intervene for fear that the creatures might do to him what he saw them doing to the scientist. As Holcomb danced helplessly more than a foot off the floor, the meat-apparitions pulled his head and his body in opposite directions. Rather than decapitating him, however, they seemed to pull his neck like taffy, drawing it into a long, unbroken strand of taut skin. Then the head vanished, leaving only a smooth stump atop the neck. Yet Holcomb flailed as if still striving to break free from the clinging globules of flesh that suspended him.

That was all Rick needed to see. He lunged toward the studio door, unwilling to acknowledge the futility of escape. Only when he felt the overbeings grasp him both outside and *inside*—gripping his heart, squeezing his stomach—did he realize how silly he was to run from an entity that could follow him anywhere and from whom he could never hide.

For an instant, they simply held him fast—long enough for him to see Holcomb's head burst through the back of his oxford shirt, surfacing from between the professor's shoulder blades. His eyes bugged wide, Holcomb yawned grotesquely, his distended jaws opening to reveal the mucus-filmed tubes of his windpipe and esophagus. As his face stretched until it became unrecognizable, the interior of his body appeared to rise from the gorge of his throat to flow out over his skin, organs bobbing on the tide of viscera. Like the Klein bottle, the professor now only possessed one surface, his inside melding with his outside in an endless loop.

That wasn't the worst of it, however. Even now, as the man's body twisted in cataclysmic agony, a light of transfiguration shone in the scientist's eyes, and Rick finally realized the extent of the scientist's obsession. Despite what he'd said, Holcomb had never cared about the Nobel Prize, or his daughter, or even his own sorry life. The monumental risk of his experiments had never concerned him, for the only thing that mattered was meeting his overbeings—to commune, however briefly, with gods he could see and hear and smell and touch.

The professor's form folded in upon itself, sucked into a ball of blood and beef not unlike the beings he worshipped. The sphere shrank, devouring itself, until it winked out of view like a collapsed star.

Rick would have screamed, but his lungs felt constricted by giant serpents. He kicked in futile terror as the soles of his sneakers lost contact with the floor, and then he was *turned*, inverted, rotated in a direction that was not up or down, left or right, forward or back. *As easily as you can flip a coin from head to tails*, Holcomb had said. And for a mercifully brief instant, Rick caught a glimpse of the spaces *between* the three dimensions of space we know—another universe superimposed upon our own and coexisting with it, a world in which every solid three-dimensional object lay open and exposed as if dissected and turned inside out. Rick's bilateral vision and two-dimensional retinas were insufficient to process his view of the entities that squirm around and among us in places we cannot look, and his mind lacked the cognition to assemble the fragmentary images he received into comprehensible life forms. All he managed to understand before his consciousness shut down was that these massive, impossibly polymorphous organisms were the overbeings in their totality, festering in their natural habitat. And that there were legions of them.

Rick came to on the floor, sprawled beside the overturned video camera, which still rolled despite cracking against the linoleum. For several minutes, he didn't attempt to move, for his guts felt bruised beyond repair. When it became apparent that he wasn't going to die, however, he groaned into a sitting position. The only motion in the studio was the lazy spin of the wax cylinder, the only sound the spindle's tick as it slowed to a stop.

Maybe it had all been some psychotic episode, Rick thought. Yes, that had to be it. He and Ozzie Holcomb had listened to that trippy recording, after which the prof had become frustrated with his failed experiment and gone home, leaving his papers, singing bowls, and other junk strewn across the floor. The scientist's bizarre theories and the freaky audio of the séance had combined with some residue of Rick's long-ago drug use to throw him into a fugue state. Why, he'd probably broken that coffee pot himself while flailing at his imaginary monsters. And yet . . . a residual aroma of electrical discharge hung in the air. And wasn't there something odd about the shape of that Klein bottle that rested in the center of the room?

Rick got to his feet and hurried over to the soundboard. Breaking his cardinal rule, he lit a smoke right there in the studio, hands shaking as he tried to steady the flame of his lighter. He'd taken the first drag before he noticed that he held the cigarette with his left hand.

He dropped the butt as if it had burned him and ran from the studio to the bathroom down the hall. As he flicked on the fluorescent bulb above the medicine chest, Rick hoped that the light might dispel his fear like the afterimage of a common nightmare.

But the overbeings had left him with proof he could not deny. Peering at his mirrored face as if at a stranger, he saw that the large mole that had once been on his right cheek was now on the left. Like Holcomb's snail, Rick had become his own mirror image.

For the next several hours, he could do nothing. He slumped in one corner of the bathroom, staring at the seemingly solid walls and ceiling and wondering if they were still watching him. Around two in the morning, however, he drove Holcomb's aging Saab to Bancroft Community College, struggling with the car's stick shift since he was no longer right-handed. He wiped his fingerprints off the car and abandoned it in the school's parking lot, then spent the rest of the night in a doughnut shop until he could take a bus home.

The police still came, of course, led to Rick Ebbers by the check he'd cashed from the missing professor. The cops didn't believe him when he told them that Holcomb had never come to his studio; but without a body, they could never charge him with the scientist's murder. Rick might have been able to prove his innocence by showing them the video file from Holcomb's digital camera, but he deleted it without watching it. He also crushed the snail shell, smashed the Klein bottle, and melted the wax cylinder and the CDs he'd made of it. Unlike Professor Tompkins, Rick was determined to leave no trace of the overbeings for future generations to find.

And when he slipped into a daze while staring at his reflection as he shaved, or when he woke gasping in the night, clutching at his stomach as if it had been clawed from within, Rick prayed to a God that he had never seen to protect him from those gods that had made him their unquestionable miracle.

Because It Is Bitter

The man lived in a small shack of rough planks and corrugated tin about two miles outside of town, and every day around noon people arrived and clustered about the shack for the day's performance. Some brought picnic lunches in wicker baskets and sat on cane chairs, chatting and fanning the flies from their faces as they waited for the man to emerge.

Each time, he came out onto the porch, blinking as if used to a cave darkness, and surveyed the gathering with an expression of resigned contempt on his furrowed face. Sometimes he sat on the porch steps for half an hour or more, the crowd silent under his stare, and rubbed his curly gray beard, muttering, making them wait, perhaps hoping to bore them into leaving. At other times he proceeded almost immediately, the sooner to get it over with.

Eventually, though, he always marched down the steps to the patch of dry dust in front of the shack where the grass never grew. Avoiding eye contact with the crowd, he slipped the straps of his overalls off his shoulders and unbuttoned his checked flannel shirt. With his pale, fleshy chest exposed, he held up his right hand and made an elaborate show of examining his fingernails, as if to emphasize to the audience that his nails were no longer or sharper than theirs. He then reached down and pressed his fingers into the skin of his stomach, just below the breastbone.

The man grunted and strained, and the fingertips sank in, followed by the whole hand as a red slit opened over the man's navel. His forearm disappeared up to the elbow as the man wormed it up under his ribcage. A moment later, with a sharp cry, the man withdrew his arm, slick and crimson, from the puckering wound, the heart in his palm still pulsing and squirting, and held it up defiantly for all to see.

The spectators, men and women alike, blanched and gasped. Even farmers seasoned by the slaughterhouse found themselves pressing their hands over their lips. But no one left. Not until the end.

The man lifted the heart to his mouth, sniffing it, his tongue flicking out for the first taste. A sigh of contentment or relief whispered out his nose when he finally bit into the red meat, sucking the pulp of the left atrium as if savoring a sour autumn apple. He cupped the quivering remains of the heart in both hands and gnawed at it, dark saliva dribbling down his beard, the lips of the slit in his stomach glistening and engorged.

When he'd swallowed the final gelatinous piece, nearly gagging on it, he wiped his mouth and smiled at the crowd disdainfully, showing yellow teeth lined with red. Licking his fingertips, he pushed the sides of the wound in his stomach closed and ran his index finger up along the gash. As he wiped his stomach clean of blood, preening like a fastidious cat, the slit vanished without a scar, though some claimed it was always there, ready to open again the following day.

No applause followed this performance. The man snorted, brusquely pulled up the straps of his overalls, and went back in his shack. After a few minutes of awed silence, the spectators found their voices and quietly murmured among themselves. The gossips split off into groups and gradually drifted away.

No one knew anything about the man. Townsfolk started peeking in his windows after two young boys came back from the swimming-hole one day with wild stories about a cannibal who lived outside of town. While few believed the tales at first, they sparked enough curiosity that some went to investigate. Those who saw for themselves told new stories of the man's strange ritual. More stories brought more people to the shack in the woods, until so many onlookers huddled around the house that the man, possibly in exasperation, began his public performances.

Rumors and theories abounded about him. He was a murderer, cursed to enact his consuming guilt. He was a saint, chosen by God to be a living testament of Christ's communion. He was a monster, he was a fraud, he was a prophet.

Town pundits speculated on how the man got a new heart each day. Some said it swelled from the stem of the aorta like a ripening fruit. Others said the man merely belched up the old heart, the bile congealing in his empty chest cavity during the night. The latter theory gained numerous supporters when spectators noticed that the man often spat out splotches of red phlegm when he'd finished his meal.

The man became so renowned throughout the area that he attracted the attention of the owner of a prominent traveling show. Something of a dandy, the impresario attended one of the man's performances dressed in his tailed coat, brocaded vest, and top hat, nudging townsfolk out of the way with his bone-handled cane until he reached the front of the crowd. After witnessing the spectacle, he became the first known individual to cross the patch of dust and enter the man's shack, pausing only to prod a stray scrap of heart on the ground with the tip of his walking stick.

No one but the two men themselves knows what transpired at that meeting, but the man soon left his shack to join the showman's troupe. They traveled through more than twenty counties, the man performing alongside clowns, contortionists, and bearded ladies. Now the audiences did applaud and cheer, and some of the men even laughed, declaring later that it was the finest geek trick they ever saw. The price of the show rose from two bits to fifty cents a head as long lines of patrons formed outside the canvas tent.

The venture was a great success, and the showman planned to take his star attraction on a national tour. However, the two men had a sudden falling out, which came to a head during one evening's performance when the man threw his freshly plucked heart right in the impresario's face. It hit the showman with a soggy slap, spattering his cheek and his ruffled white shirt, and nearly a month passed before he recovered himself enough to appear in public again.

The man returned to his shack in the woods and to his daily ritual. Though he must have made a great deal of money during his time with the traveling show, he made no change in his accustomed living habits. Many of the townspeople came to see him again shortly after he arrived, but found that they had become jaded with his act. He now seemed a carnival oddity, a juvenile entertainment. Before long, only mischievous children bothered to come gape at him.

His beard has grayed further since then, and his expression has grown darker as the skin sags and the furrows deepen. Yet, though he often plays only to the silent trees, he still emerges from his shack each day, holding his heart up for any who might wish to see, then devouring it with insatiable relish.

Revival

Brice hugged the lapels of his filthy down jacket closer around himself as he squinted down the brick chasm of the alley. Darkened doorways sulked in the walls on either side, offering neither entrance nor exit. The only sign of movement was an empty plastic bag, tumbling hollowly in the gusting draft like a shed skin.

Everything about the place felt wrong. The location was too deserted, too deep into the shunned heart of the city. Most missions stationed their soup kitchens and makeshift chapels on the fringes of the urban blight—close enough to draw the shambling needy, yet removed enough for their staff members to leave safely at night. If Brice had not been so cold and so hungry, even he, a native of the streets, could not have been lured into this district.

He consulted the crumpled flyer in his hand to check the address but could not read the small typescript. No streetlamps illuminated the surrounding grime of metal-shuttered shops and sewage-scented asphalt. All he could make out was the large heading that first captured his attention:

REVIVAL TONIGHT.

***

He'd come by the advertisement not more than an hour ago as he trudged up Main Street toward the nearest shelter that would take him in. A four-mile walk, and he wouldn't get there till well after midnight. He had no money, no food, no liquor, and the few passersby at that hour bowed their heads and quickened their steps if he so much as looked at them. In summer, he could have curled up on a vacant doorstep and slept till the cops came to shoo him away, but tonight's bitter winter wind cut right through his stocking cap and frayed jeans, and sleep would be impossible.

Without alcohol to squelch them, unwelcome memories bobbed into his consciousness like the flotsam of a wrecked ship. A job, a wife, a son whom he was no longer permitted to see. Lashed by regret for a life squandered and exhausted by the prospect of the dreary hours ahead, Brice had slumped against an adjacent lamppost, ready to collapse and die of exposure rather than take another step.

As if in commiseration, a hand grasped his upper arm and squeezed, constricting to the point of painfulness.

Brice straightened to look at the slouching figure that had accosted him. "Leon?"

The man before him wore a gray flannel sweatshirt, the face cowled completely by a pullover hood. In the static world of the homeless, however, clothing served as much a marker of identity as a face for street people to recognize one another. That hoodie certainly looked like the one Leon always wore, though mottled by new and darker stains. He stank in a way peculiar for a vagrant—a salty putrescence, like the rot of beached kelp. The smell repulsed Brice more than the fetor of sweat and urine he'd expected, and he recoiled, wrinkling his nose.

Whether or not he was Leon, the man didn't say. He simply peeled a sheet from a sheaf of papers he carried and thrust it at Brice. The latter winced with disgust as he accepted the page—its margins were sticky where the hooded man had touched it.

In the dun glow of the sodium vapor streetlight, Brice saw that most of the sheet was covered with a radiating, serpentine pattern of intertwined lines, as if a map to a labyrinth with no egress. In the ring's center, calligraphic letters promised "REVIVAL TONIGHT," with details of the event in smaller print below. Brice noted that both time and location were near.

"They got food?" Brice asked the man he assumed was Leon, but the hooded figure shuffled away without speaking. Brice rubbed his bicep, which was still sore from where the man had clenched it, and cursed when he found finger-shaped smudges where a gummy residue had clung to the sleeve of his jacket.

Leon was not the sort to have got religion. Most likely, Brice thought, someone had paid him a few bucks to distribute the flyers. Brice himself had little hope of salvation, but he'd often turned to the missionaries for a hot meal and a roof over his head. On this night, he'd settle for a cup of coffee and a chance to doze during the sermon.

***

And so he'd wended through the litter-strewn avenues of this abandoned quarter of the metropolis, advancing in the shadows to avoid being rolled by thrill-seeking gang members. Now that he was here, though, it seemed as if he'd fallen victim to some cruel practical joke. He could find no brightly lit prayer meeting, no hallelujahs and hosannas, no comfort or consolation.

As he scrutinized the flyer, a glimpse of motion in the alley caught his attention. A dim phantom drifted about halfway down the narrow lane—a shuffling figure whose gray, hooded sweatshirt appeared to float amidst the engulfing blackness. It turned through an open portal on the right and vanished from view.

Brice followed the way Leon—if it was indeed Leon—had gone. He found that the double doors there, though shut, were unlocked. They opened onto a steep stairwell that sloped into what must have been the building's basement.

Brice hesitated, for there seemed to be no light below, and he wondered if he had selected the correct entrance. As he crossed the threshold, however, he realized that a faint, bluish luminescence clearly delineated the downward steps, though its source was uncertain.

He descended to a low-ceilinged hallway and was heartened to hear music of a sort emanating from the opposite end of the passage—a solemn, sonorous hymn distorted by the odd acoustics of the structure's cinderblock foundation. The azure phosphorescence grew brighter as he advanced, until it hung like a haze in the air, although it still had no definite origin. This must be the right place after all, Brice decided.

The hallway led to a room that was much larger and higher than he anticipated. Now there could be no question that Brice had found the correct gathering, for the flyer's spiraling design of interlaced lines had been reproduced on the vast far wall, radiating blue light as if it were an enormous stained-glass window illumined from behind by a great nocturnal sun. Cerulean hues shimmered on a sea of Brice's fellow derelicts, making them appear submerged. The entire congregation stood swaying in time to the dirge-tempo psalm he'd heard.

Brice grimaced at the lack of benches or folding chairs. No chance to nap here. To avoid attracting attention, he mingled with the crowd at the rear. Slightly out of sync with those around him, he mouthed along with the chorus, whose words he couldn't quite make out, and made random vocalizations in an attempt to mimic the increasingly atonal canticle. Not like any gospel song Brice had heard before. Maybe this was one of those New Age religious orders. He only hoped they would reward him for enduring their ceremony.

Brice exchanged an embarrassed glance with the man on his left, who also faked the song. Bald crown, walrus mustache, sagging cheeks blotched with rosacea—it was Richie, a friend of his from the streets. They pretended not to recognize each other, however, as if both were ashamed they would stoop to such an indignity just for a handout.

Brice had to admit that the church, whatever denomination it was, put on a good show. As the hymn became more fervent, the pattern on the wall brightened from blue to white, the shifting, swirling intensity of color giving the design an illusion of three-dimensional depth.

When the brightness grew almost unbearable, the silhouette of a cowled figure strode in front of the glowing pattern until it stood beneath the circle's center. Brice wondered briefly if it was

Leon . . . but, no, this figure wore a robe, not a hoodie. It towered over the standing congregation, yet there seemed to be no dais to elevate it. And when it raised its arms in exaltation, the robe's sleeves slid down to reveal hands with fingers that were too long, too splayed.

Brice had no time for fear, only a stupefied astonishment. For the sinuous lacework pattern on the wall suddenly *uncurled*, the undulating lines exploding forth as gelatinous tendrils. The tip of each elastic appendage shot out and slapped down on the head of an unsuspecting congregant. A suckling mask of translucent protoplasm enveloped Richie's silently shrieking face, the membrane distending and stretching the obscured visage into a grotesque new configuration.

Only when Brice felt the soggy smack of ooze on his own head did he comprehend the miracle of which he was now a part.

The burning slime embraced his entire body, melting and molding his flesh like modeling wax. Brice shrieked with the ecstasy of religious conversion, yawned open his mouth to receive the viscous communion that poured down his throat to transubstantiate him from within. He realized that he had been touched by a real, living, tangible god—a god who would remake him in His image.

For the first time in years, Brice was no longer tempted to succumb to despair and die. Not with the purpose that now coursed through him, the mission that he must perform.

***

Hours later, yet still well before dawn, he scuffed into the foyer of the homeless shelter. Understaffed and overcrowded, the facility consisted of little more than one large dormitory room lined with cots, all of which were already taken. The sole attendant on duty sat at a desk by the entrance, reading by the light of a low-slung shaded desk lamp so as not to wake the occupants.

"Mr. Brice?" She greeted him, as she always did, with a desperate cheerfulness. Her name was Maureen, a volunteer social worker fresh out of college who hadn't been there long enough to become jaded or embittered by the intractable urban malaise. "We haven't seen you lately. Are you . . . okay?"

She obviously hadn't looked up until he'd passed her. Brice did not turn around. Paper rustled as he thumbed a sheet off the stack in his arm and passed it back to her. The page adhered to his fingers until she peeled it off with an exclamation of distaste.

Then he ambled on into the dormitory, where benighted sleepers awaited his evangelism.

Scary Monsters

"Get in, Holly," her mother said, pulling open the closet door. "Quickly."

"Can I take Misty with me?" Holly asked, cradling her doll in her arms.

"Yes, you can take Misty. Please hurry, honey."

Holly obediently stepped inside. She was tall enough now so that she had to bend over to keep from brushing her head on the hanging coats and dresses inside. She knelt on the floor and looked back up at her mother wistfully. "Mommy?"

Hands trembling, her mother was placing the key in the keyhole on the inside of the closet door. "Yes, honey?"

"Won't you stay here this time?"

Her mother glanced down at her. Though her mother's face was hidden in shadow by the light from the hall behind, her whole silhouette seemed to quiver.

"There's lots of room," Holly insisted, settling herself into one corner and drawing her knees up to her chest to leave a clear space in the closet's center. "We could both play with Misty."

Her mother bent over, kissed Holly on the forehead, and hugged her tightly. "Oh, sweetie, I wish I could," she whispered. Then she gently pushed her daughter back and started to close the door. "Remember to turn the key, Holly. And don't come out till I tell you."

Holly nodded. "Mommy?"

Her mother stuck her head back through the narrow gap of light entering the closet. "Yes, honey?"

"Is it the scary monster?"

Her mother remained silent for a moment then nodded.

"Yes, honey." She glanced fearfully over her shoulder at the thump of heavy, irregular footsteps on the front porch. The line of a

tear parted the purple patch on her cheek, but she brushed it away.
"Yes, it's the scary monster."

Then the light from the hall narrowed until the closet was sealed
in darkness. Holly turned the key.

***

She sat behind the window like a wax gypsy in an old for-tune-telling machine, waiting for me to put a quarter in her slot. Head bowed, pale face shadowed by a fall of curly brown hair, delicate china-white hands resting on an open paperback book. I rapped on the glass and she looked up, startled. The bluish light of the fluorescent lamp above made her face seem even paler, even more statuesque. But pretty. Very pretty.

"Sorry," she said, smiling nervously. "What can I do for you?" Her voice had a tinny quality due to the vent we spoke through.

"Ten on two," I answered, sliding a twenty through the steel trough below. I scanned the inside of the little hut, bounded on three sides by racks of cigarettes, chips, and road maps. "Looks co-zy in there," I added as she gave me my change.

She smiled and shrugged. "It's a living."

"What happens if you have to go to the bathroom?"

She giggled. "Don't ask."

I chuckled and turned to go back to my car. No one else seemed to be out that night—a little surprising for L.A., even at 2 A.M. I watched her in her little booth as I pumped my gas, and thought about my now-vacant love life. I decided I needed anoth-er pack of cigarettes, though I had a carton of Winstons at home. She looked relieved to see me come back.

I opened the box she handed me and shook out a smoke. "So they let you out of there once in a while?" I asked casually, light-ing up.

"Oh, once in a while. For good behavior."

Ah, I said to myself, a healthy sense of sarcasm. I like that in a woman. "I'm Doug, by the way. Deliver the *Times*." I nodded toward the newspaper dispenser across the street.

She paused before answering. Uh-oh, I thought, she's giving me the once-over. Do I pass muster?

"Holly," she answered finally. "Welcome to Insomniacs Anonymous."

I grinned. "Maybe we can share some coffee and No-Doz sometime."

She smirked back at me. "Maybe the Tooth Fairy will run for president."

"We should be so lucky," I said, and teased a laugh out of her. I decided not to rush things. This one might be a keeper. "But the *Times* they are a-callin'. See you 'round, Holly."

"I'll be here, Doug."

I smiled and waved as I left. At least she had the name. That was a foot in the door. And she seemed pretty cool.

Still, as I drove my route that night, I couldn't help wondering how someone could sit in a box for hours without going nuts.

***

The sudden darkness did not frighten Holly. The blackness was warm, close, comforting. Familiar smells embraced her: the sharp leather tang of her mother's high heels, the acrid miasma of mothballs in her grandmother's woolen coat, the stale aura of cigarettes and beer from her father's ragged military jacket. Just enough light leaked through the crack under the closet door to give soft gray outlines to the objects around her.

Holly hummed tunelessly as she and Misty explored the box of assorted knickknacks in the corner, picking up items one at a time and feeling them, imagining what they might be. Sometimes Holly played Mommy and shut Misty in the box, telling her not to come out until it was okay. Some kids at Holly's school said they were scared of closets, said there were monsters in them. But Holly knew they were just being silly. There was no monster in here.

It was outside.

She could hear its leaden, shambling tread stomping back and forth through the house. "Holly! Holly!" it called, voice slurred, now growling, now pleading. "Come here, girl! Come here and give me a kiss!"

Holly fell silent and leaned against the sturdy wooden closet door, hugging Misty to her chest and listening.

***

It took two weeks of topping off my tank at 2 A.M. and several boxes of shared donuts before Holly said she'd go out with me. I got Rick to cover my route Saturday night and picked Holly up at her place. As she opened the door, I smiled and flashed the button I'd made at the mall that afternoon: "TOOTH FAIRY FOR PRESIDENT."

"Very funny," she said, nodding as she leaned against the door frame. "You know, I could just stay home and watch cable."

"Yeah, but would you get a free meal out of it?"

"Well, since you put it that way . . ."

She locked up and followed me out to my Toyota. It was the first time I'd seen more than the top half of her. She wore a modest but elegant dress that highlighted her slight figure in black satin. Black nylons sheathed lean, smooth legs. And her face—a small red mouth, a straight aristocratic nose, perfectly arched eyebrows. Like a painted porcelain mask. Only the eyes seemed to peek from behind the mask. Brown eyes with large black pupils.

I spent the next couple of hours looking at that face as we ate dinner and danced. I twitched every time she swept back her long, full hair to reveal the pale arc of her forehead. She danced better than any woman I'd ever known, floating in the midst of the cramped dance floor without so much as brushing someone else's shoulder. I put my arm around her waist, and I could feel the delicate impression of her spine through the fabric of her dress and the almost feverish warmth of her skin.

As the crowd began to thin in the club, Holly started to tense, glancing from side to side at the vacant places on the dance floor. "Maybe we should head out," she suggested, shouting in my ear to be heard over Billy Idol's "Rebel Yell."

I looked at my watch. Only midnight—early by my standards. But that was cool. It gave us more time for what I'd planned next. I nodded, and we made our way to the door.

She smiled and seemed to ease a bit when we got back in my car. "Thanks. This was the most fun I've had in a long time."

"It's not over yet," I replied, starting the car.

Her smile wilted a bit. "Oh. Really."

I just grinned and drove. She began to fidget with her purse, snapping and unsnapping it as she peered at the road ahead. "Where we going?" she asked as concrete and glass gave way to pine and brush.

"To the top of the world." I downshifted as the road began to climb. "Close your eyes."

"What?"

"You heard me. It's a surprise."

She looked dubious, but sighed and closed her eyes anyway. "It better be good."

"It is."

The car rounded another curve, and the floodlit dome of Griffith Observatory ascended into view. "Don't open 'em yet," I said as I parked the car.

I went around and opened her door. As she got out, I put a hand over her eyes.

"Hey!"

"Just don't want you peeking till it's time." I guided her toward the rail bordering the cliff. She chuckled nervously and put an arm around my waist for support. Below us, the vast, blinking grid of Los Angeles glowed magically beneath its permanent haze of smog. Above us were as many stars as you ever see in Southern California. It was the best view L.A. had to offer.

I lifted my hand from her eyes. *"Voilà!"*

Holly blinked a moment, disoriented. Her eyes widened. She wheezed asthmatically, her gaze darting around the panoramic landscape as if seeking an exit.

My smile died. "Holly, what's wrong?"

Biting the thumb of one hand, she felt for me with the other, unable to tear her eyes from the scene. Her fingers dug into my shoulder. *"Take me home."*

"What? Holly, what's the—?"

"Take me *home!*" She beat her fist on my chest.

"*Okay. Okay.*" I glanced around the parking lot. Only a few people were left at that hour—mostly couples—and all of them were staring at us. I patted Holly's back as I guided her to my car, praying that no one would call the cops.

While I eased her into the passenger seat and turned to go around to the driver's side, I caught a brief peripheral glimpse of the view below. Suddenly, the brilliant patchwork of streets and freeways lining the L.A. basin appeared to stretch and warp upward, expanding, spreading across the horizon like some infinite web. I pictured myself falling . . . falling down between those endless threads of gold . . . into a square of bottomless black . . .

Then I looked directly at the city, and the impression was gone. I shivered and got in the car. I think I was almost as glad as Holly to be back inside.

We said nothing to each other on the drive back to her apartment. I wanted to turn on the radio, but silence seemed more appropriate.

I pulled in front of the apartment and switched off the ignition. "I—I'm sorry."

"No, it's okay," she said in a distant voice. "Really. Good night." Holly got out and walked away without glancing back.

Well, so much for that, I thought as I drove home, and felt both frustrated and relieved. She was too weird—it would never have worked out anyway.

Before I got home, though, my cell phone was already ringing.

***

"Holly!" the monster yelled. "Holly! Come when I call, dammit!" It tromped upstairs toward her closet. Holly heard the light pad of her mother's footsteps follow it.

"I told you, Ray," her mother shouted. "She's not here. I left her with Mother."

"Don't give me that crap, Marie! I'm not buying it this time!" the monster thundered. "Holly!" Its pounding came closer.

"Don't you touch her, Ray! Don't you dare—"

"Get off! I only want to give her a kiss. She's mine just as much as yours. Holly!"

Holly grabbed the tail of her daddy's army jacket and stroked it against her cheek like a security blanket. She wished Daddy were here now. All she really remembered about him was the feel of his strong shoulders as he carried her around and the gentle lull of his voice when he read her storybooks.

But surely he would know what to do about the monster.

***

"Agoraphobia."

"Niagara-*what?*" Rick's brows knit over the rims of his ever-present dark glasses.

"Agoraphobia," I repeated, explaining it to him as Holly had to me that night two weeks before. "Fear of wide open spaces. She'd freak if she came in this warehouse."

"No shit?" He clucked his tongue and shook his head as he went back to stuffing sections into the Sunday *Times*. "Doug, m'boy, sounds like you got another psycho-chick on your hands. Stoke-*moi* some more 'Calendars,' willya?"

I tossed him a bundle. "Yeah, well at least she's not a juicer," I countered, referring to Kris, my ex. I aborted that relationship shortly after Kris commented casually that, though the doctors had prescribed Valium to help her control her drinking, she'd taken thirty that day without any noticeable decrease in her desire for alcohol.

"No, she's a friggin' schizo-Niagara-phobic. She'll creep up on you in the middle of the night sometime and slice you up like Freddy Krueger." He waved his box-cutter at me for emphasis, then used it to open the newspaper bundle. "Don't say I didn't warn you."

I tried to laugh, but it came out as a snort. "Shouldn't be that bad. Long as I keep her away from state parks, stadiums, large movie theatres, rooms bigger than a breadbox . . ."

"Whoops! Scratch that honeymoon at the Grand Canyon," Dave interjected.

"What's she look like, anyway?" Stan asked.

I dug out my cell phone and thumbed up a selfie that Holly and I had taken a week earlier and passed it around. Most of the guys just nodded or shrugged. Rick sighed and shook his head again as he studied the picture. "Another flat one," he muttered as he handed the phono back. "I just hope she gives a good one, bro, know what I mean?"

My jaw tightened, but I didn't let myself say what I had in mind. I merely nodded and smirked, content in the knowledge that I had a B.A. in communications from Berkeley and they were mostly high school dropouts, so their opinions did not amount to a heap of ferret droppings. Yet I had the same lousy job they did, so who was I to talk?

Still, I felt uneasy as I climbed the stairs to Holly's apartment the following afternoon. Agoraphobia. It seemed a harmless enough handicap, as if she had diabetes or something. I'd have to make certain adjustments, but I could live with it—couldn't I? After all, Holly had.

I hesitated a moment outside her apartment door while I tried to shake off the frown that crept across my face. Then I rang the bell.

I always had the sense that she was watching me through the peephole even before I pushed the button. For a split second, I seemed to see myself as she must have seen me—my forced smile stretched wide and malefic by the fisheye lens, nose growing hideously large as I leaned in and waved, body small and squat below the harlequin face. I almost felt her flinch back as I stuck my eye right up against the peephole and said, "Hey-ho! Anybody in there?"

An awkward pause followed, during which, I suspect, she had second thoughts about letting me in. Soon, however, Holly undid the Fort Knox assortment of chains and locks she had on the door and opened it just enough to reveal her pale, smiling face. "Peeka-boo!"

"Do I pass security, or do you want to frisk me first?" I asked suggestively as I squeezed through the opening sideways.

"Hmmm. Sounds tempting." She rose on tiptoes to give me a kiss but broke it off prematurely in order to shut and lock the door behind me.

I blinked while my pupils swelled in the sudden darkness. I don't think Holly had a light bulb brighter than 15 watts in the whole place. To make matters worse, she had draped paisley fabric over some of the lampshades and most of the walls, dousing the apartment in a pinkish pall. The patches of wall that weren't coveted with cloth had posters plastered over them, as if blank space were some kind of sin.

Holly scampered toward the kitchen, and I followed her, pulling a beer from the fridge as she stirred spaghetti sauce at the stove. I stepped up behind her and lightly kissed her ear. "What's cookin', Doc?"

She giggled. "Something edible, I hope. Wellington!"

The black-and-white demon she called a cat had jumped on the counter and was stalking the strained spaghetti. She scooped him up in her arms and asked me to keep an eye on the sauce.

"He just wants some food, don't you, tiger?" She nuzzled the beast in way that made me extremely jealous. Grumbling, I set my beer on the counter and stirred the sauce.

As soon as the dear Duke had his feast of Friskies in front of him, Holly set the table for us lowly humans. I turned to grab my beer and found a shiny plastic coaster beneath the perspiring can. Coasters had a way of materializing like that around Holly's place. Like my mom, Holly was a neat freak. I chuckled and took both coaster and can to the table.

We sat down to our spaghetti, making small talk and exchanging coy glances while we ate. We got on the subject of high school, and I was fondly reminiscing about the substitutes we used to torment.

" . . . so he comes back in, slams his book on the counter, and yells, 'Where the hell is my *desk?*'" I quoted in my best Mr. Herman whine. But the expected laugh didn't follow.

In fact, Holly wasn't even looking at me. She was staring at the carpet, but her eyes seemed to focus beyond that, as if she were looking through the floor. She swept her hair back from one ear, a habit she had when she wanted to hear something better, but she didn't notice that I had stopped talking.

"Something wrong?" I asked.

"Hmm? Oh, sorry. What did you say?" She leaned forward attentively.

"You okay?"

"Yeah. Fine." She prodded her spaghetti.

"You sure?"

"Sure," she said with a nervous chuckle and a shrug.

I halfheartedly finished my substitute story while she nodded and murmured "Uh-huh." I might as well have sung "The Twelve Days of Christmas," though, because her gaze strayed around the room anxiously, as if searching for a chink in her armor of paisley prints and posters.

Finally I sighed and dropped my fork on my plate. "Holly, what is it?"

She cleared her throat and massaged her temples. "Nothing. A little headache, that's all."

Her attention wandered to the ceiling, to the floor, to the wall. I knew that look—she was having one of her "attacks." "I'm sorry, Doug, I guess I'm not feeling too good. Could you—"

"Leave? Like last week?" I asked a bit more harshly than I intended. "Is this going to be a regular thing with us? 'Excuse me while I have a nervous—' Holly, what's wrong?"

Gasping, she clapped her hands over her ears. "Don't you hear it?"

In the pause that followed, I pursed my lips and listened. For a moment, I didn't hear anything, and didn't expect to. Then I seemed to catch a muffled seashell roar coming from somewhere below us, so soft that it seemed more of an after-impression than a real sound, like the lingering whisper in your ears following a thunderclap.

Holly shrieked as if it deafened her. She jumped from her chair and ran from the room, mewling "I'm sorry, I'm sorry."

I started after her. As I got to the door, though, something about the room behind made me do a double-take. Possibly due to a change in air pressure, the paisley sheets adorning the walls seemed to have billowed outward, expanding and blurring the contours of the room. It became difficult to tell where one wall left off and the next began. I traced the chaotic pattern of the print, and it seemed to go on and on and on. I felt myself sagging against the doorjamb, gripping it tightly, because I looked and looked and the pattern never ended.

A door slammed in the bedroom, and I snapped back to reality. I had to find Holly, I told myself as I ran toward the sound. And I had to get out of that living room, though I didn't admit that at the lime.

I rushed to the bedroom, but Holly wasn't there. *Maybe she went to the bathroom instead*, I thought, but I didn't move to find out. The bedroom, like the living room, looked *wrong* somehow, as if everything in it had been subtly rearranged. The bed, the dresser, and the chair seemed to lean away from one another, leaving a spreading vacuum of emptiness in the center of the floor. Darkening gaps had formed in the tightly packed assortment of books, stuffed animals, and bric-a-brac lining the shelves, as if the objects were repelling one another to the point of exploding.

"Holly!" I called, surprised at the quaver in my voice.

She didn't answer, but I heard that muffled roar from beneath the floor again. The sound defined itself into a shout, but muted, as if the person were stifling himself with a pillow.

I was trying to make out the words when another sound caught my attention.

A tiny whimper from the bedroom closet.

"Holly?" I approached the closet door and listened.

The whimper stopped. Only a brittle silence answered, broken by the faint shouting below.

"Holly?" I tried the doorknob and found it locked. I'd never seen a closet that locked before, much less one that locked from the inside. I rapped on the door. "Holly, it's me, Doug. Open up."

Nothing.

For a moment, I got the same impression that I had outside the front door: She was in there, watching me, sizing me up . . . deciding my fate. I became irritated and knocked harder. "C'mon, Holly! It's *me*, for Christ's sake!"

Pause. The bedroom dimmed, and I fought the urge to glance over my shoulder at the pulsing blank space on the floor. A key turned in the door's lock. The closet opened a crack, and one misty, glistening eye peered out from knee-level. "Doug?"

I saw that eye and felt my stomach constrict. Needles of pity and dread pricked my skin. I wondered if Anne Frank had looked that way when the Nazis finally found her.

I forced myself to smile. "Yeah, Doug. You were expecting, maybe, the Avon Lady?"

Opening the door just wide enough for me to slip through, Holly desperately tugged my arm, pulling me down into the closet. "Come *on*, Doug—it's *coming!*"

"What? You've got to be— Holly!" I tried to yank her out into the room.

"No!" she shrieked, and let go. She was about to slam the door again, but I put my foot in the way.

"All right, all right!" I started to crawl inside. Before I could react, she yanked me off-balance and sent me stumbling among hanging skirts and blouses. The door slammed behind me, and the key turned in the lock.

I tried to sit up as best I could, scrunching myself in a corner and carelessly shoving aside the flattened shoes I'd sat on. I had to tilt my head forward to keep from brushing against the hems of the blouses above me. I blinked and rubbed my eyes, but I might as well have been blind. From the opposite corner came Holly's rabbit-quick panting.

"Well," I said to the darkness across from me, "here we are."

She shifted position but didn't respond.

I sighed. "You know, under other circumstances, I would think this is kinda kinky, but . . ."

Nothing.

I tried a different tack. "If you want to . . . you know, just talk or something, I'd—ow!" Claws sank into my thigh, and I realized that Duke Wellington, the demon cat, was in there as well. I swatted him aside and swore. *"Christ!"*

Exasperated, I put a hand out where I thought the key should be.

"No!" Holly gasped. Her delicate hand locked around my wrist like a manacle.

I shook her off. *"What?* What *is* it?"

"Don't you hear it?" she asked.

I stopped short. I knew what she meant, and, yes, I could hear it. "Someone downstairs is having a fight. So?"

"It never stops," she said wistfully. But I wasn't sure she was talking to me.

"Look, if *you* want to worry about other people's problems— fine! Let's do it outside." I grabbed the doorknob and shook it, vainly hoping I could jar the door open without unlocking it.

"Stop, please!" Holly pulled my hand from the knob and held it to her face as she began to cry, muttering "Please, please."

"Okay." I put my arms around the blackness where I felt her to be. She sank against my shoulder and hugged me. I rocked her gently back and forth. "It's okay."

But I don't think she really believed that. I know I didn't.

***

The monster roared. Glass shattered. Mommy screamed.

"It'll be over soon," Holly whispered in Misty's ear.

"Where is she, Marie?" the monster demanded. "Under here?" A wooden groan, then a crash. "Over here?" A shrill creak and a thud followed.

"Stop, Ray! Just stop!" her mother shrieked.

"Getting warm, am I? What about here?" Another crash.

"That does it, Ray! I'm calling the cops!"

"You do that, Marie. Go ahead. Get off my back."

The monster's clomp grew louder. Two lines of darkness divided the narrow thread of light leaking under the closet door. The footsteps stopped.

Holly shrank further into the corner.

The doorknob rattled violently, then fell silent.

"Holly?" the monster murmured, its voice unnaturally calm. "You in there? Open up, baby, it's me."

Holly sat perfectly still, but her heart raced. Something about that voice . . .

"Holly?" There was a tremor in the voice this time. "Come on, baby, it's Daddy. God, it's been so long."

Holly trembled. Daddy? Could it be? The voice . . . but Mommy had said—

The doorknob clattered again. "Please, Holly."

What if it was Daddy? Holly thought. What if he'd come to fight the monster? Maybe he'd even brought some of his army men to help.

She reached toward the key in the door.

"I said come out now, dammit!" the monster howled, its fury re-turned, and the whole door shook. Holly jerked her arm back as if it had been shocked. "You hear me, you little bitch? COME—OUT—NOW!"

A shuddering blow struck the door, which buckled. Holly heard its wood crackle with the strain.

"Get away from there," her mother said.

"Marie, didn't I tell you to—" The monster's shout dropped to a whisper. "Where the hell did you get that?"

"Get away," her mother repeated.

The monster laughed. "You wouldn't dare."

A small click sounded. "Don't push me, Ray, I swear I'll—"

"Come on, then. Do it." It thumped away from the closet.

"Stay back! I'm warning you!" Her mother's voice rose, shrill and thin.

"You stupid— Give me that!"

There was scuffling down the hall, toward the stairwell. Holly's mother shrieked. A loud bang made Holly's ears ring. The monster let out a pained wail. It grunted angrily, and her mother screamed. The scream ended with a dull thud.

Holly wanted to cry out to Mommy but put her hands over her mouth. It was still there.

"Oh, shit." The monster made a soft, regular wheezing sound.

"Oh, shit. Oh, shit." Holly heard it stagger and stumble, the stairs creaking as it went. "Marie? Marie?" It took a few steps, stopped.

"Marie?" It coughed and spat. "Oh, shit."

There was another thud. Then everything became very quiet.

Holly remained perfectly still. She didn't cry out, though tears streamed down both cheeks. She just sat hugging herself, cradled in darkness.

She was still there when the police pried open the closet.

***

"And they were both dead," Holly finished hollowly.

She sniffed and leaned her head against my shoulder. The Duke dozed contentedly across both our laps; I guess he'd probably heard the story before.

"And you didn't know he was your dad?" Our faces were so close now that I thought I could actually see the twitch of her thin lips, the withdrawn stare of her glazed eyes in the dark.

She sighed. "Nope. Mom never talked about him, and Grandma didn't tell me the truth until I was fourteen." She paused, and I felt a current of warm breath brush past my neck. "He left when I was two. Mom only said he had to go somewhere and might not be back for a long time. I waited and hoped. He never came." She let out a giggle that was almost a sob. "But the scary monster did."

"Jesus, Holly." I hugged her, wanting to say something wise, supportive, and compassionate, but everything I came up with sounded like the cheap sympathy of a Hallmark card. I figured it would be better just to hold her and keep my mouth shut.

We sat like that for several minutes, arms around each other, as her crying gradually exhausted itself. When it was over, she brushed my cheek with her hand. "Thank you for staying."

I touched her face and began to guide my mouth toward hers for a kiss when Wellington suddenly decided to sharpen his claws on my chest. Holly laughed, this time without tears. I grumbled, then started laughing, too. "Come on, let's get out of here."

Holly caught hold of me before I could open the door. "*Wait.*"

I waited, and we listened. The people downstairs had apparently called a truce for the night, and peace reigned once more.

Holly's grip on me eased. "Okay."

She unlocked and opened the closet. The sudden flood of light was almost painful, and a minute passed before I could keep my eyes open without blinking. The bedroom looked its usual cozy self as I squinted at it now, and I tried to remember what had seemed so weird about it when I first came in. I moved to stand up, and the crick in my neck shot an instant headache to my brain. I had to brace myself against the wall because my legs had turned to jelly.

"God," I moaned, rubbing my face. "I feel like a sardine on parole."

"Yeah, it hurts sometimes." Holly stood with Wellington in her arms, stroking his fur, and looked as fresh and relaxed as if she had just come back from a pleasant forest hike. "You get used to it, though."

I nodded and asked for some aspirin. *You get used to it, though.* I kind of hoped I wouldn't.

On the way down from Holly's later that evening, I happened to pass the apartment directly below hers. The windows were dark, the curtains drawn. On impulse, I paused at the front door and was about to knock, but chuckled and shook my head. No, I thought, better let them rest. They'd had quite a bout that night.

A little embarrassed by my own nosiness, I sighed and glanced at my feet as I turned to go. And there, sitting beside the welcome mat, were two newspapers, one leaning on top of the other.

I stared at those two papers for half a minute or more and couldn't figure out what was so God-Almighty amazing about them. As if I hadn't seen newspapers almost every night for the past eight months!

But there were *two* of them. Today's and yesterday's. On the same doorstep. Which meant that—

—*no one was home.*

I hurried away, without looking back. After all, I was late to work.

***

Holly and I grew much closer after that. She relaxed and opened up more now that she didn't have to hide her big secret. I coped with her neurotic habit the same way I'd coped with Kris's drinking at first: I ignored it. When Holly went to the closet, I went to work. Out of sight, out of mind.

Except that I still got a queasy feeling in my gut every time I stepped out of my car into a wide, flat parking lot.

We might have gone on blissfully like that for months if I hadn't had the bright idea of talking Holly into coming over to my place for a change one Friday night. Getting Holly to go out *anywhere* was a job for Superman, and it took two weeks of wheedling and cajoling to get her to come. Needless to say, I did not take the occasion lightly. I cleaned and dusted the place for the first time since the Reagan administration, and promised not to smoke for the full three hours. I even dug out Mom's old chicken cacciatore recipe, which I whipped up pretty competently once I deciphered her handwriting.

That much of the plan went swimmingly. By eight o'clock, we were cuddling on my Salvation Army sofa with Adele on the stereo. I had my lips on the warm, soft skin of her bare shoulder when I sensed that it was about to happen again. Maybe the faint quickening of the pulse in her veins tipped me off.

Or maybe *it* was happening to me, too.

My kissing got a bit hotter, my petting a bit heavier, my touching a bit rougher as I tried to bury the thought in lust. But Holly pushed me away, maneuvering her face to avoid mine.

"No . . . no, I can't . . . I've got to go," she whined.

"What?" I asked. But I knew what. I could hear them. Angry voices below us.

She looked away. "It's coming."

"Oh, Christ, Holly!" I stood up. "You're twenty-three now, for God's sake. How long is this gonna go on?"

"I'm sorry, I need to—" She tried to dodge and pass me.

I blocked her and pointed to the sofa. "No, we are going to talk about this right now."

"Couldn't we . . . later?"

"No. Look, your father is *dead.*"

Her eyes narrowed. "You think I don't know that?"

"You act like you don't. Maybe you should see someone—"

She let out a loud, humorless laugh. "I've 'seen' plenty of people. What about *you?*"

Before I knew I had done it, I slapped her across the face. Hard. I slapped her because she had agoraphobia, because my friends made fun of me for it, because she interrupted our lovemaking to go run in a closet. But mostly I slapped her because I remembered that this was my apartment, which on the ground floor, because something was now pounding up stairs that didn't exist, because the dimensions and perspectives of the room around us had swelled along with the queasy sensation in my stomach, and I wanted it all to stop.

The look on Holly's face chilled me. Not one of shock. One of *recognition.*

"Oh, God, Holly, I'm sorry," I whispered.

She glared at me, then ran past.

"Holly!" I called after her.

Holly! another voice repeated, but distorted, as if on a record played at half-speed. It came from behind me, and I whipped around to face it. There was nothing there, but I had the impression that the roof had bowed outward as something tried to pry its way in.

A door slammed to my right. I thought it might be Holly, but when I turned I found myself facing a solid wall. I suddenly felt disoriented and helpless in my own living room.

I ran the direction Holly had gone. She must have discovered that my closet didn't have a lock, for she'd sealed herself in the bathroom instead. I rapped on the door. "Holly, please let me in."

No reply. *She hates me now*, I thought morosely.

Behind me, glass smashed and furniture toppled as the voice moved back and forth through the apartment, growling semi-intelligible words like a gorilla learning to speak.

I leaned against the bathroom door, gasping. "I believe you, Holly," I said. "I believe you."

The door eased open, and I slipped inside. I hugged Holly tightly. "I never wanted to hurt you. Can you forgive me?"

After a moment, she hugged me back. "Yes." Another, longer pause followed. "Can you forgive *me?*" she asked, as the noise outside got louder and more distinct—more real.

"Yes."

But I wasn't so sure when the episode passed and we finally emerged from the bathroom. The scene in my apartment was far worse than I had imagined.

Nothing. Not a shard of shattered glass or splinter of broken furniture anywhere. The apartment was as clean as I'd made it that afternoon. Which meant only one thing.

I was going nuts.

I took several deep breaths and tried to hold back the tears of panic in my eyes. *You get used to it, though,* I thought.

"I'm sorry, Doug," Holly murmured.

***

"Looking a little pale there, Doug, m'boy," Rick commented at work the following night. "'Hot Holly' more than you bargained for, eh?" He laughed and wiped off the top of his Pepsi can with the tail of his Metallica T-shirt.

"You could say that." I massaged my forehead. Rick adding his barbs to the other thoughts needling my brain was like giving acupuncture to a porcupine.

"How is it going, anyway?" Dave asked. "You haven't said two words about her in over a week."

That's 'cause it's none of your goddamn business, I was about to say, then checked myself. Dave was an okay guy. But I still wanted to smack him and all the rest of them upside the head.

"Great," I answered as I finished stuffing another bundle of the Sunday edition. "Three months and going strong."

Rick whistled sarcastically. "Three months? Call Guinness, guys. We got a record!" Everybody laughed and clapped.

I forced my grimace into a smirk. "Yeah. And your last relationship was all of . . . twenty minutes, was it?"

Rick shrugged. "Guess I'm just a rolling stone. How's the Niagara-phobia, anyway?" he added without a beat.

I winced and ground my teeth. "Not bad. How's your coke habit?"

The snickering around us dwindled. Rick glowered at me over the lenses of his dark glasses. "Watch your mouth there, bro."

"Practice what you preach, *bro*." I licked a drop of sweat from my upper lip and narrowed my eyes against the unexpected harshness of light from the fluorescent bars above us. So bright—*too* bright.

"Hey, guys, lighten up," Pedro cut in with a forced laugh. "Or we'll have to flog you with the Image section."

The other guys gave an encouraging chuckle. Rick just stared at me.

"Rick?" Pedro nudged Rick's shoulder.

Rick shrugged and pushed his glasses back up to the bridge of his nose. "Hey, man, not my problem. He's the one with the psycho girlfriend."

I stood up, letting a pile of newspapers slide off my lap. Rick got up, too, and suddenly it seemed as if we were all alone, two gunfighters standing off on a vast plain of concrete littered with newsprint. I realized I still had my box-cutter in my hand.

Distantly, I heard Dave say, "Easy, Doug, you know he didn't mean—" Then he was drowned out by a low growl that echoed off the warehouse walls, which were very far away.

I dropped the knife and ran to the small, scummy bathroom the *Times* had thoughtfully provided us. I rushed inside the first stall and slammed the door shut, sitting on the toilet without even wiping the seat. Hyperventilating, I leaned on one side of the metal stall, savoring its comforting confinement.

I heard the bathroom door open. "Doug? You okay?" Pedro asked in a voice made hollow by the enclosed space.

I drew my legs up to my chest so my feet wouldn't show below the stall's door and sat silently until the bathroom door squeaked shut. I didn't move again for several minutes.

I got Dave to take my route that night, telling him I was about to puke. The drive home was like doing Disneyland on acid. Red stoplights dipped toward me out of nowhere. The road outside the circle of my headlights appeared to drop off into nothingness. Jagged silhouettes of buildings parted before me as if they were the teeth of a gigantic zipper. Glaring straight ahead through the windshield, I watched the dark world refract and flow around me, like a goldfish that swims around its bowl and always ends up at the same place.

When I finally made it back to my apartment, I went straight to bed, praying for a good night's unconsciousness. Instead, I lay there rigid for an hour and stared at the ceiling, which looked too far away.

I know what'll help you sleep, bro, Rick's mocking voice said in my skull. *That closet over there looks mighty comfy, doesn't it? Bet if you curled up in there, you'd be out like a light in no time.*

I wrapped my pillow around my head and hummed Beatles songs to stifle the thoughts. After an hour or so, boredom finally worked its merciful magic and I dozed off. And dreamed.

Holly and I were running down a long corridor, bordered on both sides by rows of identical doors, the passageway's end a vanishingly small point in the distance. Behind us, I heard a distant growl, like the rumble of a subway train approaching its station. I didn't look back.

Holly kept stumbling and crying as I tugged her along faster and faster. The ceiling disappeared in shadow above us as we ran, and the sides of the corridor grew farther apart, leaving us in a spreading chasm of barren hallway. I expected a huge crack to break in the floor and swallow us whole.

In desperation, I yanked open the door nearest to us. It led to a closet. I pulled open another one. Coats swung on hangers within. Holly pleaded for us to crawl inside and hide, but I held her back and dragged her across the widening hallway to another door. I twisted the knob and pulled, and the rancid smell of mothballs poured out. The growl behind us grew to a roar. More doors, more closets. Holly screamed and clawed at my face. The walls of the corridor looked as if they were about to fall off into space, letting in the surrounding void—and, with it, the thing that made the hall vibrate with its cry.

On the opposite wall, now almost a football-field away, I saw a door with a tiny spot of green light over it. Instinctively, I sprinted to it, my fingers locked around Holly's cold, frail wrist. The door receded even as we raced toward it, but the green letters above it started to come into focus: EXIT. I felt the floor quiver as another deafening wail engulfed us. I closed the gap to the door—which opened *inward*—and pushed it ajar. Behind it was a frightening, opaque blackness. But no coats. No shoes. No walls.

"Holly!" Excited, I looked over my shoulder and saw a creature of congealed darkness in her place, its burning white eyes staring at me, its bony claw still tightly gripped in my hand . . .

I woke, gasping, and the after-image of those white eyes glared down at me from the ceiling. I lay shuddering in bed and thought, *This has to stop. I have to stop it now.*

I considered not even calling her again. That had always been the easiest way in the past—no arguments, no explanations, no apologies. A month of screening the calls on my phone and that would be it. Quick. Simple. Painless. It even worked for the first four days I tried it.

Then I heard her voicemail message.

"Uh, hi, Doug, it's me," she said. "Is everything okay? I haven't heard from you all week is all." A pause followed—her real message. "Well, anyway, I only called to see what was up," she went on, a little too brightly. "'Bye." She lingered on the line a moment more, then hung up.

I almost called her back right then. But I didn't. Instead, I vegged around my apartment for the next three days, waiting for her to call again and knowing she wouldn't. She was like my mother, I thought bitterly, a master of the fine art of guilt-mongering. Oh, if I really didn't want to see her, she wouldn't complain; she'd merely cry herself to sleep in a corner someplace, don't mind her. I pictured Holly, cuddling that cursed cat, her hair hanging in front of her face in frizzy strands, her eyes watery, her nose red and runny.

So, of course, I went over to her place.

When Holly opened the door, she looked so much like my mental image of her that another jolt of guilt rippled through me. Then she brushed her hair back and beamed at me.

"Hey!" She moved forward as if to hug me, then shied back uncertainly, glancing down at her tie-dyed T-shirt and ripped jeans. "Sorry I'm such a mess. I didn't know . . ."

"Oh . . . don't sweat it. You look great." Seeing her then, I didn't know what I wanted to say. Certainly not goodbye.

The first part of the evening passed almost like normal, except that some emotional forcefield kept us apart. We ate dinner and made small talk, but we never kissed, never touched, and hardly met each other's gaze. It felt more like a blind date than a couple's quality time. Afterward, Holly conned me into playing checkers, a game she nearly always won, and I was relieved to see her giggle and gloat with her usual sprightliness.

Then I heard the shouting.

I glanced up at Holly, who averted her gaze, fidgeting in her seat. The room wavered behind her. I shook a cigarette out of my pack. Remembering that Holly hated my smoking, I sat tapping the thing on the table as I scanned my hopeless position in the game.

An overturned piece of furniture thudded below us, and a woman screamed.

Holly inhaled sharply and rubbed her forehead. As our eyes met, she gave a wan smile but didn't leave her chair.

Shadows deepened and grew longer as the walls retreated. Irregular but purposeful footsteps pounded up unseen stairs.

I chose a checker at random and moved it. As I leaned back in my chair, my hands gripped the armrests as if they were the safety bars on a roller-coaster. Holly mumbled something to herself that I didn't catch.

"Your move," I said.

A door slammed outside the apartment's curtained window, the sound pulsing in my ears with dream-like resonance. The paisley sheets shivered as darkness seeped over them. Holly stared at the table, eyes brimming with restrained tears, and muttered softly, "Not tonight. Please . . . not tonight."

I wanted to cry, too. She was trying so hard.

So was I.

"Holly . . . " I began.

Holly! an angry voice echoed.

That did it. She bolted for the bedroom. I jumped from my chair and managed to grab her around the waist. We pitched forward and landed on the floor in a wriggling embrace.

"No!" she shrieked. *"Let me go!"*

"Holly, wait—*listen* to me!" I turned her to face me. "We can't live like this—"

She grabbed a fistful of my hair and yanked. I yelped in pain, and she squirmed free. Before she even got to her feet, she scampered toward the bedroom on all fours.

Part of me wanted to leave. But I think if I had, I would only have ended up in another closet.

I scrambled after Holly. The bedroom seemed about to dissolve, its walls undulating like a mirage. Holly was half-inside the closet as I came and pushed her the rest of the way, shutting the door behind us.

We sat for a minute, hyperventilating and listening to the stomp of footsteps, the smash of glass. It was like huddling in an air-raid shelter, with the muted din of sirens, planes, and bombs reminding you that your world was being destroyed.

"Well," I said, my voice quavering as I tried to sound cheerful, "here we are again."

Holly giggled and sniffed. "Yep. We've got to stop meeting like this." Then her head drooped onto my shoulder. "I tried," she whispered.

"I know."

The doorknob rattled.

"Do you want to try again?" I asked gently. I felt her body go rigid in my arms.

Holly? a reptilian voice outside murmured. *You in there? Open up, baby, it's me . . .*

She whimpered and didn't move. But she didn't say no.

"Holly?" I prompted.

Holly? the voice oozed. *Come on, baby, it's Daddy. God, it's been so long . . .*

Her fingers tightened on my arm. "You can go. It's okay."

"I won't go if you stay."

Please, Holly . . .

I leaned closer until my lips almost brushed her earlobe. "I'm scared, too." And then I whispered something else.

I said come out now, dammit! You hear me, you little bitch? COME—OUT—NOW!

The door shook with the words, and we cringed. As I extended my arm toward the doorknob, I could feel Holly's heart speed up—or maybe it was mine. She caught hold of my hand and pulled it away. Her skin was hot and damp. I sat back, resigned.

Then Holly drew a deep breath and threw the door wide open.

The bedroom had vanished. We saw only a strip of wooden flooring and, beyond it, a wall of darkness.

And we looked up into the blazing eyes of the scary monster.

The creature towered over us. Bloated and black, yet surrounded by an incandescent white radiance, like an overexposed film negative. Cold white fire shone from its blank eyes and from behind rows of needle-like teeth, light that signaled an emptiness that could never be filled. Rivulets of shining mercury drool dripped from its jaws.

It was the bogeyman Holly had made of her father.

Grinning, the thing swiped its open claw toward us. Our backs pressed to the wall of the closet, Holly and I were too paralyzed even to shiver.

Get away from there, Ray, another voice said sternly.

The thing swiveled toward the woman who appeared next to it. She had a bruise on one cheek and a bleeding cut above her eye. Holding a pistol straight out in front of her with both hands, she aimed the barrel at the monster's misshapen head.

"Mommy." Holly started forward, eyes glistening.

The creature advanced on the woman, jeering at her and snatching at the gun with its talons. She backed away and cocked the pistol. *Don't push me, Ray, I swear I'll—*

Holly crept forward onto the wooden flooring and stood. I reluctantly followed her. The thing had cornered the woman against the banister of a stairwell that bordered on a limitless cavern of empty space. They grappled. The gun went off like a cannon blast, the shot impacting the monster's chest. Howling with rage, the thing seized the woman and lifted her, writhing, from the floor.

"Mommy!" Holly screamed and darted toward the two figures.

I tried to catch her. "No! You can't—"

But she was already there. The monster hurled the woman over the railing, where she vanished in darkness. Holly came up behind it, shrieking, "Stop it! Stop it!" And she laid her hands on its back.

The thing's black hide burned red, then orange, then blindingly white beneath her touch. It wailed as its massive head deflated and collapsed into its torso. Its legs and arms shriveled and shrunk like burning matchsticks, and it sank to its knees.

The white light dimmed and disappeared. Holly covered her mouth with her hands. Before her kneeled a gaunt, unshaven man with thinning brown hair who wore a pair of shabby fatigue pants and a tank top with a growing spot of red on it. He gazed up into Holly's face with brown eyes that were infinitely tired.

I had seen eyes like them a hundred times before. The eyes of a Larry Talbot or a Henry Jekyll. They pleaded: *Let me die.*

The man mouthed some words, but only a wheeze came out. Then he fell back against the railing and lay still, eyes open. Although I can't read lips, I like to think he tried to say "I'm sorry."

Quaking, Holly bent to touch him, but her hand passed right through his chest. Her fingers touched shag carpeting instead of wooden floorboards. She sat down where he had been and wept.

I seated myself beside her, yet I didn't put my arm around her; this was something she couldn't share with me, much as I wanted her to. The walls of Holly's bedroom shimmered back into view, and I wondered if Holly even noticed. She sobbed longer and harder than I had ever seen her cry before. This time, however, she was sad, not afraid.

When she quieted to the hiccupping stage, I whispered in her ear. She sniffled and smiled. We got up and went to the apartment's front door. Hesitating only a moment, she opened it for me, bowing gallantly.

We laughed, then went out and stood under the limitless canopy of the night sky. Even in L.A., it's something to see.

Menagerie of the Maladapted

The glare off the bone-gray asphalt of the I-5 was so bright that, even with my dark glasses, I had to squint to make out the broken black lines that marked the lane I was in.

I grunted and shook my head. And to think some idiots in Sacramento had actually proposed paving the highways in bright white to reflect a few more degrees of heat back into space. Who were they kidding? Did they want to blind us all?

I was just barely old enough to remember when the roads were black and the stripes down the middle were white, back before the asphalt in L.A. got hot enough on an August afternoon to melt the soles of your sneakers. Back before the cops had to scrape up the sun-stroked remains of the homeless as if they were fried eggs in a pan. Back when L.A. didn't look like Phoenix. Back when human beings could still live in Phoenix.

With relief, I veered my truck off onto the 605 freeway. The sooner I made the delivery, the sooner I could get out of this hellhole. The route took me past the new desalination plant that they'd built where Santa Monica was now submerged. *Water, water everywhere . . .*

Southern California was such a mess now, I sometimes wondered why I ever bothered to come back. Most of my customers were rich enough to live up north—Minnesota, Canada, places like that—where they could let the "pets" I brought them roam among real trees and green grass. Nowadays, you'd be lucky to find a living cactus growing wild in Los Angeles.

I knew perfectly well why I kept coming back, though: Jules. She paid me less than any of my other clients, yet she was worth more than the rest of the lot put together. And she was the only one who didn't make me feel like a common criminal.

Like the rest of the buildings on campus, the exterior of UCLA's Terasaki Life Sciences Building was tiled in solar panels, most of them devoted to powering the central air conditioning that ran almost continuously year-round. Out front, the facility featured a Japanese-style rock garden of raked gravel and serene stones of the sort that had become fashionable since California freshwater conservation regulations had outlawed grass lawns. But I drove the truck around back, where large loading bays made the rear wall resemble an industrial warehouse more than an academic institution.

I needed to make this delivery indoors, and not just because my cargo couldn't take the hundred-fourteen-degree heat outside. If the Feds found out what my shipment was, Customs would have me in jail faster than you could sizzle bacon on the hood of your car.

I pulled up to one of the roll-up bay doors and videoed Jules with my camera phone. "Here I am!" I flashed a big grin as I held the phone in front of my face. "You miss me?"

As usual, she chose not to let me see her. "Only 'cause my aim is bad," her voice replied. "Gimme a sec to let you in."

A moment later, the door rose, and I parked in the bay's cool interior. The door lowered almost immediately, yet as I got out of the truck's cab, I still felt a furnace-blast of parched air gust inside before it closed, as if the heat wanted to infiltrate the air-conditioned haven.

Perforated with air-holes, the polymer cage in the back of the truck was big and heavy enough that I had to use a pallet jack to move it. Even as I rolled it down the ramp, I could see the cage quiver as its contents stirred and slithered within.

I guided the jack down a long corridor of laboratories and classrooms until I came to the pair of double doors at the end with a sign that said "STAFF ONLY—No Admittance." I pushed on through into a barn-sized room that smelled like a pet store but looked like a pharmaceutical testing lab. Metal cages on every wall rattled as the animals within them pressed up against the grating to see and sniff me.

But these weren't the usual rhesus monkeys or white rats. A three-tailed cat hissed from my left, while on the right an albino fox peered down at me with unearthly pink eyes. Other creatures—ones whose deformities were too severe to allow them to survive—floated, almost unrecognizable, in jars of formaldehyde. Jules fondly referred to the collection as her "Menagerie of the Maladapted."

Her long brown hair knotted in lazy bun, she wore her usual blue jeans and black tank top. When no one was around, she walked around the lab barefoot, and her skin had the moonlight pallor of someone who seldom went outside. She didn't look up as I entered, but continued to stroke the shell of a two-headed tortoise that scrabbled across her desk.

"Is he a new addition?" I asked.

"You mean 'they.' Conjoined *females*, in case you're interested." She let the left head drag the body a few inches to one side, then pulled the shell back so the right head could waddle in the opposite direction. "And they're so *pretty*, aren't you?"

I leaned on the cage in front of me and grinned. "That's one of the things I love about you, Jules. Always the champion of the evolutionary underdog."

She didn't crack a smile, nor did she call me "Ray," as I'd been trying to get her to do for the last ten years.

"In natural selection, you learn about the winners by studying the losers," she remarked softly, and her expression became even more glum than usual. That was one of things that got me about her, I think: pretty as hell, but she always had this sad, worried look that made me want to tickle her until she forgot about the fate of the earth for a few seconds.

"So, Mr. Gaynor, you finally bring me my dodo bird?" A dodo would have been the pièce de résistance in her exhibit of extinction, so she always asked, even though she knew perfectly well there were only a handful of dodo skeletons in the entire world, each of which would fetch exorbitant sums at auction.

"If only," I sighed. "Maybe then I could retire."

"What about a quagga?" she asked. The rather goofy-looking African herd animal, striped like a zebra in front, brown like a horse in back, had died out in the late nineteenth century.

"Nope."

"Tasmanian tiger?" Jules always had to run down the entire list of the failed species she coveted. It was her way of flirting.

"Sorry," I said. "But my supplier assures me that he's got something very special for you in here." I rapped on the lid of the cage and felt an answering thump from within.

Jules eyed me skeptically, then set aside her conjoined tortoises and came over to inspect the merchandise. A flap on the side of the cage opened to reveal a clear plastic window, and Jules peeped through it. She rolled her eyes. "You brought me an *anaconda*? It's not even albino."

"That's just the wrapping." I pointed to a large lump in the snake's body. "The real prize is inside."

She frowned. "You mean I have to . . . ?"

"Afraid so, Dr. Pierce."

"This better be worth it, or you don't get paid." Although Jules had dissected hundreds of animals in her career, she clearly didn't relish having to kill one. Nevertheless, she plugged all but one of the air-holes in the cage, then gassed the reptile with chloroform.

Even I had to admit that Cazador's security measures were extreme this time. Emulating drug couriers who seal their heroin in plastic bags and swallow them, the poacher had sealed a dead specimen in plastic and tied it to a live dog, then fed both to the anaconda. The snake gulped the shipment whole, but the plastic kept it from digesting the merchandise with the dog. Cazador knew that few Customs agents were bold enough to search inside a living serpent. Whatever he'd wrapped in that package must be special, indeed, for he'd gone to great lengths to keep anyone from discovering it.

Jules not only put on shoes, she donned an entire set of scrubs, latex gloves, and a surgical mask before arranging the dead anaconda on a dissection table. As she slit the snake's abdomen with a scalpel, the lump split open like an egg-sac, disgorging a blue bundle. Jules removed the anaconda and cleaned the steel table before slicing open the azure plastic package as delicately as if incising skin. Inside, chemical ice clustered around the dead specimen to keep it from decomposing.

When Jules plucked the blue ice bricks from around the specimen, I took it for another reptile. It curled in a shriveled ball, its leathery hide a mosaic of large, scaly diamonds and trapezoids. Its stubby, withered-looking appendages were folded close at its sides as if used to scrabbling, lizard-like, over the ground. Even when Jules rolled the thing on its back, the mere stub of a nose and nonexistent ears gave it the flattened, featureless visage of a salamander.

Then I saw the navel on its belly, which still dangled an inch of a carelessly cut umbilical cord. Below that, a hairless vulva peeked from the crux of its stubby legs. The thing was a girl—a baby girl.

My face went cold, my stomach sour. I'd trafficked in hundreds of species, both dead and alive, but never a human. It was a new level of crime that made me dizzy with dread.

"I swear, Jules," I babbled, "I didn't know—"

"Hush." She bent over the dead infant, exploring it with her latex-sheathed fingers, her eyes aglow with fascination.

Her enthusiasm made me squirm. "What happened to her?" I asked.

"I'm not sure. It *looks* like ichthyosis."

"Which is?"

"Alligator skin. It's a congenital condition. But this doesn't seem to be a buildup of dead skin cells as in ichthyosis. The thick skin tissue seems to have been alive and had a normal, healthy lipid layer underneath. I've never seen anything like it—in humans, at least. Nor this."

She lifted one of the infant's arms. A gelatinous film of what I assumed to be pus appeared to cling to the baby's side. As it fanned out, however, I saw that it was actually a translucent membrane finely threaded with veins and capillaries. The network of vessels had blackened with congealed blood.

"Wings?" I lamely suggested.

Jules shook her head. "Too thin, too fragile."

Peeling off the gloves, she hastened to her desk and pawed among the hanging file folders in a lower drawer. She yanked out a dog-eared college composition book and leafed through it. I read over her shoulder as she selected a page and ran a pen down a scribbled two-column list:

Environ. Change	Possible Adapt.
rising sea levels	amphib.?
lack of fresh water	higher saline content in blood?
excessive heat	nocturnal?

There were many other entries, but the pen stopped at "excessive heat." Below "nocturnal," she scrawled the word "thermoregulation," circled and starred it.

"Not a very successful adaptation if it killed her," I remarked.

"The mutation didn't kill her." Jules gently lifted the baby's chin with the tip of the pen. The wrinkled red line that ran between the scales on her neck suddenly gapped open to reveal the rictus of a knife slit. "Your supplier do that?"

Jules awaited my response with the patience of a prosecutor during cross-examination. I thought of Cazador and found I couldn't answer right away.

"No," I said without conviction.

"In that case," she replied, "I need you to take me where he got this. Now."

***

Manaus, Brazil, had become a ghost metropolis. Overlooking the dry bed of the Rio Negro, the city's high-rises jutted from the earth like fossilized bones. Their corporate tenants had all fled, vacating offices as commerce collapsed. Supermarkets had given way to a handful of ramshackle street vendors. With no running water, sanitation consisted of any patch of unused pavement in the fetid back alleys. Only those too poor to relocate had remained, and from our helicopter we could see them speckling the empty streets like dust motes. A few trudged on listless errands, but most clung to the shadows, unwilling to move in the daytime heat. It was late August—mid-winter in the southern hemisphere—and a quarter-to-nine in the morning, yet the temperature was already 112° Fahrenheit.

"This is exactly the kind of environment that sparks adaptation," Jules commented, shouting to be heard over the swooping of the rotor blades.

We'd hired the chopper because the local airport had shut down more than five years ago. Besides, it made it easier to land at our appointed rendezvous location, right in the middle of what had once been among the largest tributaries of the Amazon.

The skids barely sank into the hard, cracked soil as the copter touched down beside four custom-made off-road vehicles parked in the dry riverbed. Five men awaited us beneath a makeshift canopy between the two cars. As we alighted, four of the men came forward to help us with our gear. I immediately knew who the fifth man was, dressed in loose-fitting linen clothes and calmly waiting for us in the awning's shade.

"So you finally come to visit me, eh, my friend?" Cazador grinned as we approached, his teeth wide and white beneath his thick black mustache.

A compact man, he made up in bravado what he lacked in height. His nationality and ethnicity were almost impossible to place; his olive skin and glossy, jet-black hair might have been *mestizo*, or Italian, or Arabic, or Sikh. He'd trapped rare animals on every continent on the planet and spoke so many languages with smug fluency that his accent had smoothed into a polyglot gentility. He freely admitted that Cazador was no more his real name than any of the others on his many passports. But he was the best poacher in the business. We'd made a lot of money together, he and I, but I did not like him, and he was *not* my friend.

"This is business, not a social call," I reminded him.

"But of course, my friend! That last one, it was special, just as I told you, no? And you have brought me this lovely creature in trade."

He extended his hand to Jules. She didn't take it. "Did you kill it?" she asked.

Cazador laughed. "Dr. Pierce, isn't it? Tell me, doctor . . . why would I slaughter my own profit? The living beast would have been worth a thousand times what you paid for it."

She crossed her arms. "Then I can assume that, if we ever find another one, you won't slit its throat?"

"I promise you, doctor—I will kill only the person who tries to keep me from taking the creature alive." He smiled to let Jules know that his statement included her.

She nodded coolly. "Then let's do it."

Cazador's men barely had time to take down the canopy before we climbed into the off-road vehicles and tore off up the dry riverbed, the oversized tires pluming dust in our wake. As large as armored personnel carriers, the vehicles emulated the design of the classic VW Beetle with air-cooled engines to avoid overheating. One of the four contained our gear and food. One contained Cazador's tranquilizer guns, traps, nets, and collapsed cages. The other two were filled with nothing but plastic jugs, tanks, and bottles of water.

The journey up the Rio Negro was surreal, for the cracked soil on which we drove was at least thirty feet below the river's former water line. Fourteen years of unrelenting drought had reduced the once-mighty tributary to a trickle of mud. Nevertheless, slack-limbed men and women crowded the bottom of the enormous gully, attempting to scoop what sludge they could into buckets and pails in hopes of filtering a few gallons of drinkable water from the contents. On either side of us, the abandoned derelicts of boats from the once-thriving fishing industry lined the inlet, their spars jutting over the dry shores like the tusks of beached narwhals.

As we made our way upriver from Manaus, the banks became littered with the detritus of the dying Amazon rain forest. The thin layer of fertile topsoil had mostly dried up and blown away, denuding the jungle vegetation's shallow roots. Fallen samauma trees that once wove the forest's canopy lay in jackstraw heaps, their trunks either bleached gray by sun or blackened by wildfires.

After passing through this wasted landscape for miles and hours, Cazador abruptly ordered the vehicles to stop. Jules and I scanned the wreckage of deadwood along the river's edge but could find little life of any kind, much less human habitation.

Jules frowned at Cazador. "You said there'd be a village."

He checked his satellite GPS. "There is."

Stepping out of the climate-controlled vehicle felt like sticking my face in a convection oven. "At least it's a dry heat," I quipped, but even I didn't laugh. The brutal air thickened around us like hot pitch, clinging to us, resisting every movement of our muscles, so that even shouldering our backpacks seemed an exhausting task. Even before we had crested the modest slope of the nearest riverbank, we oozed perspiration, but it brought no relief. The ambient temperature cooked our bodies faster than evaporation could carry the heat away, and the sweat only made our skin itchy and miserable while leeching the moisture from our mouths. Already, I craved a swig of the coffee-warm liquid in my canteen, but

Cazador had set a strict rationing regimen for our water supply.

As we ascended over the Rio Negro's parched lip, Cazador and his men in the lead, I saw the corrugated tin roofs of what might once have been shanties strewn about like scattered playing cards, but still no inhabitants. Yet the air reeked of humanity, the stench of people who could no longer afford to squander water to wash away their own filth. And there was a worse smell underlying the sewage and sweat—a curdling odor of putrefaction and decay.

I gagged and tried to hold every breath as long as I could. Jules took out a jar of Vicks VapoRub and dabbed a bit of the mentholated ointment under each of her nostrils, a trick she'd learned to deal with the decomposing animal cadavers that she had to dissect.

Cazador stalked ahead of us and shouted down into a pit that resembled a giant mole's burrow. A gaunt man in a broad-brimmed hat, his brown skin and ragged beard greasy with grime, thrust his head and shoulders out of the hole, making it appear that he stood inside an open grave. Most likely, he was a *caboclo*, a rubber harvester from back when there were living rubber trees to tap. I realized then that this hole and the others I saw around it were in fact hovels that the villagers had dug in the ground, seeking the coolness of the earth's natural insulation. The whole town had been buried alive.

Cazador and the man exchanged rapid conversation in Portuguese, a language I don't speak. I knew enough Spanish, however, to understand why the local man's eyes widened when Cazador inquired about the *cidade de crianças mortas*. The City of Dead Children.

The man waved his arms and yelled, attempting to shoo Cazador away. He fell silent, though, the instant the poacher took a gallon jug of fresh water from his backpack. Cazador dangled the jug from one crooked finger, and the man rubbed his mouth with the back of his hand and nodded.

He climbed from the pit and motioned for us to follow him

on a path among the logs of the ruined forest. Along the way, we passed one of the wells that either the Peace Corps or the Brazilian government had drilled in the wilderness in order to tap groundwater for the natives. Their clothes stained yellow like our guide's, a long queue of people with pails awaited their turn at the single faucet with the joyless determination of panhandlers in a Depression-era breadline.

As it turned out, we didn't need the local man to show us how to find the City of Dead Children. We could simply have traced that terrible stink of ripening meat to its source, for it grew more rank with each stride we took. Finally, our guide halted, as if he refused to get any closer. He simply made a slicing motion across his throat and pointed ahead of us. Cazador held out the jug of water as payment, and the guide snatched it from his hand, greedily hugging it to his chest.

The spot he'd indicated was another earthen pit, as wide and deep as a swimming pool. The putrid hole had attracted the most wildlife we'd yet seen in the Amazon. A haze of flies as thick as coal smoke churned above the cavity, so many that I was afraid to open my mouth for fear of swallowing some. Perversely beautiful dung beetles jeweled the forest floor with an undulating carpet of iridescent blue and purple carapaces, all trundling toward the pit. King vultures swirled and dove and swooped up again with unidentifiable scraps caught in their orange beaks. Enterprising villagers threw rocks at the birds, hoping to land an easy meal.

As we got close enough to peer over the rim, I saw that the villagers would soon need to dig another pit, for this one was nearly full. Tiny corpses flopped on top of one another in a heap, like fish spilled from a net. Some had already been reduced to skeletons with little toothless skulls, indistinguishable from those of any human infant. But others still retained enough ripped and ragged skin to show the distinctive diamond-shaped scales we'd seen on the specimen I'd brought to Jules—and the grinning slashes at every child's throat. Gas bloated their little bellies, and their complexion ranged from gray to blue to black depending on how long they'd been left to rot.

Cazador's mercenary game hunters made the sign of the cross at first sight of the mass grave. It was Auschwitz in miniature.

"No," Jules said aloud. Then again, her voice rising to a shout. *"No!"*

I assumed she was aghast at the carnage. But no—she gaped straight across the pit at something on the other side. A local woman approached the opposite rim, clutching a caterwauling infant. From the way the baby clung at her breast, it was obvious the woman must have been its mother, yet she pried it loose with revulsion as if it were a giant leech. I could now see the bald head, earless and nose-less, etched with interlocking scales like jigsaw puzzle pieces. The child bawled louder, its wail rising to a scream as it kicked and flailed in its mother's grasp as she drew a machete from a belt around her waist. With the stoic ruthlessness of the women in ancient Sparta who hurled malformed newborns off cliffs onto the rocks below, she slashed the baby's throat, nearly severing the head, and cast it into the *cidade de crianças mortas* as if tossing garbage into a landfill. The child flopped onto the other infant cadavers, gushing blood, and before it had ceased twitching, the vultures flocked to pick at its puny carcass.

Cazador whipped out the Desert Eagle .45 that he wore as a sidearm and leveled it at the woman, seemingly intent on carrying out his threat to kill anyone who prevented him from obtaining a live specimen. Then he cursed in Hindi and holstered the weapon again. He'd always prided himself on mastering the profanity of every country he'd ever been to.

"Why?" Jules yelled at the mother who'd just butchered her own offspring, as if the woman could understand her. When the woman simply walked away, Jules stalked back to our guide, who took minuscule sips from his water jug as if savoring a fine Bordeaux. "You!" she commanded Cazador. "Ask him why they do this."

The poacher snorted with annoyance, but repeated her inquiry in Portuguese. The guide responded with an angry outburst, spitting words and gesticulating fanatically as Cazador translated.

"What do you expect us to do? This land . . . she is cursed. We have nothing . . . no work, no food or drink . . . and our women only give birth to devils. Are we . . . supposed to feed these monsters . . . when we can't even feed ourselves?"

I didn't realize until then that I hadn't seen a single child since we arrived. Not in the village, nor in line at the well. There didn't seem to be anyone under the age of twenty in the vicinity, and I began to wonder just how deep the *cidade de crianças mortas* went, how long they had given birth to nothing but monsters.

"Why don't you leave?" Jules demanded of the guide, gesturing for Cazador to pass on the question.

The *caboclo* gave her an incredulous look. "And go where?" he retorted through Cazador. He spread his arms to indicate the wasteland of the Amazon, but he might just as well have meant the entire planet.

***

Cazador exchanged words of his own with the guide, negotiations that I couldn't understand but which involved the exchange of several more gallons of water. As a result, we secured lodging for the night in the dug-out hovels of our guide and his extended family. Cazador put Jules and me together in one of the underground shelters, more because we were the only gringos in the group than because we were longtime friends.

I could hardly call the place a room, for it was little more than a crawlspace, ten-by-ten, with a ceiling so low I had to squat to keep from hitting my head. Rough branches from fallen trees were bound together and used to reinforce the hard-packed dirt walls. The place stank, but by then so did we, so the smell didn't bother us as much.

The setting of the sun and the insulation provided by the soil around us had cooled the interior temperature from intolerable to merely uncomfortable, so we sat cross-legged on the dirt floor to wolf down our dinner of dry sausage and trail mix, which we washed down with extravagant gulps from our canteens. Jules stripped down to a tank top and boy shorts, and the light of our fluorescent lantern glossed the sweat-dewed skin of her lean legs and pale shoulders with silver. It was like a wet dream come true, except that I was too exhausted and malodorous to do anything about it.

"Ordinarily, I don't pry into my customers' business," I said, for the sake of making conversation, "but what exactly is going on here? Some weird disease? Pollution?"

"No. Evolution." Jules looked straight at me for the first time since leaving the mass grave that afternoon. She seemed as glum as if that pit brimmed with her own fetuses. "We're seeing what may well be our species' only hope of survival."

I jerked a thumb over my shoulder. "You mean those things? You gotta be kidding me. And anyway, isn't evolution supposed to take, like, a zillion years?"

"That's the prevailing wisdom, yes. But back in the eighteenth century, a French naturalist named Jean-Baptiste Lamarck suggested that species mutate in order to better adapt to their environment. Giraffes need to reach the leaves on tall trees, so giraffes develop long necks.

"Then Darwin came along and said, no, mutation is random. It was just a happy accident that some giraffes happened to be born with long necks, allowing them to thrive while all the short-necked giraffes died off."

"You don't believe in natural selection?" I eyed her with mild surprise; she'd always seemed like one of those hard-nosed, no-nonsense science types. "Do think it was—gasp!—*intelligent design?*" I whistled the *Twilight Zone* theme.

She frowned and fidgeted. "Look, all I'm saying is that, in some sense, Lamarck must have been right. When a comet hits your planet and causes an Ice Age in less than ten thousand years—or when greenhouse gases raise the average temperature by a dozen degrees in only a century—you don't have time to roll the dice. You need an adaptive mutation, and you need it *now*. I think there's some unknown biological mechanism in our DNA that senses changes in the environment and alters us to survive in that environment."

I leaned back against the wall and crossed my ankles. "You think those dead kids are *homo superior?* Please!"

Jules started to get mad. "*If they were allowed to live*, they'd be way more suited to this climate than you and I. I mean, look at us!" She tugged on the straps of her perspiration-soaked tank top. "Sweat is a great way to cool off, but look at how much water it wastes. Not good if you're going to be living on a desert planet in the near future.

"Rather than squandering precious moisture on evaporative cooling, those children circulate their blood through that thin, wing-like membrane beneath their arms. The tiny capillaries release heat into the surrounding air before returning the blood to lower the body's internal temperature. All without losing a drop of water."

I chuckled. "Like Cazador's air-cooled car engines." Her ideas were incredible, but they made a crazy kind of sense. "But if these are the future of the human race, why worry about them? Why not just kick back and wait for them to take over?"

"Because, as we saw today, humans are the only species that can choose *not* to adapt. They're afraid of change, even if that change is necessary for their existence. That's why we have to protect these new mutants before they're exterminated by their own parents or penned up in zoos by humanitarians like your friend Cazador."

"Okay, for the last time, Cazador is *not* my friend—"

Speak of the devil. Cazador chose that very moment to jump down into the hollow of our underground shanty and stick his head inside. I don't know if he heard me disavow him, but he made a harsh gesture for silence as he entered, then motioned for us to follow him. He carried his dart rifle in the crook of one arm.

We scrabbled out of the dirt hovel and onto the level ground of the village. The night was clear but still hot, the air as thick as sorghum around us. The rays from a low, full moon made the crisscrossing lattice of dead and dying trees into a black-and-silver bas-relief of shadow and light. We trailed Cazador as he soundlessly zigzagged from one pool of darkness to the next. From behind another tree about ten yards ahead, I saw the *caboclo* who'd served as our guide that afternoon. He beckoned and pointed excitedly at the incline of a tilted samauma.

A small silhouette, about the size of a Doberman, scaled the trunk's diagonal on all fours. When it reached a height almost level with our view of the moon, it stood on two feet. Now it appeared to have the proportions of a five-year-old boy. Then the figure raised its arms to pull taut the translucent membranes on its sides. Illuminated by the moonlight shining through the rubbery skin of the wings, the delicate tracery of veins pulsed with liquid life.

At least one of us gasped. It might even have been me. I remembered one of the other notations in Jules's list of possible adaptations: *Nocturnal.*

Cazador raised the barrel of his rifle to eye-level, angled up at the strange prodigy perched on the tree trunk. Just as he squeezed off his shot, however, Jules let out a shout. The creature leapt off into darkness as the dart whistled into oblivion.

Cazador expended only a split-second to glare at Jules with murderous fury before charging up to the spot where the thing had disappeared. With a small LED flashlight, he scanned the ground until he located a set of small, human-like footprints. We didn't have to track the prints far to see that they looped back toward the village.

For a minute, Cazador appeared to be muttering to himself in Portuguese. Then I saw him adjust the earpiece of his headset and realized he must be communicating with his men via shortwave. Next, he questioned the *caboclo*, whom he'd evidently recruited as his personal ferret. I caught enough to glean the gist of their exchange.

Was there anyone in the village without a family? Cazador wanted to know. Someone who could hide such a monster from the neighbors.

Yes, the *caboclo* replied, there was a widow who lived alone, whose husband had died about four years earlier.

Take me to her, Cazador commanded.

A few minutes later, we were all arrayed outside one of the village's dugout shanties. Cazador's four hired thugs had already stationed themselves around the hole. Each of them held a tranquilizer gun. Despite their stolid stance, they betrayed a restless anxiety I'd noted ever since they'd seen the mutant creatures in the pit that afternoon.

"*You* stay here," Cazador said to Jules when she tried to accompany him into the widow's home.

He nodded for me to join him, however, so together we descended into the hovel without bothering to announce ourselves. Almost immediately, a panicked woman appeared in the beam of Cazador's flashlight as he ducked through the threshold. She shook her head frantically, pleading in a barrage of syllables and flailing her hands this way and that to indicate the empty floor and vacant corners.

Cazador ignored her. Advancing in a crouch, he swept his flashlight beam around the perimeter of the room. A few filthy rags of clothing, some meager piles of food in wooden bowls— nothing more. Struck by a sudden impulse, he shone the light straight up at the low roof above him.

In a recessed cubbyhole, a small face patched with large scales flinched at the sudden glare.

Cazador fumbled to aim his rifle into the cramped space, but the creature pounced right on top of his head. He floundered and fell to the floor as the thing scurried out the door.

"*Foge tu, Nando, foge tu!*" the woman shrieked.

Nando, she called it. Short for Fernando. Unlike the mothers who had cast their offspring into the waste-heap of the *cidade de crianças mortas*, she had named her extraordinary child and nurtured it as her son.

Cazador clambered out of the widow's hovel and looked at his men. When they looked back at him with dumb, abashed expressions, he exploded, berating them for allowing their quarry to escape. Then, with frightening ease, he reassumed his affable swagger.

"Well, my *friend*," he said to me, stressing the word, "it seems we may bring back our live specimen after all, eh? We begin the hunt at first light." He gave an ingratiating bow to Jules. "Dr. Pierce, I can have one of my assistants drive you back to Manaus—"

"I'm coming with you." She crossed her arms to cut off debate.

A hint of menace sharpened Cazador's tone. "I do not think that would be a good idea. Out in the woods, with no one around for miles—almost anything could happen. I would hate for any harm to come to you."

"I paid for this expedition," she retorted. "And I'll top any fee you're getting from someone else."

I doubted she had that kind of money, but she didn't blink as she said it.

Cazador silently sized her up. "Very well, then," he concluded, as if accepting a challenge to a duel. "Tomorrow, at dawn."

While the rest of us went to grab a few hours of fitful sleep, Cazador's four thugs lingered behind, whispering to one another with worried faces and nodding. I should have known something was up. They were ne'er-do-wells whom Cazador had most likely pulled from the streets of São Paulo. Deeply superstitious, they had taken the job thinking they would be hunting an animal, not a chimera that resembled a demon from a Hieronymus Bosch painting.

In the blood-orange light of morning, when Cazador returned to the dry gulch of the Rio Negro to ready his gear, he found that all four off-road vehicles were gone. No doubt they would fetch a good price for the mutinous henchmen—as would the water they contained.

Cazador gaped at the empty gully in a state of strangled outrage, then called the thieves bastards in Swahili, Farsi, Afrikaans, and Quechua—and those were just the languages I recognized. Although he was a master at anticipating the wiles of animals, the actions of human beings often confounded him.

"We can probably make it back to Manaus on foot," I suggested when he calmed down.

"*You* go to Manaus." Cazador shouldered his backpack. "I will capture the creature."

"But you have no traps. And no water."

He patted the canteen strapped to his pack. "I have more water than *it* has."

I turned to Jules, hoping she would listen to reason.

"If he's going, I have to go," she said. She waggled her half-empty water bottle. "Maybe we can top off at the well."

I groaned. If she went, then I had to go.

We set out sleep-deprived and dehydrated, muscles screaming with every step, and I knew it would only get worse. As it turned out, Jules and I didn't get a chance to top off at the well, because Cazador hiked at such a relentless pace that we had to keep up or lose him entirely.

For a while, I nursed the vain hope that Nando had so much of a head start that Cazador would lose the trail and give up. But the poacher was as keen and tenacious as a bloodhound, and every time the dotted line of small footsteps petered out, Cazador would scour the vicinity until he found some telltale droppings or a papery peeling of sloughed-off skin. We traveled during the heat of the day because Cazador needed the light to check for signs of his quarry. Since he believed Nando to be nocturnal, the poacher planned to catch the mutant asleep during sunlit hours.

Nando's path led inland from the dried-up river, and the further we followed it, the more arid the environment became. There were no wells here, for there were no longer any people to need them.

"It will work to our advantage," Cazador assured us with unshakable hubris. "We are herding it to where it must come to us for water or die."

In retrospect, I think the truth was just the opposite: Nando was instinctively luring us onto *his* turf, where his natural adaptation would give him the edge against us.

Our rations of water diminished from a capful an hour to one every four hours, to one every six hours. Even when we got a drink, it seemed as if we didn't swallow the mouthful of liquid so much as absorb it directly through our cotton-numb tongues. By the end of the second day, Jules had drained her water bottle, and I shared what little I had left with her. We licked sweat off our unwashed forearms to reclaim what moisture we could and hobbled along, leaning on each other like contestants in a demented three-legged race.

Cazador marched on in front of us with the implacability of a machine. But by the third day, I could see him falter. His gaze lost its focus at times, and he would stagger a step out of line. On those rare occasions when he permitted himself a sip from his canteen, he took a drunken swig as if from a flagon of whisky. Hours passed without any of us saying a word, our mouths too raw for speech.

With our water exhausted, I thought Cazador would have no choice but to turn back. Even if he didn't, I urged Jules to leave him to his fate. The mutant child was most likely already dead, I told her as we talked every night before dropping into unconsciousness. Even if the creature was still alive, Cazador would die looking for it, and there was no reason we should perish with him. I think she was about to relent when Cazador gave a rusty but triumphant shout.

Before us, the tiny footprints we'd been tracking veered into a niche formed by the canted trunk of another collapsed samauma tree. For a hunt, it was an anticlimactic ending, for no cornered monster with gnashing fangs lay in wait there. Only the forlorn figure of a small, naked boy, his legs and arms drawn up to his chest, his eyes shut in the sweet blankness of innocent sleep. He may have had strangely veined membranes under his arms and a thick, reptilian hide, but he was simply a little boy for all that.

Nando.

Cazador laid down his dart rifle, for he could tell that he would have no need of it. The child remained a petrified lump as the poacher dragged the immobile form out of its crevice and onto the bare, parched ground. The body looked desiccated, gray and stiff with dehydration as if mummified.

Cazador muttered something in Mandarin Chinese that I knew must be an obscenity. Then he rasped a laugh and turned to me, wearing a wan semblance of his usual cocksure grin.

"I guess we do not bring the creature back alive this time, my friend," he croaked. "But we do not leave empty-handed, eh? A nice specimen here, and not too heavy to carry. I think it might even fit in my pack, no?"

Jules hung her head, her face in her hands. If she'd had enough water in her for tears, I think she would have wept. Cazador calmly started emptying his pack to make room for his consolation prize. I just stood there, knees quivering as I struggled to remain upright, too wrung out to feel much of anything except thirst. Maybe that was why I was the first to see the forest move, as if it were stirring back to life.

Initially it seemed like a heat mirage—a slight wavering of the moribund landscape around us. Then pieces of the dried wood and arid ground detached themselves and unfolded to full height, the earth-tones of their skin shifting tint, chameleon-like, to visibility. Yet another advantageous adaptation: camouflage.

Cazador had made a crucial miscalculation. He was not hunting a lone animal, as he thought, but rather one member of an entirely new race.

More than two dozen of them surrounded us. They were all fully grown, the broad chests of the males and the full breasts of the females all plated with the rough but supple diamond-shaped scales. Obviously, Nando hadn't been the only—or even the first—mutant child to survive and escape to freedom. Perhaps their stunted noses had scented some pheromone signal that one of their kind was in distress, or perhaps Nando had called to them in some private tongue that we would never understand. Whichever it was, they had come to his aid.

As one, they raised their arms and fanned out their veined membranes, panting in unison. Whether it was a gesture of greeting or of warning was impossible to tell from their smooth, expressionless faces. Many of them held weapons: wooden spears and large machetes that they had either fashioned themselves or stolen from the scattered conclaves of humans in the area. The peculiar grandeur of the sight inspired such awe that, for a moment, Cazador himself could only gawk in dumb amazement.

Then he must have sensed either overwhelming danger or a perverse opportunity to bag a live specimen, for despite the fact we were grossly outnumbered, he dove to retrieve his tranquilizer dart rifle. Jules moved faster, though, kicking the gun out of his reach.

Cazador howled and drew his .45. If they had been alone, I'm sure he would have shot her. But the circle of mutants contracted around us, spear- and knife-points raised, and he had no time. He wheeled on them and fired, his unerring aim sending a bullet smack into the ridged chest of one of the young males. The thing reeled and dropped.

I knew Cazador would take down another creature for every cartridge left in his pistol. I also knew he didn't have enough bullets left to shoot them all and that he would get us all killed in the process. With the last of my strength, I sprang on him, grabbing hold of his gun arm and letting my overbalanced weight slam us both down to the ground.

We'd barely hit the dust when I felt scaly palms seize my biceps, tugging me off Cazador. *Well, that's it*, I thought with some relief, expecting the sting of a machete across my Adam's apple. A fitting punishment, really, given how many of their throats we humans had slit.

Instead, they merely dragged me back a few feet and left me sitting in the dirt. Their mercy did not extend to Cazador. As the poacher thrashed and cursed them in a dozen different languages, four of the beings each took hold of one of his limbs and held him, supine and spread-eagled, on the ground. A fifth, the largest and beefiest of the males, raised his machete over his head and arced it down on Cazador's neck in a crisp chop. It took two more hacks before the head finally came off.

Before too much blood could jet out of the severed neck's straggling arteries, the creatures picked the decapitated corpse up by its ankles and inverted it over the papery bundle of skin and bones that had been Nando. The instant the first spatters rained upon the crinkled hide, capillary action within the skin absorbed the moisture. A stain spread out from around the expanding puddle of liquid as the pallid gray scales darkened to a healthier brown hue. Shriveled wattles filled and rounded to smoothness, and the curled limbs stretched out as if released from the confines of a chrysalis. It was then that I remembered the African lungfish—how it can remain in a state of suspended animation for up to four years during a time of drought, then revive as soon as it comes into contact with water.

Nando soaked up every drop of Cazador's blood so thoroughly that, by the time the boy opened his tight-lidded eyes, his hide was not even damp. He jumped to his feet, his gaze as bright and restless as any toddler who has just awakened from a nap. A female extended her hand to him, and he scampered to embrace her thigh.

The mutant warriors carried Cazador's carcass away on their shoulders, for what purpose I hesitated to speculate; no doubt, such fresh meat would not go to waste. The large, stocky one picked up the head and held it out to me, neck tipped up, as if offering a cold beer.

Jules doubled over, dry-heaving. She clapped both hands over her mouth to keep herself from retching, however. Good girl. We couldn't afford to lose a drop of fluid under these conditions. How far was it back to the nearest well? Two days' journey?

Getting up onto my knees, I peered at the head. Cazador's eyes had rolled up under the open lids, and I imagined that his mouth still bobbed for breath. I tried to swallow, but my throat felt like sandpaper all the way down to my gut. Refusing this token of goodwill would not only be a bad move diplomatically; it might deprive us of our only source of water for the return trip. Recalling stories of shipwrecked sailors who survived by drinking their dead comrades' blood, I scrambled to grab the empty canteen from my pack. I'm ashamed to admit that, as the creature decanted the head's blood into my flask, I couldn't help but lick my chapped lips.

Still clutching Cazador's scalp by the hair, the creature gave my shoulder an indulgent pat with his free hand and walked off beside his fellows. Only little Nando lagged behind, cocking his head to peer at Jules and me in our sweaty, thirsting exhaustion. Not with fear, for we were no longer a threat. Rather, with curiosity and a little puzzlement, the way we would look at a quagga or a dodo, clucking our tongues and shaking our heads, wondering at how such ungainly, hapless creatures ever came into existence. The newest exhibit in the Menagerie of the Maladapted.

Then Nando ran off to be with his own kind in the world they would one day inherit.

Street Runes

As Andrea drove to work that morning, she saw that the taggers had struck a house north of Sequoia Avenue.

Almost in reflex, she slowed the Toyota and peered out the dirty driver's-side window at the marked house as if passing a mangled auto wreck. A plump Mexican woman stood on the front walk and complained in frenetic gestures and staccato speech to the white cop beside her, who nodded and took notes on a clipboard. The woman pointed with agitation to the spaghetti-tangled patterns of black spray paint that covered the face of the cottage-style house behind her. Against the pink stucco of the wall, the marks bore a perverse resemblance to tattoos.

They're moving in, Andrea thought as she drove on. This was the first house she'd seen them strike on this side of the freeway overpass, which crossed Harper Boulevard. It wouldn't be long before they grew bold enough to invade the upscale neighborhoods north of Longview.

As she pulled into the teachers' parking lot at Morrison High, she wondered if any of her students were involved, but quickly suppressed the idea. She found it hard enough to maintain her enthusiasm without suspecting all her kids of delinquency.

Clusters of teenagers loitered on the concrete walkways between the rows of classrooms. The girls struck poses of supermodel insouciance as hormonal young males clowned and competed for their attention. Some of the boys wore their baggy pants low around their hips, which elongated their torsos and stunted their legs until they looked like the distorted figures in carnival mirrors. Andrea saw several of the kids hide their lit cigarettes as she approached them, but she pretended not to notice—she needed to save her disciplinary energy for later in the day. Mocking smiles on their faces, they whispered to one another in conspiratorial mirth as she passed by. Clutching her file folders to her chest, she kept her gaze downcast until she entered the sanctuary of the faculty lounge.

"—the heck am I supposed to do? Hold back the entire ninth grade?" Brent Waller, the English department chairman, complained as she stepped through the door.

Curt Martin, the chemistry teacher, shrugged and took a swig of coffee from his I ♥ FRIDAYS mug. "Hey, that's what the curve is for. If I flunked all the ones who deserved it, my class size would double every semester."

Not wanting to get drawn into the discussion, Andrea headed straight for the copy machine to run off some worksheets.

"Hell, I'd send the seniors back to grade school if I could," Waller went on, running a hand through his collar-length gray hair. "These kids should be reading Dick and Jane, not *Romeo and Juliet.*"

"Oh, well. Nothing a few thousand dollars of computer equipment can't fix." Martin flashed a taut grin. His eyes pivoted toward Andrea, the slate gray irises peering out from the sagging draperies of his eyelids. "But hey—young turks like Andie here are gonna drum some knowledge into these kids. Isn't that right, Andie?"

"Or die trying." She gave a smile that felt more like a grimace, grabbed the stack of worksheets that had accumulated in the copier's out-basket, and left the lounge without even retrieving her original from the machine.

She hated being called "Andie."

A bank of lemon-yellow lockers along one wall of the English department bore a meaningless squiggle of black paint similar to the one on the house she'd driven past that morning. It had been there almost a month now, for the janitorial staff had tired of painting over the marks, which inevitably reappeared within days after the most recent lemon-yellow coat had dried. Andrea shook her head, more out of puzzlement than disapproval. What was it supposed to mean? If it said "School Sucks" or "Metallica Rules" or even "Fuck You," it would at least make sense. Instead, it looked like the crayon scribble of a frustrated four-year-old. The thought that these kids couldn't even write well enough to vandalize properly depressed her further, and she succumbed to an increasing sense of futility as she floundered through her first five classes.

A late September heat wave had descended on Southern California, and the air in the classroom was thick and stagnant. Her sixth-period students slouched in their seats, too listless even to talk among themselves. Sweat collected in the small of her back, and the loose fabric of her dress clung to her skin as she stretched to write on the top of the blackboard.

"Now that we know how to separate subjects and predicates, can anyone tell me what the dividing point is in this example?" Andrea asked in a tone of strained cheerfulness, pointing with her chalk to the sentence she'd just scrawled.

They looked back at her with the unseeing eyes of beached fish, the dulled gaze of dying brains. No one spoke a word.

Scanning the rows of blank faces, she saw Luis at the back of the room, slumped over his desk and doodling in a ragged spiral notebook. He'd been one of her favorite students ever since she'd read "The Tell-Tale Heart" aloud in class at the beginning of the year. Luis did an amazing sketch that depicted the narrator burying the old man's dismembered body under the floorboards with the glistening heart looming large in the background. It was morbid, but at least it proved that he'd actually listened to her. The fact that he wasn't paying the slightest attention to her now focused the irritation she felt toward the whole class, and she directed her vexation at him.

"Luis, can you read this sentence and tell us its subject and predicate?"

He sat up and blinked at her as if waking from a doze. "Huh?"

A ripple of laughter ran through the room.

Andrea stalked back to Luis's desk and attempted to snatch

the notebook away from him. In a sudden panic, he crossed his arms over the notebook and held it fast to the desktop. "No, Miz Thomas!"

Her jaw tightened. "Let me see," she commanded.

Luis regarded her for a moment with large brown eyes that were quick and liquid, then took his hands off the notebook and slumped back in his chair with a defeated look.

There on the dog-eared, college-ruled paper was a curlicued snarl of heavy black lines, traced in ink with calligraphic care.

The figure's resemblance to the graffiti Andrea had seen on the house rekindled her suspicion that her own students might be the vandals. Her annoyance with Luis deepened into a sense of betrayal, and she ripped the page out of the notebook and crumpled it in front of his face. "Don't you ever waste class time on this crap again! You understand?"

He nodded, mute.

She threw the wadded paper into the wastebasket by her desk in disgust, then returned to the chalkboard. "Since no one seems to know how to divide this sentence, I guess I'll have to start from the beginning . . ."

She ended the class with the threat of a pop quiz later in the week, and spent the rest of the afternoon in a sour mood. Though she headed home with a six-inch stack of papers to grade, she seriously considered blowing off the chore that night and drowning her sorrows in white wine and *Seinfeld* reruns.

The marks marring the house on Harper had blackened like dried scabs in the smog-stained sunlight of late afternoon. They tugged at Andrea's peripheral vision as she drove past.

She abruptly stomped on the brake.

Rolling down the window, she squinted at the squiggle spray-painted on the house's front door. A large loop rose from the central tangle of lines, rather like the top of a cursive "S," while two matching spirals curled at the base of the figure.

With a inexplicable sense of urgency, Andrea hung a U and

headed back to Morrison.

When she returned to the English department, she saw the janitor's cart parked two doors down from hers and knew she was probably too late. Nevertheless, she dug her keys out of her purse, let herself into her classroom, and rushed over to the wastebasket.

It was empty.

Disappointment mingled with relief. The familiarity of the graffiti on the house gnawed at her, and now she'd never know if her suspicions were correct. Unless . . .

She stepped back outside and looked toward the janitor's cart. A large trash can lined with a plastic bag sat on its front end.

With a self-conscious glance to either side to make sure no one was watching, Andrea approached the cart and peered into the can. Wrinkling her nose, she gingerly nudged aside some crumpled Taco Bell wrappers and a leaking soft drink cup to see if she could spot a wad of notebook paper somewhere amidst the mass of discarded photocopies at the bottom of the can.

"Help you with something, Miss Thomas?"

Andrea flushed as she lifted her head from the garbage can to see the elderly janitor grinning at her. "Oh, I'm sorry, Alvin. I . . . thought I'd thrown away a student's paper by mistake. I was hoping it might still be here."

"Well, go ahead and look all you want," he urged, an amiable North Carolina twang to his voice. He bowed and gestured to the can with one grimy hand. "My trash is your trash!" She chuckled and thanked him, and Alvin obligingly dumped the can's contents on the pavement for her. A tightly crushed ball of notebook paper rolled out and came to rest on one side of the heap.

She took the ball and picked at its tucked edges until it unfurled.

"That it?" Alvin asked.

Her heart sank as she stared at the figure on the crinkled sheet. A knot of twisted lines with a loop like the top of a cursive "S" and two matching spiral tails. "Yeah, this is it."

***

Andrea looked forward to sixth period the following day with both impatience and dread. She didn't want to risk alienating Luis, the only student with whom she'd established a real connection; but if he was involved in a gang, she felt obliged to confront him about it before he ended up dead or in jail.

The bell rang to end class, and the students crowded toward the door. While the rest of the kids chattered to one another, Luis lagged alone and silent at the back of the bunch, clasping his dog-eared notebook to his side. As with most adolescent outcasts, a small circle of isolation seemed to surround him.

Andrea positioned herself in the battered wooden office chair behind her desk, fixing her gaze upon him until he happened to make eye contact. "Luis, I want you to stay after for a few minutes."

The end-of-class chatter dropped three decibels, and the empty circle around Luis widened. "I gotta go, Miz Thomas," he pleaded, his feet shuffling as if ready to leave without him. "I gotta help my mama."

"It'll only take a few minutes. Have a seat." She indicated the small chair beside hers, which the kids called "the Deep Shit Seat."

Chewing on his upper lip, Luis trudged to the chair and sagged onto it.

Andrea waited for the rest of the class to exit before speaking. "First of all, I want to apologize for tearing that page out of your notebook the other day. I shouldn't have done that."

Luis didn't respond.

She opened the top drawer of her desk and pulled out the rumpled sheet of paper, now pressed and smoothed to the texture of shed snakeskin. "I like this design," she said, pointing to the cursive pattern on the page. "How did you come up with it?"

He remained as immobile as a manikin, his eyes focused inward.

"I saw one just like it on a house the other day. What does it mean?"

His gaze shifted abruptly, but not toward her. Instead, he peered out the open classroom doorway. Andrea went to the door to see what had caught his attention.

Outside, two of her "problem children" leaned against the opposite wall, watching her classroom. A failed senior with spiky bleached hair, Eric was merely killing time until his eighteenth birthday freed him from school and unleashed him on society at large. Beside him stood Miguel, a short, quick-tempered Chicano. His biceps ringed with tattoos of barbed wire, Miguel compensated for his lack of height with bodybuilding and machismo. Together, they looked like L.A.'s answer to Laurel and Hardy. She scowled at them and kicked up the doorstop. As the door eased shut, cutting them off from view, she saw Eric point at her and whisper in Miguel's ear.

Andrea turned back to Luis, who waited with the resigned dejection of a dog expecting punishment. "Are they part of your gang?" she asked.

He shook his head, and his mouth opened as if he wanted to correct her, but he didn't speak.

"Come on, level with me! What is this?" She thrust the drawing in front of his face.

He shrugged. "Nothing."

"What does it mean?"

"Nothing! Okay? It don't mean nothing! I just made it up."

"*Doesn't* mean *anything*. And if you made it up, then you put it on that house." She cast the paper aside and reached for the phone on her desk. "I'm going to have to tell your parents about this."

"*Mamacita!* No!" Dropping his prized notebook, Luis leapt from his chair and seized hold of her hand, pushing the receiver back into its cradle. "You can't!"

Andrea felt his hands trembling as they touched her, and she let go of the phone. She glanced from his pleading face to the notebook, which had fallen open on the floor.

Its pages teamed with ornate, incomprehensible designs.

She stooped to pick it up, but he snatched it and hugged it to his chest.

Placing a hand on his shoulder, Andrea knelt until the two of them were eye-level. "Luis, I want to help. But if you won't let me, I'm going to have to call your mother."

He considered the alternatives a moment, and his expression turned sly. "You won't tell nobody, will you?"

"Anybody." She shook her head. "No."

"If anybody asks, we talked about that test I flunked last week, okay?"

"Whatever you say." She lowered her hand to the notebook, gently prying it away from his chest. "May I see?"

He grudgingly lowered his arms. Andrea surveyed the web of intersecting curlicues on the open page, different from the one she'd seen before. "What is this? Is this your gang's symbol?"

Luis actually laughed at that. "Nah. It's a sentence."

Andrea's scalp prickled. "I don't understand . . ."

"See?" Luis pointed to a twist on the upper right side of the figure, then zigzagged his finger from loop to curl throughout the design as he translated. "'The . . . time . . . of . . . the . . . New . . . Lord . . . has . . . come.' Betcha can't divide that sentence, can you, Miz Thomas?" He gave a condescending little snicker.

Andrea frowned as she retraced the path his finger had drawn through the maze of lines. "Luis, this isn't funny."

"No, really! That's what it says. Here, look—" He flipped a few pages, then held the open notebook out for her to see. "I started to rewrite that story we read—the one about the guy who gets walled up in the cellar. Pretty cool, huh?" He grinned with pride.

The page he displayed was nearly black with ink, the inter-locking lacework of lines so dense that it gave the sheet the tex-ture of parchment.

"I didn't know a lot of the words, so I had to make some stuff up," Luis explained. "Like the name of that wine."

"Amontillado," she murmured absently, squinting at the drawing as though it were an eye chart which refused to come into focus. "Where did you learn to . . . write like this?"

"From Him." Luis pointed to the crumpled sheet on her desk.

Andrea shivered as she looked again at the symbol. "Who is 'he'?"

"The New Lord." Luis indicated the paper. "That's His Name. He don't let us say it, though."

"Who is 'us'?" she asked, her own grammar faltering.

"You know—everybody." He swept his hand toward all the empty desks where her students sat.

"But your mom doesn't know about this . . ."

Luis shifted in his chair. "No. He don't like us to tell nobody like mothers and teachers and shit. That's why you gotta swear not to tell nobody. They'd hurt Mama if she knew." His face darkened. "They'd hurt you, too."

"I see." Andrea folded her hands so Luis wouldn't see them quiver. "I'll promise that, if you promise to stop spray-painting people's houses. Deal?"

The boy mulled over the proposition. "Okay."

"All right, then. You may go now."

Notebook in hand, Luis moved to leave, but paused at the door. "Miz Thomas?"

"Hmm?"

"Could we do some more of that Poe guy?"

She gave him a slight smile. "Sure. If you want."

He allowed her a brief glimpse of his big front teeth in return and opened the door. Sticking his head out like a wary tortoise, he scanned the exterior walkway before stepping outside. As the door clicked shut behind him, a breeze blew across Andrea's desk, rustling the Name of the New Lord.

She was about to ball up the rumpled sheet and throw it back into the trash, but, nagged by a intuitive unease, she set it to one side of her desk. As she graded a stack of worksheets she'd collected earlier that day, she glanced back from time to time at the labyrinthine figure on the parchment-like page and shook her head. A new language? These kids couldn't even spell plain English, much less some script that made Arabic seem simple by comparison. Luis's imagination had turned gang vandalism into a secret culture.

Still, even as she lay in bed that night, Andrea couldn't keep the images of Luis's strange script out of her head. Above her, the stuccoed ceiling resembled a page of manic Braille, its patterns pulsing with indecipherable intelligence.

She didn't sleep much that night.

The following morning on her way to work, she almost rear-ended the car in front of her when she nodded off while waiting at a stoplight. Her eyes felt swollen and sticky, and every time she blinked, the promise of cool unconsciousness washed over her. She downed three cups of sludgy coffee in the faculty lounge to try to wake up, and the caffeine made her gaze quiver and her stomach constrict.

The day's first five periods crept past with narcotic monotony. Listless in the stifling atmosphere of the classroom's bottled air, Andrea droned through her lessons on auto-pilot. Fanning themselves with folded worksheets, the students watched her with all the comprehension of monkeys in a zoo. Or maybe she was the monkey, gibbering pointlessly while they regarded her pathetic attempts to communicate with amused contempt.

As she scrawled on the chalkboard, Andrea heard a couple of the girls giggle behind her.

"All right, that's enough," she snapped, turning to face the roomful of smirking faces. "Open your literature books to the story called 'The Lottery,' which you should all have read by now . . ."

Surveying the room, Andrea spotted a note that was working its way to the rear of the class. When it got to the last row, Josie, the resident fashion-plate, actually put down her nail file for a moment to slide the slip of paper onto Luis's desk. Luis tensed in his chair as he glanced down at the note. The whites of his eyes grew large, and his nut-brown skin appeared to pale three shades.

"Ah! Let's see what we have here." Andrea stalked forward and seized the slip. It was a page ripped from the literature book, its text obscured by a twisted figure that someone had superimposed on the script with a thick black marker.

"All right! What's this supposed to mean?" she demanded, displaying the page.

The class erupted in laughter. Luis was the only one to remain silent. He sat frozen in the chair, motionless except for a tiny tremor which ran through his bony frame.

"I'm not kidding! I want to know who did this."

The laughter swelled, and Andrea's voice cracked as she shouted over the din. "Okay, that's it! Everyone turn in your books right now! When I find out where this page came from, one of you is gonna spend a week in detention!"

She stood watch as the students filed past and tossed their copies of the text onto a haphazard pile on her desk. Eric, she noticed, lagged at the back of the line, and when the bell rang to end sixth period, he headed straight for the door.

She moved to block his exit. "Where's yours?"

He shrugged. "I lost it."

"Find it. By tomorrow."

He leaned forward, emphasizing the difference in height between them, and challenged her with cold, flat eyes. "Or what?"

Instinctively, Andrea took a step backward. The reality of his towering figure and broad shoulders fully impressed itself upon her for the first time. This wasn't a schoolchild standing in front of her, she realized—it was a seventeen-year-old man, a foot taller and sixty pounds heavier than she was. During the day, she could send him to the vice principal's office, maybe even make him stay after school and copy definitions out of the dictionary. But what about at night, on the streets? What power did she have over him then?

She fought to keep her gaze and voice steady, but both betrayed her anxiety. "Just find it. Or else."

Eric stretched his thin lips into an icy smirk. "Yeah. Sure."

He shouldered his way past her and left the room. She saw him glance back and grin at her as he walked away, as though he knew she was watching him.

Andrea let out her pent-up breath and looked down at the crumpled page in her hand. *Much madness is divinest sense . . .* The rest of Emily Dickinson's words had been buried by the crisscrossing web of the black glyph.

"Luis, do you know what this means?" She held the figure up for him to see, but found herself alone in the room.

She stayed after school for more than two hours, a vague apprehension making her reluctant to leave the shelter of the classroom. She first went through all the literature books heaped on her desk to see if she could find the one that was missing a page of Emily Dickinson. While the incriminating text never turned up, she discovered to her dismay that pages of nearly every book bore the same sort of infantile scribbling, defaced with pens, pencils, even crayons.

Disheartened, Andrea graded papers in a desultory manner until Alvin poked his head into the room for the fifth time to see if he could come in and clean. Finally getting the hint that it was time to go home, she collected her work, told Alvin the trash was his for the taking, then headed out to the parking lot.

There, just a few yards from her Toyota, lay Luis's notebook, its pages ruffling in the wind like the splayed feathers of a dead bird.

Andrea glanced around the deserted parking lot in a sudden panic, as if she had found Luis's severed hand lying there on the asphalt instead. Miguel and Eric must have really frightened him to make him drop his artwork, she thought, as she stooped and picked up the notebook. Well, she'd put some fear into those boys tomorrow.

She idly flipped through Luis's drawings and rococo designs, smiling when she came across the "Tell-Tale Heart" illustration. The other sketches, all done with a black ball-point pen, were equally macabre: a wolf-headed demon raking a naked woman's body with talons shaped like switch-blades; a swarm of gnomes gleefully piercing an emaciated junkie with dozens of syringe needles; a gaseous wraith swooping over a cityscape, trailing a cloud of contamination that blotted out the sun. Above the heads of each of these figures rose comic-strip balloons that held more of those cryptic scribbles, some punctuated with the inverted exclamation points used in Spanish.

Andrea shook her head, her smile gone. Poor kid must have been abused to wind up with such a morbid imagination. No wonder the violence of street gangs attracted him.

As she thumbed past sections filled with incomprehensible scribbles, the notebook, as if by habit, opened to a central illustration of a looming, hooded figure. Luis had painstakingly filled in the entire cloak of its body with black ink save for the eyes, which were a vacant white. The figure stood before what appeared to be an old Spanish church or mission whose walls were tapestried with ornate graffiti, and at the spectre's feet a mass of tiny supplicants raised their arms in adulation.

Brainwashing, she told herself, her scalp prickling. Worship the gang leader as though he's a god. Wasn't that how all cults worked? They probably even had their own rituals, their own initiation, their own catechism.

Their own language.

The picture crystallized the concern she'd felt for Luis all afternoon, and almost without realizing, Andrea turned around and headed back to her classroom, her stride quickening to a run.

Once inside the room, Andrea hurriedly flipped open the grade book on her desk and scanned her student list as she picked up the phone. She dialed 9 to get out of the school's system, then punched in the number she'd recorded beside Luis's name on her roll sheet.

The phone at the other end rang six times, giving Andrea ample time to feel like an idiot for calling and to consider hanging up before anyone could answer. She held on, however, until a gruff male voice came on the line. *"Bueno."*

Andrea's mouth hung open, and she felt her face flush. "Um— is Luis there?"

"Que? Luis? Quien es?" The voice sounded suspicious.

Andrea hastily attempted to stitch together a few fragments of the high school Spanish she could remember. *"Soy . . .* uh *. . . maestra.* Ms. Thomas. *Esta Luis?"*

Andrea evidently convinced the voice that she knew the language, for it rattled off a rapid series of questions, then waited for her reply. She understood maybe one word out of five, tops. *"Lo siento—lo siento!"* She hung up the receiver, and covered her burning face with her hands.

That went well, she thought with a sigh. What next? Call the police? And tell them what? "I think one of my students is in trouble, officer. I don't know where he is or what he's doing, but he likes to draw disgusting pictures. Look into it, won't you?" The only real evidence she had that Luis was in any actual danger was the fact that he had dropped his prized notebook. With no more than that to go on, she'd done about all she could do. Sorry, Luis, but you're on your own now, kid.

God, she was beginning to sound like Curt Martin. There had to be *something* else she could do. If only she could give the police some real information about the gang: who was involved, what they did, where they hung out . . .

Prompted by a dim recollection, Andrea snatched up the notebook and pawed through it to the picture of the robed figure and its adoring congregation. She scrutinized the background behind the ominous form, the building with its Spanish-mission architecture and graffiti-covered walls. The cupola on its roof displayed a pockmarked clock-face with Roman numerals. The hands of the clock stood at twenty past ten.

She knew this place. It was the abandoned San Martin train station in the old downtown district. A few years back, the city had considered restoring the thirties-era building and making it part of the Metrorail system, but they ultimately discarded the plan due to the cost of the project and the crime in the surrounding area. The landmark continued to remain vacant and in disrepair. If she could confirm that this was the gang's meeting site, she might have enough information to get the police involved.

The sun was already sinking below the horizon by the time Andrea finally left Morrison. She skipped her usual turnoff toward home and kept heading south on Harper, descending into the underpass that separated the city's newer, more affluent suburbs from its aging urban district. The freeway bridge arched over her like a triumphal gateway, its concrete columns and embankments decorated with a dizzying patchwork of multi-colored hieroglyphics.

As the car climbed the incline on the other side of the underpass, the stark change in the surrounding landscape made Andrea feel as if she'd just entered a foreign city. Green yards and pleasant houses gave way to gloomy gray façades of brick and cement. Once home to the town's major banks and businesses, the shabby grandeur of these Depression-era buildings now housed thrift stores, cheap hotels, and porn shops. The sidewalks were vacant and the windows were dark.

Instinctively, Andrea rolled up her window and locked her door. The deeper she drove into the downtown area, the more graffiti she saw. Spray-painted snarls adorned each street sign and store front, eclipsing the words they intended to exterminate. In the purple twilight of the city, these symbols seemed to hold the same arcane significance as Chinese characters, Arabic calligraphy, Celtic runes. They made Andrea think of the time she got lost in Koreatown, where every incomprehensible sign she came across served as a reminder that *she* was now the stranger, the outsider, the illiterate.

Situated near the heart of the old city, the train station sulked in the center of a vacant lot, surrounded by a chain-link fence. Its fake adobe face gleamed orange in the light of the street's sodium-vapor lamps. Black patches of graffiti spread over the plaster like a creeping cancer. The clock on its cupola had frozen at twenty past ten.

Andrea parked her car across the street and observed the place for several minutes through her passenger-side window, hoping that she might learn enough from there so that she wouldn't have to leave the safety of her locked vehicle. The site remained silent and deserted as the last ambient light faded from the sky, and Andrea decided that she would need to take a closer look now before it became too dark.

Before she got out of the car, however, she pawed through her handbag and pulled out the can of Mace she'd carried ever since she'd moved to L.A. It wasn't much, but it reassured her nonetheless.

After only a few minutes of searching, she found a place where the skirt of the fence had been peeled back to allow passage underneath. She obviously wasn't the first person to trespass on this property. As she crouched to pass through the opening, though, a disturbing thought occurred to her: if this was the only way in or out, she could easily become trapped.

Shivering, Andrea stood and surveyed the vacant lot, a rectangular patch of hard-packed dirt littered with beer cans, fast-food wrappers, and a few scattered weeds. The fence bordered the entire lot, then disappeared from view behind the train station. While she couldn't see another opening from where she stood, she figured a gang the size of Luis's would have a wider entrance hidden somewhere.

If the gang existed. If she could find the actual location Luis drew in his notebook, that would be proof enough for her. Then she could get the hell out of there and leave the rest to the cops.

Turning her attention toward the station, Andrea guessed that the mural shown in Luis's drawing must be on the rear wall, out of sight of patrolling police cars. She tightened her grip on the Mace can and edged her way around the building.

Luis's black ink sketch could not have prepared Andrea for what she found on the rear wall. A collision of labyrinthine characters exploded across a plaster surface thirty feet high and fifty feet across, covering the boarded windows and chained doors in that side of the building as well. Overlapping twists and filigrees of glaring red and gold and orange meshed into a fresco of frustrated fury, a visual rendering of the animal howl of ignorance. Branded in black on the center of the mural, the now-familiar Name of the New Lord was the eye of cold calm around which the chaos swirled.

Even in the growing darkness, the artwork appeared to possess a stroboscopic phosphorescence, creating the illusion that its intertwining lines shifted and writhed like snakes. Transfixed, Andrea almost failed to hear the murmur of approaching voices, the shifting of gravel beneath many, many feet.

Retreating into the shadows at the side of the building, Andrea peered around the corner at the crowd of silhouettes that advanced toward the station along the rail-bed. They followed the tracks up to the broad platform beneath the mural, and as they drew closer, Andrea recognized several of her students.

But there were many more whom she had never seen. Hundreds more.

All teenaged boys and girls, they clustered into a semicircle around the mural as if awaiting a pronouncement. Having seen more than enough, Andrea was ready to run to her car and drive to the nearest police station.

Then they brought out Luis.

Two burly boys, one of whom she recognized as Miguel, dragged Luis into the center of the gathering and forced him to his knees as he writhed and kicked and let out a strange keening shriek. Andrea next saw Eric emerge from the crowd of spectators to inspect the prisoner. In his right hand, Eric held a can of spray paint, idly shaking it as he circled around Luis, grinning. The crowd grew quiet, and Luis's shriek diminished to a whimper. For a moment, all Andrea could hear was the rhythmic clacking of the paint can. Then Eric lifted the can over his head and shouted a series of sneering nonsense syllables, to which the crowd responded with whoops and whistles.

As they cheered him on, Eric leaned toward Luis and sprayed black paint into both of the smaller boy's eyes. He added a black slash across the mouth, a perverse clown's grin, turning Luis's visage into an ironic smiley face. Miguel dug his fingers into Luis's side to make him scream so that Eric could shoot paint into the boy's open mouth, coating his tongue and teeth.

"STOP!" Startled by the volume of her own voice, Andrea stepped out of hiding to confront the suddenly silent gathering. She knew she didn't stand a chance against all of them, but she had to do something to keep them from killing Luis. With the can of Mace held out at arm's length as though it were a .38 special, she moved toward Eric and Luis's other captors. "Get away from him," she commanded.

Eric grinned, then nodded at Miguel and the other boy. They let go of Luis, who dropped onto the cement, his painted mouth bobbing open in a rasping, asthmatic gasp.

Struggling to mask her fear with cool authority, Andrea surveyed the multitude of mute, impassive faces which regarded her. "I already called the cops," she lied. "They should be here any second."

No one moved to threaten her, and Andrea briefly wondered if her bluff had actually worked. Her hope evaporated as a torrent of laughter rolled through the crowd. It was just like in the classroom, she realized, angry tears welling in her eyes. Only now they didn't have to wait until she turned her back to jeer at her.

Still, none of them tried to attack her. Instead, they began to chant a succession of discordant, slurred squeals and clicks and screeches, like the chittering of a locust swarm. At first, the din sounded as formless as white noise, the verbal equivalent of radio static, but as the teens' voices rose in chorus, Andrea discerned a pattern in their vocalizations, a mantra.

An invocation.

Andrea dropped her can of Mace and clamped her hands over her ears. Their alien tongue sent surges of visceral nausea throughout her body, as if the grating of chalk against a blackboard had been amplified a hundred million times. And as she stared aghast at the rapture on their faces, Andrea understood that they had been waiting for her to join them. Indeed, Eric and Miguel must have left Luis's notebook in the school parking lot as her invitation to the mass.

Tonight, she would receive her education. Tonight, she would learn the language of the New Lord.

Its alphabet was born of shattered windows, cracked pavement, and tangled freeways. Its speech was the cacophony of car horns, sirens, and gunshots. It offered hope of a higher intelligence to children left half-sentient by a society that had allowed its own language to wither with disuse.

And, like every language that preceded it, it had fostered its own deity.

A sudden glare bathed the chanting congregation in bluish-white light, and Andrea turned to see what had caused it. She found that the ebony symbol in the center of the mural now shone with a luminescence that seemed to emanate from deep within the wall.

Sinking to her knees, Andrea quoted the Bible in her mind: *In the beginning was the Word, and the Word was with God, and the Word was God.*

A black mist billowed from the glowing insignia on the wall before her.

And the Word was made flesh.

***

Andrea didn't notice when dawn came.

Hours passed uncounted in the deserted classroom, the silence broken only by the hum of fluorescent ceiling panels and the whisper of chalk on slate. Andrea scrawled each slash and swirl as if by rote, as though she were copying definitions from a dictionary. Oblivious to the numbness of her legs and the stink of her sweat-stained blouse, she didn't stop even when she heard the door open behind her.

"Andrea? You're here early." Brent Waller's voice. "I saw your light on and wanted to make sure— What the hell is *that?"*

She paused in mid-stroke and cast a pitying glance at the bewildered expression of the English department chairman, who stared, uncomprehending, at the anarchy of lines that covered the entire chalkboard. She smiled, but didn't speak. He wouldn't have understood her, anyway. There was much he didn't understand.

But he would learn. Soon, they all would.

School was now in session.

Prisoners

"These are my abortions," Price announced matter-of-factly as he opened the door to the darkened room.

We stepped into the blackness of the studio, and the sodden smell of wet clay seeped around us, like the chill, calcifying draft from a cave. Price tapped a light switch, and two parallel bars along the ceiling flickered into fluorescence, one of which shimmered uncertainly and emitted a high-pitched mosquito hum. The institutional black linoleum of the floor turned the silver light into a miasma of gray.

Price had once taught classes in this room, but he'd now pushed all the students' desks into a haphazard jam at the perimeter. In the center of the floor stood a Druidic semi-circle of six tall, glistening stalagmites of clay. A viscous plasma of water and silt pooled at the base of each figure, staining the plywood squares upon which they sat.

I looked to Price to give me the guided tour of his new exhibit, but he merely stared through me, toward the sculptures. After an awkward pause, I moved to get a closer look at the first of the figures, all of which towered over me by at least a foot. "Big suckers," I murmured over my shoulder. "Wood?" I gestured to indicate the statue's internal support.

"PVC pipe and chicken wire." He still didn't look at me.

I forced a chuckle. "Some things never change."

The lame attempt at camaraderie got the reaction it deserved. I turned back to gaze up at the smeared face above me, if you could call it a face. Its features had been wiped smooth, obliterated, until only an amorphous ghost of an expression remained. If not for the deep, empty sockets of its eyes, I might not have even realized the figure was human.

I made my way around the circle of half-formed statues, stopping to examine each in turn, as though I actually knew something about art. This one raised its arms in distress, that one hunched over some item clutched in its open palms, but all were shrouded in sheets of blank clay. Here and there details abruptly burst forth, as if piercing a curtain—a thick-veined hand, a drooping earlobe—but the rest of the figures dissolved into obscurity, like melted waxworks.

Except for the eyes. Each possessed a pair of black hollows that seemed to stare toward the center of the circle.

"Not bad for a start." I inched backward, out of the statues' view. "How long have you been working on them?"

"Three years."

I looked at Price in shock. This was the man who sculpted ten statues in two months for his senior project in college.

"Oh, not these exact figures," he replied in answer to my unspoken question. "The clay goes bad after a while, even when you wet it down. I must have thrown away a ton of the stuff."

He shuffled past me to stand before the nearest work. "I can't do it anymore, Richard." His voice faltered. "I can't make them live."

He reached out to lay a hand on the slick clay and raised his eyes to meet the statue's gaze. It glared down at him with the impatience of a dormant golem.

Price turned to me, his puffy face pleading. "I need your help."

* * *

Back in our Berkeley days, I thought Price survived solely on coffee and nicotine. A skin-covered skull stuck onto the broomstick body of a mime, he either couldn't afford a decent meal or had decided that eating was a chore not worth his time. The only portion of his anatomy that suggested any sort of strength or health at all were his restless, knobby hands, their fingertips wrinkled and tinged a permanent shade of gray from constant immersion in clay. I'd often find him in his dorm room at three A.M., the burnt-out butt of a cigarette pressed between his thin lips as he perched on a stepladder beside his latest expressionistic effigy of despair. He'd greet me with his death's-head grin, and we'd head off together to the local Denny's to spend the rest of the night drinking coffee and trying to out-bullshit each other with our intellectual pretension.

He was the only genius I'd ever known.

Now, the sharp edges of his cheekbones and jaw had become buried beneath the jowls of a premature middle age. He blamed the weight gain on the time his ex-wife forced him to quit smoking; he had taken up the habit again since their divorce, but he lacked the nonchalant facility with a cigarette he once possessed. He puffed with desperation rather than conviction, as though he were an unstudied actor portraying his former self.

"I got scared," he admitted, flicking ash into a tray heaped with extinguished Marlboros. "I was thirty years old, and I was still living in my parents' house and working graveyard at a convenience store."

"So you took the job at Hilliard." We sat in the Spartan living room of his apartment, where Price had invited me for coffee after the tour of his studio at the college.

He shrugged. "Seemed like easy money at the time. I had the degree and they liked my stuff."

"And what about Karen?"

He grimaced and sighed smoke, stubbing his butt out in the tray. "Being poor wasn't the only thing I was afraid of."

Adopting my best father-confessor voice, I attempted to absolve him of his failure. "You can't always live up to your expectations. Everyone has to make concessions to reality."

Price just laughed. "Boy, you have that shrink shit down pat!" He spoke out of one side of his mouth as he lit another cigarette. "Pays better than social work, though, don't it?"

I leaned back in my chair and crossed my arms. Price knew he wasn't the only one who'd sold out. "You obviously don't want my sympathy," I remarked, "so what *do* you want?"

His sardonic expression turned sober. "I'm dying, Rich," he said softly. When he saw the shock on my face, he tapped his chest for clarification. "In here."

I relaxed a little. A typical Price overstatement. "Look, every artist has creative blocks—"

He shook his head. "You don't understand. I've systematically destroyed my soul. Buried it under students' term papers. Anesthetized it with lectures on nineteenth-century neoclassicists. Poisoned it with prime-time sitcoms and TV dinners. I've killed the only thing that made me worth a damn in this world."

"So if that's your problem, why not just chuck it all? Go to Tahiti and screw native women until your muse wakes up."

"It's too late for that." He sank back on the sofa, the heels of his palms pressed against his eyes. "My job is already hanging by a thread. The department *made* me take a six-month sabbatical."

"How'd you manage that?"

"Oh, I just forgot to turn in my grades last term." He smiled, and a shade of the old Price shone through. "The extra time didn't help, though. You saw those things in the studio. I can't finish them—I don't know what they want to be."

I regarded him in silence for a moment. He wore the nervous despair of a schizophrenic who feels the inexorable tide of insanity effacing his personality. The only difference was that Price had always been crazy, and now a flood of normalcy had washed away the madness he treasured.

"What do you want me to do?" I asked.

Fishing in the pocket of his jeans, he pulled out a compact rectangle of folded notebook paper, opened it, and presented it to me. I scanned the jagged handwriting on the page and glanced from Price to the paper and back again. "You've got to be kidding."

He met my stare without blinking. "Power of suggestion."

"Yeah, but ... " I pointed to the scribbled notes, quoting.

"'You are becoming part of the clay. You feel its inner life. It is merely an extension of yourself, a physical representation of your being.' You really believe this crap?"

"I used to." Gazing at nothing, he rubbed absently at the fleshy pouch of his cheek with the thumb of his cigarette hand. "You once told me that hypnosis only works because the subject wants it to. Well, I *want* this." His eyes shifted and focused on me. "I want it more than anything else in the world."

I chewed my lip a moment, then nodded. "Okay."

We did the first session that night. Once I put him under, I murmured the script he'd drafted for me, embellishing it with my own improvisations, as Price lay limp on his bed. Despite their bizarre content, his sculpting mantras seemed innocuous enough, the sort of visualization techniques Method actors use to get into character for a role. When I woke him up, I cautioned him not to expect an immediate effect, for it sometimes takes several sessions for these mesmeric suggestions to imprint themselves on the subconscious. For convenience's sake, I planted a code word in Price's mind that would automatically induce a trance on future occasions. "Pygmalion"—it seemed appropriate.

As I anticipated, Price phoned me several times during the following month, asking me to come to his apartment to "refresh" his hypnotic conditioning. Though I sensed that he was disappointed with the results of our experiment so far, he swore to me that his work was improving, that all he needed was some psychological reinforcement and he would return to his old, artistic, manic-depressive self.

When two weeks passed without a word from him, I assumed he'd either found the inspiration he'd been looking for or had given up on the whole project. Then he called me late one evening, frenetically excited, and demanded that I come to his studio immediately. "I want to try something a little different," he said. "Total immersion. You'll see—it'll be cool." He hung up without waiting for me to respond.

Despite my better judgment, I obediently went to the studio that night in the hope that one more session might convince Price to end this strange course of "therapy." As I arrived at the studio door, I heard a muttered conversation going on inside and briefly wondered if Price had invited a third party.

When I entered the room, however, I found Price standing alone among his statues, nervously gnawing on his thumb and nodding, as if in agreement with something someone had just said. His complexion had grown more pasty than ever during the past few weeks and his eyes were dim and dilated, yet he welcomed me with a broad grin, beaming with enthusiasm and gratitude.

"Well—what do think?" He swept a hand toward his creations.

"Mmm . . . yeah, they're really coming along." Actually, they looked almost exactly the same as the first time I'd seen them. I noticed subtle changes in position in several of the figures—the turn of a head, the bend of an arm—but they remained cocooned in sheets of clay. The contorted effigies seemed to strain at the earthen veils that enveloped them, and I remembered how Price had once referred to his sculptures as "prisoners" waiting to be released.

"With your help, I think I can free them," Price mused, as though he had overheard my thoughts. "Shall we?"

He handed me a new script he'd written for the occasion and directed me toward a nearby folding chair. He then stretched out upon a rumpled bedroll in the center of the floor. Judging by the empty Coke cans, pizza delivery boxes, and flattened cigarette butts strewn around the sleeping bag, I guessed that Price hadn't stepped outside the studio in at least a week. Fortunately, the scent of wet clay in the room overwhelmed the odor of Price's unwashed body.

Once he'd settled his head upon his sweat-stained pillow, I positioned my chair at his side and leaned toward him, propping my elbows on my knees.

"Pygmalion," I said.

All tension instantly drained from Price's limbs, leaving him in a state of rag-doll repose. Unlike our previous sessions, though, he kept his eyes open, fixed on the face of the statue at the foot of his bedroll, and I wondered if he'd truly entered a trance.

"Price? Can you hear me?"

"Yes." Voice lethargic, distant.

"Are you asleep?"

"Yes."

Satisfied, I continued, using Price's new script as my guide. "Do you see that statue in front of you?"

"Yes."

"I want you to become that statue. I want you to feel its form and essence. Its flesh is your flesh."

His limbs stiffened to rigidity.

"What are you, Price?"

"I . . . am . . . a . . . sta . . . tue." The words sluggish, viscous.

"What are you made of?"

"I . . . am . . . clay."

"That's right—soft, pliable clay, that you can make into anything you want. Picture your ideal self. Fix the image in your mind. What do you want to be?"

"I . . . want . . . to be . . . *freeee*." His hands clenched into fists, and he began to shudder. "I . . . want . . . to be . . . *alive* . . ."

"Good. Now let's imagine how Price the *sculptor* will—"

"I want . . . to be . . . *freeeee!*" His body convulsed as though struggling against paralysis. "I want . . . to be . . . *alive!*"

I rose from my chair. "Okay, Price, listen carefully. At the count of three—"

"I want—to be—*FREEEEEE!* I want—to be—*ALIVE!*"

"*At the count of three*, I want you to wake up as yourself, okay? One—"

"I WANT TO BE FREE! I WANT TO BE ALIVE!" His hands flew up to his face, dirty fingernails digging into his cheeks and forehead. Droplets of blood sprouted along the red trails of grazed skin.

I dropped down beside him and grabbed his wrists. "ONE—
TWO—THREE!"

Price abruptly stopped struggling and sagged back onto his pillow, whimpering. I patted his shoulder. "It's okay. You're going to
be all right."

He thrust my hand away and shrieked in my face. *"Why did
you stop me?"*

"What? Are you nuts?"

"God damn you, I almost made it!"

"That does it!" I got to my feet. "I'm outta here."

"You bastard!" he bawled as I stalked out of the studio. *"Why
did you stop me?"*

Fear and anger scourged me as I drove home that night, and I
cursed myself for agreeing to Price's insane plan in the first place. I
only wanted to help him achieve the art I knew he was capable
of, and instead I'd led him to the brink of complete psychosis. If I
got Price the psychiatric treatment he needed, I'd have to confess
my own role in his mental breakdown, destroying my career in
the process. If I didn't get him some help, he might off himself at
any time. A devil's choice if there ever was one.

Yet, while my conscious mind dwelt on such selfish concerns,
an entirely different anxiety simmered in the dim recesses of my
brain, a sickening disquiet that made me run away from an old
friend who was on the verge of suicide: when Price screamed at
me, I noticed that his tongue had turned gray.

The persistent afterimage of that pale tongue lingered in my
memory as I went to work the following morning. It lolled in
front of my eyes while Mrs. Thompson droned on and on about
how her father had never *really* loved her. I gave her some per-
functory words of consolation to hurry her out of my office, then
ordered my receptionist to postpone my next appointment.

I picked up the phone and dialed Price's apartment; I knew he
wouldn't be there, but I didn't have a number for the studio. The
phone rang twice before sending me to Price's voicemail.

"Life is a meaningless charade of existential despair," the re-cording said, "and I'm currently contemplating slashing my wrists. Leave your name and number after the beep, and if I find a reason to live, I'll return your call."

Price's usual greeting, which I took as a good sign. If he'd really killed himself, he would have told me so in his outgoing message, just to rub my nose in it.

"Hey, buddy," I replied after the tone. "Sorry I walked out on you last night, but you freaked me out a little there. Hope you're okay. Give me a call when you get the chance—I'd like to talk."

A futile gesture, I thought as I hung up. Price would just laugh at the transparent insincerity of my apology; to be perfectly frank, it even nauseated me. I somnambulated through the rest of the day, Price's gray tongue licking at my conscience.

By the time I got home, I found that Price had left me a voicemail in reply.

For a single, evil moment, I considered deleting the message without listening to it. Reluctantly, I retrieved the recording.

"Hey, b-buddy!" Price sneered. His voice sounded strangely liquid, almost as if he were speaking underwater, and he enunci-ated with the deliberateness of a drunk. "B-bet you're surprised to hear f-from me. W-well, here's another surprise: I d-don't need you anyway." He gave a guttural laugh. "'P-pygmalion.' That's cute! J-just call me 'P-pyg,' for short!"

The message ended, and I felt the blood drain from my face. Price shouldn't have been able to remember my code word. If he knew that, then maybe he really didn't need me.

But how could he continue the hypnosis on his own? I asked my-self as I hurried back out to my car. I discovered the answer when I arrived at Hilliard and heard my own voice filtering through the door of Price's studio.

"You are becoming part of the clay," my voice murmured. *"Feel its inner life. Soft, pliable clay, that you can make into any-thing you want . . ."*

A wail of panic resounded from inside the studio, and I burst into the room to find Price squatting in the center of the semicircle of statues, sobbing, his face buried in his hands.

A soundbar sat nearby, still reciting my own mesmeric incantations. He must have secretly recorded each of our sessions, then dubbed selected excerpts together to create his own personal self-hypnosis soundtrack. I yanked the extension cord that powered the stereo out of the wall socket, and the soundbar cut off. Then I turned to Price to see what he'd done to himself.

At first, I thought he had merely smeared his cheeks with clay while crying, for his arms were sheened with gray slime and gray sludge oozed from between his fingers. Then he lifted his head, and I saw that his face had become an almost featureless mass of clay. His fingers frantically clawed and kneaded the putty of his skull, vainly attempting to reconstruct his hooked nose and rounded chin, as the vacant thumbholes of his eyes wept trickles of silt.

My mind rationalized what I was seeing: Price had tried to make some kind of life-mask of himself, and now he couldn't breathe. I ran over to him and moved to pull the clay off his face. "Here! Let me help—"

"Naaaaaa!" He batted my hands away and turned his back toward me.

I grabbed his shoulder and, with a surge of nausea, felt my fingers sink into his flesh. Gray fluid seeped through the thin cotton of his bowling shirt and flowed over my hand.

He lurched forward on his knees, even as his torso sagged and began to collapse. His hands tore at the pouches of his cheeks, ripping the earthen flesh off in clumps, and I suddenly realized that he was trying to sculpt the high cheekbones and bony jaw of his old face. But the corners of the slit that formed his mouth drooped into a shapeless grimace, a moan gurgling from lips that leaked muddy drool.

I wanted to shake him, but I was afraid to touch his doughy body. "This isn't the way!" I shouted in the wilting flap of his ear. "For God's sake, let it go before it's too late!"

I don't even know if he heard me at that point. I doubt that it made any difference if he did. Though he continued to claw at his unmade face, his fingers begin to lose their definition as well, until his hands degenerated into mushy stumps.

Prostrate before one of his hulking, half-finished masterpieces, Price stretched a flaccid arm up toward the figure, whimpering. Each consonant he attempted to speak threatened to seal the soggy slash of his mouth forever. "Hhhep-p . . . p-pease!"

The statue seemed to quiver in response, but I attributed the tremor to the stroboscopic flicker of the faulty fluorescent lighting. I didn't see—couldn't accept—that the figure was slowly raising its arm, until it held its heavy hand out to Price. In a pathetic imitation of God granting life to Adam, the creation reached toward its creator, trying to give Price a spark of the passion that had once defined his existence.

Its hand faltered and froze. With a face as unformed as that of a fetus, the statue gazed down at Price with the helpless longing of a child for its parent. Incomplete, it possessed no life of its own.

Price pawed the air, nearly touched the figure's fingers. Then his arm dropped off and fell to the floor with a slap, spattering the linoleum with splashes of gray. Gray bubbles filled the pits of his eyes, his jaw went limp, and his head sank into his chest. His bowling shirt deflated as gray flesh poured out the sleeves to clump in a pile at his knees. A moment later, nothing remained of Price but a hill of muck and sodden clothes.

In disbelief, I crouched beside the ruin of my friend and put a trembling hand out to touch the soft mass of clay.

It was warm.

My fingers recoiled from the contact, and bile rose in my throat.

As I staggered to my feet, a strangled, mewling sound rose in the room. All around me, the prisoners writhed in their shrouds of clay, each like an insect trapped and dying in its own chrysalis. The keening cry of earthen throats crescendoed in my ears as they mourned the loss of the only man who could set them free.

I ran from the studio without looking back.

It was some weeks later, shortly before fall semester was due to begin, that I first heard some mutual acquaintances speak of Price's sudden disappearance. It caused a small scandal at Hilliard Community College, but no one suspected foul play or even found his absence all that mysterious. He was a notorious eccentric, dissatisfied with his job, and everyone assumed he'd done a Gauguin and run off to some exotic foreign locale to ply his art in isolation. As his only heir, his ex-wife auctioned off the unfinished works they found in his studio, some of which fetched impressive prices.

I never told anyone what happened, of course. I'm a psychiatrist, after all—I know what sounds crazy. I've almost convinced myself that I hallucinated the whole thing.

Yet sometimes, after a day of prescribing antidepressants to confused teenagers and listening with bored detachment to the lamentations of lonely housewives, I'll look in the mirror and see a visage devoid of features, eyes recessed into layers of mud, and then I, like Price, yearn to tear off this mask of clay and exhume the face I used to have.

A Tour of the Catacombs

Please watch your step as we descend. As you can see, these stairs were cleft into solid stone, and their slant has become treacherous from the tread of so many feet.

And I hope there shall be no stragglers among you. As we say in the Abbey, only two sorts enter the Catacombs: the quick and the dead.

The crypt predates the Abbey, of course, by many centuries. You can see for yourself the difference in construction. Medieval artisans, however clever they might have been, could hardly hope to have burrowed into impenetrable metamorphic rock in this fashion. The early Church often constructed its edifices on top of pagan architecture, both to take advantage of the existing structures and to make a rather presumptuous attempt to usurp the places of older gods.

I apologize for the cold. At this depth, the temperature remains a constant 56 degrees Fahrenheit, whether in the furnace of summer or the icebox of winter. I'm afraid the damp makes it worse, as well. You can smell it here—the dripping, seeping odor of silt and sediment. But I promise that you shan't suffer the chill for long.

A few of you are already gasping for breath, so let us rest here in order that I may demonstrate another aspect of these Stygian hollows. I shall briefly turn off this electric lantern, and I strongly advise that you all remain absolutely still when I do so. To shift even an inch under such conditions could be catastrophic.

What you are now seeing—or not seeing, depending on your perception—is a *cave darkness*, the absolute absence of all light. I think you'll appreciate the paradox of how it makes the cavern feel unimaginably vast and oppressively close at the same time.

I can hear some of you panting with panic, so I'll switch on this nuisance of a light. There! Again, mind the worn steps as we continue down. On the lower, older stairs, the shallow bevels of parallel footsteps meld into a single deep groove, as if from the dragging of a saurian tail rather than the shuffle of human soles.

What was that? Yes, those markings on the wall are indeed a form of writing—a language sadly lost to all but us initiates of the Abbey. I could translate the passages for you, but you would probably find them tedious. *Most* of you, I should say.

Voilà! Did I not promise you it would grow warmer? Where before you were shivering, you now are sweltering, and the clammy drafts of the sepulcher have become the hot, humid mineral breaths of a sauna. As I mentioned earlier, this rock is volcanic in origin, the petrified strata of what was once boiling magma. We are fearfully deep into the earth now. You can feel it, can't you? The weight of it compacting the very air around you . . .

Please note, as we pass, the hexagonal excavation of these cells in the walls, exquisite workmanship that I believe to be unique to this location. Yes, there *are* an incredible number of them—thousands upon thousands. No, those ovoid chrysalises you see in each cell are not sarcophagi. This is a place of incubation, not entombment. Not a grave, but a cradle.

Ah! We've reached the final flight of these winding steps. As you can see, the tunnel opens into an immense abyss. Would that this paltry light could plumb the farthest reaches of this titanic chamber! There you would view a city of living rock the scale and splendor of which would beggar the most extravagant fantasies of the pharaohs, its colonnades and cornices teeming with the multitudes whose melodic shrieks are even now resonating in the stone around us.

But this lantern is obviously quite useless, so I shall turn it off. Those of you who are like me—who have felt the Abbey and its underside calling to you in your dreams across miles and millennia—will have little need of it. Your cells, the cocoons of your larval renaissance, await you.

As for the rest of you, well . . . recall what I said about the quick and the dead. You will probably not wish to see what is coming.

This concludes our tour. Don't forget the guide as you depart . . .

A Woman Absent

To men a man is but a mind. Who cares
What face he carries or what form he wears?
But woman's body is the woman. O,
Stay thou, my sweetheart, and do never go,
But heed the warning the sage hath said:
A woman absent is a woman dead.
—AMBROSE BIERCE

Sheree gazed out the kitchen window at the early morning sky as she did the dishes, and thought, as she always did, about leaving Dan.

Today was different, though. Today she knew she would.

She pulled her hands out of the dishwater, shaking the suds off them, and gently rubbed the tender areas of her right palm. The hot water made the burns sting. She'd tried wearing rubber gloves, but her skin stuck to them and tugged at her sores.

Still, she didn't have anyone but herself to blame for that, did she? She'd been so afraid of burning the garlic bread for Dan's spaghetti that she'd reached in to pull the tray out of the oven without a potholder. Dan didn't get mad at her, at least not then. He chuckled and called her a ditz.

Sheree sighed and hurriedly finished the dishes, ignoring the throb in her hand. She then cooked Dan his favorite breakfast; the smell of scrambled eggs and bacon grease congealed in the tiny kitchen. Behind her, she could hear Dan pissing in the toilet with the bathroom door open.

He came in a few minutes later, wearing his orange vest over his bare, tan chest, and sat at the table. His mouth twisted as she set the bacon and eggs in front of him. "Thanks."

Avoiding his glance, she poured him some coffee. "What time

155

will you be home tonight?"

"I don't know. We're supposed to finish that intersection on Lincoln this week. There might be some overtime in it." He stirred the eggs with his fork, then shoveled some into his mouth when he couldn't think of anything else to say.

Sheree packed his lunch while he ate. As she handed it to him, he ran his fingers gently along her forearm where the bruises stained her skin. "Sorry."

She'd known he would say that, but hadn't steeled herself against the sincerity in his boyish blue eyes. "I know."

She touched his strong, smooth arms, felt her resolve weaken. He kissed her cheek, and her soul seemed to tug against itself, trying to split in two.

I'm leaving, she reminded herself.

***

Sheree waited about half an hour after Dan went to work, then took a new garbage bag into the bedroom and started throwing her clothes and other belongings into it. She balled up her blouses and stuffed them in the bag before the hangers had stopped swinging in the closet, and scraped her makeup bottles off the dresser with one sweep of her arm.

She wasn't going to give herself the chance to change her mind this time. Memories of the night before whipped her on.

C'mon, baby! Give me a break! What do you mean, you don't feel like it? Christ, I gotta work outside all fuckin' day, when it's ninety degrees, and I can't even fuck my own wife when I get home? Bullshit! Get down on the bed, now!

She hadn't struggled long. She knew better than that by now. Though Dan hadn't loosened his grip on her wrists, she wouldn't have moved even if he'd let go entirely.

Afterward, he ripped the arms off Jerry Bear, just to teach her a lesson.

She picked up the stuffed teddy from the nightstand, but

paused before putting him in the bag, stroking his matted polyester fur. He winked at her with his one remaining black-button eye, still wearing the same goofy grin he'd had when she was three, his red velvet tongue lolling from one side of his snout. He didn't seem to mind the fact that his shoulders ended in torn cloth and dangling thread.

Sheree often cuddled Jerry Bear at night to help her sleep. Last night, however, Dan had snatched it out of her hands.

I swear, sometimes I think you give this goddamn toy more head than you give me! He grabbed one stubby paw and yanked.

Sheree had never seen Dan's anger focused on anything but herself before. It was like standing outside herself, watching him thrash her.

***

"I'll fix you," she promised Jerry Bear, nestling him in her sack with his detached arms beside him.

She took the small wad of cash she'd saved from its hiding place inside the vacuum cleaner bag and stuck it in her purse. Then she slung the purse and garbage bag over her shoulder and headed out to the bus stop in front of their apartment building.

The bus didn't arrive for almost an hour. Sheree shifted her weight nervously as she waited, terrified by the thought that Dan might drive by and see her standing there at the curb.

Some teenagers in shorts with Boogie boards under their arms came up to wait with her. She tried to smile. "Going to the beach?"

They didn't answer, only laughed and talked among themselves. Not surprising, she thought. It was a pointless question. She'd spent so much time with Dan, she'd forgotten how to talk to strangers.

When the bus finally came, she got on with the teenagers, dropped exact change in the fare box, and settled herself in one of the hard plastic seats. Though she felt as conspicuous as an escaped convict, no one even glanced her way. As she watched the apartment house recede behind her, Sheree felt a fear and exhilaration she hadn't known since she was eighteen.

She was on her own.

She sighed and stared through the window at the people and buildings flowing past outside. She'd pictured this moment in her head so many times it hardly seemed real.

On a whim, she let the bus carry her all the way to Newport Beach, the end of the line. Her sack on her shoulder, Sheree followed the teenagers out onto the sidewalk and inhaled the soft salt breeze. She walked up the street past souvenir shops and fast-food places until it dead-ended at the pier, then she turned right.

When she reached the fringe of the beach, Sheree slipped off her sandals and let the warm sand pillow her bare feet. She strolled along the shore for a little way, looking out over the ocean to avoid watching the smiling couples who lay on parallel towels. After awhile, she set her bag on the sand, sat down, and hitched her skirt up past her knees.

It shocked her to see how pale her legs were. She and Dan used to come down here all the time when they were dating in high school. Dan even talked about getting a beach house someday, about eating dinner out on the patio with the sunset and the sound of the surf . . .

Sheree chuckled dryly. She felt like an old lady the way she was reminiscing. Christ, she was only twenty-three! She could go to college, get a job, buy her *own* beach house. Her mother would put her up until the divorce went through and she decided what to do. Mom was going to be so proud of her!

Holding up her left hand, she took off her wedding and engagement rings and considered throwing them both in the sand for the first lucky old man with a metal detector. She decided she should probably sell them instead and put them in her purse, wondering how long it would take the banded "scars" around her ring finger to fade.

Sheree lay back and put her head on the sack, giggling as she thought what a gypsy she must look. This was Southern California, however, so it didn't surprise her when no one paid her the slightest notice.

The tension and doubt of the morning evaporated as the sunlight bathed her face. Though she'd hardly eaten all day, she didn't feel hungry, just pleasantly lazy.

***

She woke with a start to find the crowd on the beach had thinned, and the sun sat lower on the horizon. Blinking, she stood and shook the sand from her skirt.

A chill breeze made Sheree shiver; she dimly worried about having a sunburn, though her arms looked as white as ever. An anxious sensation seized her: a feeling of being late for a rendezvous she'd forgotten, of being where she shouldn't be.

She had to get to Mom's before it got too late. She had to get *home*.

The shadows of the shops and palm trees stretched over the sidewalk as she walked back to the bus stop, where only a few people now waited. She rode with them toward her mother's place as the surrounding cityscape turned orange, then purple.

The bus passed her stop.

Sheree pushed the gray plastic strip by the window to ring the bell and alert the driver, but no sound came. She cursed and stood, steadying herself as the bus accelerated. "Excuse me. That was my stop."

The driver drove on complacently.

An older man behind Sheree pressed the gray strip, and the bell rang. The bus pulled to the curb. Carrying her bag, Sheree joined the man as he positioned himself in front of the door. She turned to him with a grateful smile. "Thanks. I don't know what's wrong with that driver."

The man didn't answer. The door opened, and he descended to the street without looking at her.

Sheree got off after him, a wounded expression on her face. She walked the extra block back to where she was supposed to have disembarked and proceeded into a dark neighborhood.

The yellow porch light over her mother's front doorstep gleamed like a beacon. Sheree set her purse and bag at her feet, swept back her tangled hair, and rang the doorbell. She didn't hear the familiar chimes, even after several tries, and no one answered. When she rapped on the door with her fist, her knock sounded strangely deadened.

Sudden desperation prickled the nape of her neck. What if Mom was gone? But no—her car was in the driveway. She had to be there.

The front door opened to the length of its chain, and Sheree almost cried when she saw her mother's concerned face peer through the gap.

"It's me, Mom," she said. "I did it. I left him."

But her mother didn't meet her gaze. Instead, she peered around the front step suspiciously, as if to see why the neighbor's dogs were barking. Then she eased the door shut and locked it.

"Mom? *Mommy!*" Sheree pounded on the door again, but she suddenly felt as light and insubstantial as the evening breeze.

She leaned against the door jamb, sobbing. A new thought occurred to her, and her crying quieted to a hiccup.

It was a dream. She had fallen asleep on the beach and was having a nightmare.

Or maybe she was still in bed with Dan . . .

She bolted from her mother's house in a panic, leaving her things on the doorstep. As she ran, the city smeared by her in a blur, a strip of celluloid that had come loose from its sprockets. A succession of stoplights and street signs guided her back where she'd started.

Home.

The apartment house loomed cold and comfortless in the night, a few of its small windows lit from within. Sheree stopped in front of it, breathing hard, hoping to wake up on the beach. Her throat tight, she reluctantly shuffled forward. She had to be sure.

The apartment seemed alien to her, as if she'd never been there before. She wanted to unlock the door, but remembered that her keys were still in her purse, which she'd left at her mother's. She was about to knock, but hesitated.

What if it wasn't a dream? What if Dan could see her . . . touch her? How would she explain where she'd been all day?

That was stupid, she told herself. It had to be a dream. Her own mother had looked right through her.

Nevertheless, she lingered by the door, biting her thumb. Then she noticed that the light was on in the bedroom. She crept up and squinted through the parted curtains, her breath not even fogging the window's glass.

Two figures lay on the bed in the room. Dan bucked on top of the woman, rearing back to moan in pleasure. The woman cupped his buttocks with her hands to help him thrust, her face lost behind long brown hair.

In spite of herself, Sheree felt the sting of jealousy. Had he replaced her already?

Dan bent down to kiss the woman's throat, and she rolled her head toward the window, looking at Sheree with empty, hopeless resignation.

Sheree clawed at the windowpane, whimpering. The woman's face was her own.

"No . . . no, *please.*"

Sheree watched Dan lick the breasts of the body beneath him, watched the body simulate the shudders of ecstasy. He didn't even know she was gone.

No! We did it! We got away!

Sheree beat her fists against the glass, wanting to smash it to shards. It didn't even vibrate beneath her blows.

Her vision clouded, and she glanced at the nightstand by the bed. There sat Jerry Bear, still armless, still smiling.

"I'll make it real," Sheree whispered. "I'll put us back together."

And she would have walked into the room right then, but she still believed in walls. So, instead, she sat down outside the window, hugging her knees and sobbing softly.

Waiting for her chance.

Inside, the body reclined with Dan in the bed. It would carry on without her. It would cope.

Voodoo

"Chartres," Blaisdell said as he climbed into the cab. He pronounced the street name as if it were the celebrated cathedral, with a soft *sh* at the beginning and a trilled *r* at the end.

"I beg your pardon, sir?" The driver, a young Arabic man, glanced at Blaisdell's frown in the rearview mirror and laughed. "Oh! You mean 'Charters.'"

"I suppose I do." Arlen Blaisdell, who'd conversed in French on five continents—from Haiti to Guiana to Switzerland to the Côte d'Ivoire to Vietnam—could not fathom how a metropolis that called itself New Orleans could so mangle the Gallic tongue. Even the local name for the French Quarter—the *Vieux Carré*, or "Old Square"—had become slurred into "Voo Carré." In the land of the Cajun and the Creole, Blaisdell had found that speaking *le vrai français* was more of a hindrance than a help.

Ce n'est pas Paris, n'est-ce pas? he heard Garston chuckle in his memory. It was their running joke back when they were grad students in Port-au-Prince every time the roof of their hostel leaked rain onto their anthropology texts or fleas infested their mattresses.

At the thought of Garston, Blaisdell stopped fanning himself with the manila envelope he carried, which contained the crime scene photos of his late friend's remains. Even inside the cab, the mid-August humidity broiled Blaisdell until his skin crawled with festering sweat. Though any breeze was welcome, he laid the envelope on his lap out of respect for the dead.

"We had nothing to do with this," the priestess had told him, her brown face stern, when he'd visited the nearby temple and showed her the images. "Our spirits would never command us to do such a thing."

Blaisdell flattened his hand on the envelope. Spirits may not have done such a thing, but someone had, and he needed to find out who and why.

The taxi slunk through narrow lanes constricted by ranks of manses in the vintage Louisiana style, Spanish iron grillwork masking Greek Revival masonry. Some of them were original, others merely tarted-up facsimiles. Souvenir shops sold Mardi Gras costumes and plastic beads, voodoo dolls and gris-gris bags, most imported from China. Pop culture had long ago appropriated New Orleans's style, and in turn New Orleans had done its best to mimic what the culture expected it to be, until the real city lay veiled beneath a veneer of the phony and the fatuous. Perhaps, Blaisdell fretted, he'd come all this way for nothing . . .

The cab disgorged him on a desolate corner of "Charters." Hardly anyone walked the streets. It was the off-season, when tourists abandoned the city to its heat and palmetto bugs. No jazz billowed from the bars to freshen the air, which congealed in stultifying silence. A lone black man strode down the opposite side of the lane. Despite the heat, he walked quickly, glancing up at the jaundiced haze of the late afternoon sky as he went.

Blaisdell could almost feel the barometric pressure plunging. The National Weather Service had reported a tropical storm brewing in the Gulf and said it might achieve hurricane strength by the time it made landfall. Of all the ghosts that haunted New Orleans, the only one the locals truly feared was named Katrina. He knew he ought to dispense with this nonsense and get back to his hotel, but he would feel like a complete fool if he left without any of the answers he sought.

He consulted the small map of the French Quarter he carried in the breast pocket of his light linen suit. The cab had overshot his destination by about three blocks, so he backtracked along Chartres to the appropriate cross street and turned right. The praline shop on the corner had already rolled down its metal doors an hour ahead of its scheduled closing time. Next to that, Blaisdell saw what he at first mistook for a dilapidated thrift store. So much dust filmed the front window that its tableau of manikins seemed to perform its dumb show in a permanent fog. Only the painted circus-font letters on the glass distinguished the establishment from its neighbors: "LEGRASSE MUSEUM of NATIVE BELIEFS."

Blaisdell rechecked both the location on the map and the name and address he'd researched online, hoping there was some mistake. He couldn't tell if the place was open—the interior looked dark, deserted. With a sigh, Blaisdell pulled on the glass door of the entrance and found it unlocked.

A bell bobbed on a coiled spring as the door swung open, its jingle jarring in the afternoon's thick stillness. Blaisdell entered a cramped foyer lit by a single incandescent bulb overhead. An iron ceiling fan stirred the sodden air, as useless as the propeller of a sunken ship.

A fat man with a wispy brown mustache sat at a folding card table beside the open archway that led into the museum's main chamber. He bowed his head over a notebook, motionless, and sweat had so glossed the pocked surface of his bald scalp that Blaisdell at first mistook him for a wax figure, a diorama dummy like those he'd seen in the front window. Perspiration stained the underarms of the man's short-sleeved oxford shirt.

"Five dollars," he said without looking up. "And we close in twenty minutes." He had the accent of a New Orleans native— not the Tennessee Williams drawl they used in movies, but rather a clipped, nasal tone with flattened vowels, like something you'd hear in Boston or the Bronx.

"Ah! Of course." Tucking the manila envelope under his arm, Blaisdell took a ten from his wallet and offered it to the proprietor. The man ignored it and kept scrawling in his notebook, so Blaisdell left the bill on the card table without waiting for change.

Not knowing how to broach the real subject of his visit, Blaisdell milled about the miserable little museum and despaired, for it seemed merely another lowbrow tourist trap, exploiting regional culture with cheap sensationalism for the curious and clueless. Clumsy effigies stood in for the *loa*, the mercurial spirits of Haitian tradition. There stood Baron Samedi and Maman Brigitte, master and mistress of the dead, with their painted skeletal faces and thrift-store funereal finery, as stiff as figurines from a giant wedding cake. The cruel and fearsome Marinette, a sorceress of fire and the protector of werewolves, might as well have been called Marionette: her spindly arms were flung above her head as if dangling from strings as she posed amongst flames of red aluminum foil. A stuffed Siberian husky stood in for one of the *loup-garous* at her command. An ancient, emaciated black man with a wide-brimmed straw hat—apparently intended to represent Papa Legba, the fatherly *loa* who served as an intermediary between the human and spirit worlds—had what must have been a nylon Santa beard glued to his face. The Legba figure bowed its head, evidently preparing to possess a counterfeit *houngan* priest, who writhed in religious ecstasy on the floor before him.

The displays all looked so slapdash and ill-kept that they seemed to express a silent contempt for their subjects. The entire building smelled of plaster dust and mildew, and the flecked dust on Baron Samedi's black frock coat bore a discomfiting resemblance to dandruff. Blaisdell spared only a cursory glance at the yellowed, typewritten placards taped to the wall that gave terse explanations of each exhibit. Only after skimming several of the paragraphs did he realize what struck him so odd about them.

Like the peculiar name of the museum itself, the capsule descriptions never used the word "voodoo."

Dispirited, Blaisdell moved toward the exit. As he passed through the archway, he glanced toward the man at the card table again, and his gaze happened to fall upon the man's open notebook. Rows of glyphs cramped its graph-paper pages: a mélange of wedge-shaped hash-marks and spattered dots that looked like a cross between cuneiform and Braille. Despite a lifetime of study of languages both living and dead, Blaisdell had seen writing like this only once, among the papers that Garston had left behind after his death.

"Mister . . . Legrasse?" Blaisdell ventured.

The museum proprietor slapped his pulpy hand over the text he'd scribbled, like a schoolboy who fears a classmate might be copying him. "*Doctor* Legrasse," he corrected.

"Yes . . . of course." Blaisdell cleared his throat. "I believe you corresponded with a colleague of mine from Princeton. Morris Garston?"

Legrasse's pale gray eyes narrowed. "I recognize the name."

"He consulted you about certain voodoo rituals—"

"*Rituals*, yes." Again the remonstrative tone.

"Did any of them involve . . ." Blaisdell did not want to be melodramatic but saw no way around it. ". . . human sacrifice?"

Legrasse gave him a withering look. "There is no history of human sacrifice in either Haitian or Louisianan native beliefs. Good day, Mister . . ."

"*Doctor* Blaisdell. I heard as much from the priestess at the voodoo temple."

Legrasse hacked out a laugh. "Ha! *Voodoo*. A handful of half-truths cluttered with a bunch of Catholic claptrap. Even the name is a corruption."

Blaisdell pursed his lips to keep from commenting on the arrogance of a white man denouncing and dismissing an entire ethnic religion. He presumed Legrasse sneered at the word *voodoo* because he favored one of the many variant spellings and pronunciations: *vodou, vodun, vodoun, voudoun, vodú*. There was some debate over which term was the most historically appropriate, and it was the sort of thing academics loved to argue over at cocktail parties.

"Still, regardless of whether you agree with their beliefs, you can't deny that this region has spawned some unusual cult behavior," Blaisdell said, striving to remain respectful. "I understand that your own great-grandfather found—"

"My great-grandfather was a fool. He glimpsed a cosmic truth, then spent the rest of his life trying to forget it. And the followers of 'voodoo' are no better." He jerked a thumb toward the displays Blaisdell had just viewed. "They take the elemental entities of the universe and turn them into anthropomorphic cartoon characters. They want to peep beneath the world's veil, but they're too afraid to cast it off."

"Morris Garston wasn't." Blaisdell took the manila envelope from beneath his arm. "I don't know how much he told you about his work. After it was discovered that zombification had a scientific basis in the use of neurotoxins by voodoo priests, Morris became convinced that psychoactive drugs also played a role in rituals involving possession by the *loa*."

"Yes, your friend Garston understood better than most." For the first time in the conversation, Legrasse seemed interested. "Voodoo teaches that the *loa* come from outside, that they 'ride' us like horses. But Garston knew the truth—the *loa* come from within. The space inside." He tapped the center of his forehead. "You need the proper words to focus your mind, though, and call them forth. The Old Language." He stroked the open page of his notebook absently.

"I gather that's what you provided Morris." Blaisdell opened the envelope, pulled out the 8 × 10 black-and-white prints. "He had just come back from research trips to Africa and Haiti, very excited. He was certain he'd found the key ingredients with which to formulate the drug, a psychedelic entheogen that he believed stimulated the pineal gland in the brain.

"Then, about a week after his return, this happened."

Blaisdell flipped the first photo around for Legrasse to see. It depicted an aerial view, taken from police helicopter, of a stand of pines in the Herrontown Woods Arboretum near Princeton. The center of the grove resembled a miniature version of Russia's Tunguska impact site, with tree trunks flattened like matchsticks, fanned out in a circle around a tiny form that was just barely visible at the center.

Legrasse feigned nonchalance, but a vein throbbed visibly on his brow. "And Garston . . . he was involved somehow?"

"You tell me." Blaisdell turned over the second photo, which was a closer shot of the vaguely humanoid figure at the circle's center. Man-shaped but flat, like an Egyptian hieroglyph, it could have easily been mistaken for an item of discarded clothing, a rumpled outfit laid out to dry in the sun. Only upon closer scrutiny did one see the face, the genitals, the arms with hands like flaccid gloves. The flayed flesh of a sloughed human skin. A ragged tear split the hide from crown to crotch. The body itself had, as yet, not been found.

The circumstances of the death nonplussed the police, but as soon as they heard about the strange, secret drug Garston had been seeking, they assumed he must have run afoul of drug dealers. They dismissed as mere tabloid sensationalism any speculation that the murder might have been some sort of cult killing.

Blaisdell wasn't so sure.

"Do you know who might have done this?" he asked, handing Legrasse the third and final photo. It was a close-up of what was left of Garston's face, its nose and ears and chin pancaked into what looked like a Cubist portrait. Despite the deformation, Blaisdell still recognized his friend—the curly, unkempt hair going to gray, the patchy stubble on the jaw that never quite became a full beard.

"Oh, yes, I know who did it." Legrasse reddened as he pored over the pictures, sweating more than ever, fat cheeks quivering with outrage and an expression of bizarre, petulant envy. "Forty years I searched—forty years—and *Garston* gets to it first. He promised me if I helped—he *swore* . . ."

Legrasse cut off his muttering, looked up at Blaisdell. His gaze cooled to freezing. "This drug. Do you have it?"

Blaisdell almost blurted the truth. No, of course he didn't have it. Morris had bragged about the drug but had never even shown it to him.

"I don't have it with me," Blaisdell said instead. "But I have some at my hotel."

Legrasse moistened his lips. "If you bring me the drug, I'll do better than tell you what happened to Garston. I'll *show* you."

Blaisdell's heart stuttered. He did not want to see another man butchered, particularly if *he* was that man. Legrasse might well be insane. Yet he clearly knew something about Morris's death, and this might be Blaisdell's only opportunity to find out what it was.

"I can be back in twenty minutes." He barely waited for Legrasse to nod before bolting out the door.

Blaisdell exited in such haste that he collided with a hulking individual on the sidewalk just outside the museum. The figure he'd run into was so tall that Blaisdell had to crane his neck upward to see its face. A Venetian-style mask of glazed white porcelain peered down at him with blank black eyeholes, its expression neither tragic nor comic, merely impassive.

Though Mardi Gras was the traditional time for Carnivale-style masquerade, New Orleans hosted so many parties and festivals that one might see costumed revelers there nearly any time of year. The masked figure was clearly one of them. Its size had startled Blaisdell, but it wore what seemed to be a harlequin's outfit crisscrossed with diamonds of green and purple, the city's trademark colors, with a matching coxcomb from which four belled tassels curled. As Blaisdell gazed up at the blank porcelain visage above him, he saw that in addition to the two conventional eyeholes, another had been added in the center of the forehead, as if to accommodate the spiritual "third eye" of Hinduism and other Eastern religions.

"Excuse me," Blaisdell apologized, and attempted to step around the costumed stranger.

In reply, the figure seemed to turn its head *all the way around*, so that another, identical white mask now peered down at him.

Perhaps the stranger had his back to Blaisdell before. It was difficult to tell . . . the harlequin outfit appeared to be a shapeless cassock, with neither sleeves nor legs to indicate the orientation of the body. But Blaisdell was sure that only the head had twisted, owl-like, while the rest of the figure remained still. The effect must have been part of the costume—a clever gimmick, like those trick boxes he'd seen magicians use to create the illusion that their heads could rotate full-circle.

Yet, as he stepped around the queer jester, he could not shake the uncanny impression that the three eyeholes on each of the thing's two false faces all glared at him as he passed. The sensation was so strong that he had taken fewer than a half-dozen steps before he glanced back, certain he would catch the harlequin staring at him.

The sidewalk behind him was vacant. A bell jingled as the glass door of the museum eased shut. Either the bell on the door or the bell of a fool's coxcomb—Blaisdell couldn't be sure. Perhaps both.

He had little time to wonder, for he needed to find some phony drug to bring back to Legrasse. Blaisdell considered going to a pharmacy and buying a bottle of some nutritional supplement but felt sure Legrasse would see through such a ruse immediately. It couldn't be a prefabricated pill. No, it had to look like a botanical intoxicant that a native of Haiti or Africa could find in the forest, something akin to peyote or psilocybin mushrooms.

Blaisdell stepped out into the nearly barren lane and felt the first spittle of rain on his face. Peering up and down the street in desperation, he spotted one of the French Quarter's lurid souvenir shops, the sign above its door promising "VOODOO" in giant letters that looked like dripping green candles. A young black woman in a tank top with a skull on it stood before the entrance, pulling the metal security door shut with a chain.

"Excuse me! Miss?" Blaisdell waved and ran up to her. "Wait!"

"Mister, we gotta close." She nodded toward the sky, which

had darkened to the color of soot.

Blaisdell fished out his wallet, pulled what cash he had from it. "Here . . . here's eighty-four dollars. I'll only be a couple of minutes."

She rolled her eyes, but took the money and opened the metal door again.

The shop still smelled of patchouli from recently extinguished incense. In addition to T-shirts and candles, the place sold cellophane envelopes of herbs and roots for casting spells and making gris-gris bags, and Blaisdell selected the first item he saw that could pass for a controlled substance. It turned out to be mugwort, a handful of dried brownish-green leaves that resembled a hybrid of hashish and parsley. Would Legrasse recognize it for what it really was? Would he want to sample the "drug" before telling Blaisdell about Garston's death?

Perhaps, but Blaisdell didn't have any better plan, so he asked the shopkeeper for a small glass phial into which he poured the flakes of mugwort leaves.

Wind lashed Blaisdell's face with raindrops as he ran through the vacant avenues back to Legrasse's museum. He yanked the glass door open and skidded over the threshold, his water-slicked shoes slippery on the cement floor. No one answered the jangling bell, however, and the card table in the entryway was bare. Even Legrasse's notebook was gone.

Blaisdell checked the museum's other small rooms including the lavatory, but the building's only residents were the shabby *loa* manikins. Thinking Legrasse had stepped out for a smoke, Blaisdell blustered back out into the street, hoping to catch him.

Rainwater drizzled into his eyes, so that he could barely keep them open. Through the shimmering curtains of precipitation, he could just distinguish two figures far up the lane, making their way northward toward Basin Street. Blaisdell could not be certain that the shorter of the two individuals was Legrasse, but there was no mistaking the taller, hulking form in its motley robe and belled cap.

He sprinted after them, cutting across intersections and plashing through gutters to keep them in sight. The rain sheeted down, gusting into his face, saturating his suit until it clung to him like seaweed. When Blaisdell rounded the corner of Basin Street, the two figures had disappeared. All he saw were the ghostly ramparts of the white wall that bordered St. Louis Cemetery #1.

Ordinarily, a phalanx of vagrants would have lined up outside the wall to cadge a handout from the tourists who visited the city's oldest and most famous graveyard, but the torrential downpour had driven the panhandlers away. Even the cemetery's guard had apparently locked up and left in advance of the storm. But the entrance stood open and unattended, its right-hand gate now canted on one hinge, the padlock hanging from broken chains.

Blaisdell advanced into the cemetery warily, afraid of losing his quarries, afraid of finding them. Unlike its more affluent sister cemeteries, St. Louis #1 looked more like slum housing for corpses. Rather than grassy, cypress-shaded family plots with carved angels and Greco-Roman tombs, the densely packed mausoleums were tenement blocks of graffiti-marred brick with mud and gravel on the narrow paths between.

Lagging at a discreet distance, Blaisdell spotted the two figures he'd seen earlier. They wound their way between the crypts, the taller one in the lead, until they neared the tomb that may or may not have held the remains of Marie Laveau, who was renowned as a voodoo queen but may have been simply a clever hairdresser. The tall harlequin stopped, and its shorter companion stripped naked and knelt before it in the pelting rain.

Crouching behind a mausoleum several yards away, Blaisdell could clearly see from the bald pate and fleshy paunch that the supplicant was Legrasse. They must have come here because it was the nearest spot in the city where they could be sure their meeting would not be interrupted.

The harlequin emitted a sonorous, wavering hum—a vibration that Blaisdell could feel in his back molars—punctuated by guttural clicks, and Legrasse did his best to imitate the sounds with his own crude vocalizations. The costumed figure lifted a fold of its robe, and Legrasse reached up to take a proffered object: a hypodermic syringe.

Blaisdell let the phial of mugwort slip from his clenched fist. The genuine drug had to be in that needle, and it could only have come from one person.

He promised me if I helped—he swore . . .

Garston had always been a man of his word.

"Morris!" Blaisdell shouted.

As before, the harlequin turned its head so that one of its blank faces peered at him with its three hollow eyes.

But the ritual did not stop. Legrasse now had his chance to be more than a seedy dime-museum impresario, and Blaisdell could tell he was determined to go through with it. No more funhouse fakery; he would see the real *loa*.

Legrasse plunged the hypodermic's needle into a vein of his left arm and shut his eyes in an expectant ecstasy, still murmuring the strange invocation. He remained that way for several minutes after the injection, seemingly suspended in a religious trance. Then his eyes popped open in an expression of terrified surprise, such as a puppet might have made if it could feel the hand moving inside it.

A red split opened on the crown of his scalp, and Legrasse's face peeled away like cheap latex. What emerged was not the blood, bone, and sinew one would expect, but rather a viscous crimson ectoplasm that squeezed out of Legrasse's flesh like paste from a tube. It welled up and unfolded into a rose whose petals consisted of forked red tongues. A three-lobed translucent orb bobbed on the liquid surface of the coagulating creature, the eye migrating this way and that to survey its surroundings. The tear in Legrasse's skin unzipped his belly, and a thicket of quivering burgundy cilia spilled out, clicking and humming. As the remainder of Legrasse slid off into soggy heap, the *loa*, if that's what one could call it, surged in stature to the height of its companion. At the same time, the thing that had once been Morris Garston evidently saw no need to perpetuate its charade of humanity, so the prehensile cilia tore free of the motley robe and the two-faced porcelain mask shattered as its tongue-petal rose burst forth. The tasseled jester's cap tumbled off with an incongruous tinkling of bells.

At that point, Blaisdell might have fled. But, really, where could he go? If such things existed, there could be no escape. Deep in the pit of his being—in the "space inside"—Blaisdell fancied he could sense something gnawing and champing, yearning to shed the costume of his flesh.

Now he understood what Legrasse had meant when he called the word voodoo a "corruption." Time and misuse and human denial had slurred the word in the same way that *Vieux Carré* had become "Voo Carré."

Voodoo.

Vieux Dieux.

Old Gods.

Weakened with nausea, Blaisdell clung to the wall of the mausoleum and watched the two monstrosities converse in their unfathomable dead language. Far worse than their awful appearance was the impression that the greater portion of their bodies were hidden from view—that their alien forms penetrated down into the ground or, more accurately, extended into regions unseen. Blaisdell had the horrid notion that they were not separate entities at all but rather parts of a greater whole, like giant fingers dipped into the shallows of our world to feel and grope and seize. Perhaps all humans were nothing more than nascent sensory ganglia in the service of some vast, inscrutable *corpus universalis*.

His theory received dreadful confirmation an instant later, when a curtain parted in the scene before him. A yawning gap appeared in his view of the cemetery, as though the walls and tombs and sand-strewn paths were merely matte paintings on a theatrical backdrop. And through the dark rift, he glimpsed the reality that underlay the stagecraft of the visible world: a cosmos of galactic, glistening viscera, of mammoth pulsing veins and twitching, unidentifiable organs.

The things that had been Legrasse and Garston filed into the open gash in space, which then slammed shut like the door to Valhalla. A sonic boom detonated the air, and the resultant shockwave blew the surrounding crypts into a hail of bricks and bones. The explosion burst Blaisdell's eardrums and threw him back as far as the cemetery's main gate, where unconsciousness gave him a respite of blessed oblivion.

***

It was nearly a week before he awoke in the LSU Medical Center, and by that time the cataclysm in the famous St. Louis #1 Cemetery had made national headlines. Local authorities attributed the incident to a lightning bolt from the tropical storm. Blaisdell, temporarily deaf and still recovering from a concussion, said nothing to disabuse them of that theory.

As soon as he was able, he returned to Princeton and immediately retired from his position in the anthropology department. The locals saw him seldom after that. Occasionally one would find him in a local diner, hands pressed to his head as if holding it in place.

For he had peeped beneath the veil and, try as he might, he could no longer see the world around him as genuine. With dismal mien, he awaited the day when every mask, every comforting false face, would be ripped away—from him, from the world, from the new gods we created in our own image, from the universe itself—and there would be no cherished illusions to cling to. Nothing left but those things . . . the ones whose true name he could not bring himself to speak . . .

The Voodoo.

Mr. Casey Is in the House

Martin swirled the cockroach around in the popcorn cup, watching it skitter in circles, and slowly tilted the cup upside down. The insect scrambled for purchase as it slid down the slick-coated wall of the container, then dropped into the sizzling oil of the popper with the crackle of frying bacon.

Another thrilling Saturday night at the glorious Royale Cinema, the city's last remaining second-run movie theater.

Charlene snapped her gum. "That is *so* gross."

"Just doing my part for pest control." Martin peered down at his test subject, which, amazingly, still scuttled around the circumference of the popper's metal tub, seeking a way out.

Charlene leaned against the candy case and went back to daubing puce polish on her fingernails. "I read that torturing small animals is one of the telltale signs of a serial killer. You wet your bed, too, Martin?"

He bugged his eyes and leered at her. "Only when I dream about keeping your head in my fridge."

"Freak!" The girl recoiled to the opposite end of the concessions stand. "I hope Ms. Sprague cans your ass." Although barely older than her teenaged employees, the manager insisted on being called *Ms.*

"B.F.D. if she did." Martin nodded toward the vacant lobby and chucked the popcorn cup in the trash. "This place is doomed anyway."

The Royale's October "Slasher Classic" Fright Fest was a bust. Serves 'em right for playing wussy crap like the original versions of *Psycho* and *Halloween*, which had, like, what? three drops of blood between them? As resident expert on splatter films, Martin had tried to tell Sprague to go for the *Saw* and *Hostel* movies if she wanted some *real* horror, but did the manager listen to him? Of course not. No wonder the owners were planning to bulldoze this firetrap and put up condos.

"Yo, Martin!" Randy called from the box office. "We got a couple green tickets here!"

Martin abruptly snapped to attention. He slapped the lid on the popper shut to hide the frying cockroach, then buttoned up his grease-spotted red vest. "Green tickets" was their code word for cute chicks.

Two girls in their late teens entered through the theater's swinging glass doors, one in a miniskirt and platform shoes, the other in low-rise jeans and a camisole. Martin leaned forward as they approached the concessions counter and smiled.

Charlene intercepted them. "I can help you over here."

The two girls veered toward her to place their order. Charlene filled their fountain drinks with her right hand while waving the left back and forth to dry her nails.

Martin glared, clenching his jaw. She did that just to tick him off . . . and she did it a *lot*.

A flat, toneless voice pierced his brooding. "Popcorn. Large."

Martin looked over and found a gaunt man with stringy black hair standing at the counter. The guy was pale even for a Goth, and his bony frame all but disappeared in the shapeless drapery of a black trench coat. He looked only twentysomething, but his hard, flat expression seemed etched by far greater experience.

Martin pulled a fresh popcorn cup from the dispenser behind him and scooped it into the mound of white kernels they'd made before the first feature. He glanced up at the guy's reflection in the mirror mounted on the back wall of the concessions stand. "Want butter on that?"

The man stared at him with unblinking eyes, whites filigreed with bloodshot capillaries, pupils dilated to hollow blackness. His lips formed soundless words.

Junkie, Martin decided. He pumped greasy "Golden Flavored" oil onto the popcorn and passed the cup across the counter.

The dude handed him a twenty and suddenly snickered for no reason at all. "Thanks, Martin."

That creeped him out. How did the freak know his name? Then he remembered the stupid name badge pinned to his vest. *Duh*.

"Good movie, *Martin*," the dude went on. "George Romero. Ever see it?"

At that, Martin had to grin. "You bet I have. Wish we were showing it now." He fished the guy's change out of the register and jerked his head toward Charlene. "Idiots here wouldn't know real horror if it puked on 'em."

The dude smiled his appreciation. "You can say that again."

He grabbed the popcorn and wandered off without taking the change.

"This is your brain on drugs," Martin chuckled and shoved the cash in his pocket.

A few other teenagers showed up before the start of the second feature, mostly couples hoping to make out in the darkness of the near-empty theater. As always, the moment the opening credits started to roll, Ted, the projectionist, came down to the lobby and thrust his plastic tumbler at Martin. "Half Coke, no ice."

Martin half filled the cup with undiluted soda, leaving plenty of room for Ted's rum. The gangly projectionist grabbed it and headed back toward a door marked "Employees Only."

Martin ground his teeth as he unbuttoned his vest. Damned if he was going to get stuck working in this dump like that lush. Having to live with his uptight parents and brain-dead sister was already driving Martin nuts.

Bored to the point of unconsciousness, Martin filled a cup with Coke for himself. "I'm going in to watch the movie."

Charlene rolled her eyes. "Like you haven't seen it a zillion times already!"

Ignoring her, he stepped out of the concession stand and pushed through the double doors leading into the auditorium. The aroma of beer and pot smoke saturated the theater's darkened interior. That was another advantage of the Royale: lax security.

Navigating through the shifting illumination reflected from the screen, Martin made his way down the center aisle toward the front rows. As he slouched in a seat upholstered with crushed velvet, he shared the viewpoint of little Michael Myers, staring through the eyeholes of a clown mask as the boy stalked and stabbed his older sister. Fortunately, the film was dark enough that the picture camouflaged the large tear in the Royale's screen, a flap of fabric lolling from the hole like a lascivious tongue.

Wussy as the original *Halloween* was, Martin enjoyed filling in the movie with his own gory details. He pictured Mikey driving the blade right into his naked sister's navel and nipples: with some decent makeup effects, that would be awesome. Rob Zombie had done an okay job putting some guts into the remake, but even that kind of splatter had started to bore Martin. So cartoony and fake, he could tell the girls getting killed weren't being hurt at all. Martin wanted to know what it *really* felt like to do someone like that. How do you hold someone still while you're cutting 'em up, anyway? What if a dead girl gets all rigor mortis on your erection while you're still inside her? And what does a human liver taste like, with or without fava beans?

To satisfy his curiosity, Martin had been checking out some really gnarly autopsy photos online, and had gone from watching cheesy low-budget flicks about Berkowitz and Manson to poring over true-crime books about them. He fantasized about one day collecting serial-killer memorabilia like the lead singer from Korn, stuff like Gacy's clown drawings or Bundy's VW Bug. Man, that would be *sick!*

Not that Martin could bid for those kinds of trophies anytime soon, especially if he couldn't even hold onto a slave-wage job at the Royale. He didn't want Sprague, She-Wolf of the S.S., to catch him loafing, so he joined the crowd that left during the closing credits, before the house lights came up. As the patrons filed out the auditorium's double doors, the manager emerged from her office in her usual pantsuit and pumps to supervise the Royale's closing ritual. Martin pretended to tidy the concessions stand so she wouldn't ask him to help sweep the theater.

"Go ahead and cash out, Charlene," Sprague said. Barely out of high school herself, she'd made manager before she was twenty by having a bug up her butt the size of Missouri. "Randy, why don't you start on clean-up?"

"You got it!" He propped open one of the theater's double doors and wheeled a garbage can into the auditorium.

Martin saw Randy return to the lobby just a few minutes later, before Sprague had even finished counting Charlene's register drawer. The ticket seller clutched at his stomach, his face ashen as he shuffled over to the manager.

Sprague glanced up from thumbing through a stack of fives and frowned. "What is it?"

Randy scanned the lobby, where a few audience members still lingered. The two green tickets gossiped with Charlene, while another girl waited for her boyfriend to get out of the bathroom.

Randy leaned closer and spoke in a low, unsteady voice. *"Mr. Casey is in the house."*

Martin saw Sprague blanch and felt the hair on his own scalp prickle. "Mr. Casey is in the house" was the code signal cinema employees used to inform management of an emergency, such as a fire in the building, so the patrons wouldn't panic and trample one another stampeding toward the exits.

Sprague hastened Randy into her office, out of earshot of any customers. Unobserved, Martin sauntered over to the open door of the auditorium and stepped inside.

Brass lighting fixtures with fluted chimneys of frosted glass, relics of the Royale's heyday in the thirties, illuminated the theater with a dim, jaundiced glow. Once bright crimson, the carpeting along the center aisle had blackened to maroon, and soft drink stains and pancakes of dried chewing gum dotted its length. A fresh yellow splat marked the spot in the aisle where Randy had barfed.

Only one audience member remained in the cavernous auditorium: the dude slumped in an aisle seat, second row from the front, his head lolling over the edge of the backrest. It was not unusual at the Royale to find bums or druggies who'd passed out during the show. The spreading wetness under the guy's chair might simply have been a sloshed soda or beer.

Martin halted halfway down the aisle. Beside the overturned popcorn cup at the man's feet, white kernels had scattered over the spilled liquid and turned scarlet. A knife lay on the floor by the figure's limp right hand, the blade drizzling redness. Martin didn't need to see the freak's face to know who the dude was, for he had already recognized the stringy black hair and pale skin.

***

"Did you see him that night? I mean, see his *eyes*, up close?" Charlene hugged herself, as if the stuffy lobby had become a mortuary freezer.

Randy shook his head. "Not until . . . you know. They were still open."

"Well, you could tell he was a freak." She shuddered. "The cops say he killed those girls they've been finding along I-5. He found out they were onto him, so he cut up his mom, then came here to off himself."

Randy looked at his feet and shrugged. "Guess he did us a favor."

"Yeah, but why did he have to come *here?* I'm so creeped out I didn't even want to come to work."

Sweeping up the flattened popcorn kernels that littered the lobby, Martin paused to grin at her. "Hey, he's the closest thing to a celebrity we've had here. I think it's cool."

She made a face. "You would."

After the psycho committed suicide, the Royale had closed for a couple of days to allow the police to conduct their investigation. Tonight the staff had reopened the theater, and naturally the killer was all they could talk about. "And how do you know so much about the dude, Charlene?" Martin jeered. "Been Googling everything you can about him, haven't you? Admit it—you're just as into the whole thing as I am."

"Whatever." Unable to think of a snappier comeback, she took a sudden interest in wiping down the candy case.

Martin's grin widened. He'd never actually managed to shut her up before.

Although he'd said it to tweak her, Martin honestly *did* think it was cool that, after months of reading about guys like Henry Lee Lucas and Jeffrey Dahmer, he'd met an actual serial killer, face-to-face. The guy sounded like a top-notch sicko, too. The local paper gave his name as Virgil Aldon Barnett, and the cops figured that he'd murdered at least sixteen women before butchering his mom. Although the reports withheld details "out of sensitivity to our readers," the stuff they hinted at was juicy enough. The articles mentioned that at least one victim had been decapitated and that semen samples had been recovered "from inside the body cavity" of another. Detectives and reporters speculated that self-loathing over the viciousness of his final crimes may have driven him to take his own life.

Now Martin wished he'd talked to the dude more while he'd had the chance. At the very least, he should have gotten a better look at Barnett's body. Maybe even grabbed the guy's knife before the cops got it. Heck, Martin would have settled for the murderer's empty popcorn cup. That's one souvenir you'd never find on eBay! Damn! When would he have an opportunity like *that* again? If only he hadn't been so squeamish about getting close to the corpse.

Ironically, the killer's suicide gave the Royale such notoriety in the local press that the "Slasher Classic" Fright Fest became a huge overnight success. Local teens lined up around the block to be part of the first audience in a theater where a genuine slasher bled to death. The packed house resulted in a bumper crop of trash, and Ms. Sprague asked for a "volunteer" to stay late, clean up, and secure the premises. Charlene immediately said she wouldn't go anywhere near where the dead guy had been, while Randy peered down at the carpet, his mouth twisting, evidently hoping the manager wouldn't notice him.

Martin gave a crooked smile. "I'll do it."

Everyone looked at him as if horns had sprouted from his forehead. Ordinarily Martin would never have offered to work late.

But tonight was different—it might be his only chance to see the remaining bloodstains before they cleaned everything up.

"Look, you want me to do it or not?" he snapped when no one said anything.

Ms. Sprague spread her hands to indicate the empty lobby. "Hey, it's all yours. But I better find it clean in the morning. And don't forget to block the doors before you go."

Randy and Charlene punched out on the time clock and left with Sprague, who locked the Royale's entrance behind her and took the keys. The push bars on the doors would allow Martin to exit, but once he did he'd be shut out of the building. Only a few lights remained on in the lobby for his benefit; his final duty for the evening would be to flick the switch in the circuit breaker box that would turn them off.

Relieved to be rid of the others, he popped in his earbuds and blasted Cannibal Corpse and Psycroptic into his skull while he shuffled around and bagged garbage. He worked just long enough to be sure that Sprague wouldn't come back for something, then went through the double doors to see Virgil Aldon Barnett's blood for himself. Martin swore that the theater still reeked of it—a rusty odor he could taste on his tongue as he drew closer to the aisle seat in the second row. Once the cops had finished their investigation, Sprague asked Randy to swab the floor with a cou-

ple gallons of bleach, but the stain beneath the chair had permeated the cement so badly that the usher could not mop it away.
Sprague said she might have to call in a special crime-scene cleaning service to sanitize the place.

The ruined seat was still bolted to the floor, and Maintenance
hadn't sent anyone to remove it yet. Randy had covered the chair
with a black plastic trash bag and stretched thick strips of silver
duct tape across the armrests to keep people from sitting there until
it could be replaced. These precautions hadn't deterred some thrill-
seeker from occupying the corpse's seat. The duct tape dangled
from its sides in curlicue tangles, and the shifting weight of the
chair's recent occupant had rent a large hole in the plastic cover.

Martin told himself that he wasn't going to wimp out this
time. He probed the open lips of the tear with quivering fingers,
until he touched the velvet upholstery. The cushion was still
sticky, gummed with what felt like the trail of a giant slug. Martin
recoiled, cursing, and wiped his hand on his vest with prissy anxiety.

A bead of sweat dripped into his eye, and he brushed it away.
It certainly wasn't heat that was making him perspire. Sprague
had lowered the thermostat to keep the larger audiences comfortable during the Indian summer weather. With only Martin's body
to warm the cavernous space, the theater had turned numbingly
cold, yet he stood motionless in front of the forbidden aisle seat.
An overwhelming urge seized him to rip off that stupid plastic
bag and sit in Virgil Aldon Barnett's place.

The fact that he wanted to cozy up to that gore—wanted it
badly—tripped Martin out. He busied himself with his closing
chores to keep from thinking about it. Ms. Sprague would have been
astonished at how quickly he cleared up the half-empty soft drink
cups and crumpled candy wrappers. He just wanted out of there.

From the utility closet in the lobby, he grabbed two L-shaped
wooden blocks from a stack in the corner and returned to make a
final check of the auditorium. Local homeless people often

viewed the Royale as a dirt-cheap motel, so Martin gingerly checked behind the threadbare, red velvet drapes hanging on either side of the screen, searching for hidden vagrants. He didn't know what he'd actually do if he found one, but he kept hold of the wooden blocks as possible weapons, just in case. Last of all, he checked the dark niche beneath the screen.

Satisfied that only he and the cockroaches remained, Martin crossed over to the fire exit. Testing to make sure the door was firmly latched, he wedged both blocks in between the door and its push bar handle to keep anyone from using a coat hanger to open the door from the outside. Now all he had to do was get the other pair of blocks from the closet, jam them in the door handle on the front entrance, and leave this dump.

He got about halfway up the center aisle when the house lights went down.

Total darkness engulfed Martin. Not even the exit sign stayed lit.

He groaned. Randy's little joke, no doubt. Ha-ha, very funny. Martin put his hands out at arm's length and inched his way forward.

A circle of light flickered on in the square window of the projection booth, a cone of dancing cinema light frosting forward to the movie screen. As the soundtrack slurred up to speed, a girl's shriek cleft the air. *"Get offa me! Oh, God—"*

The scream made Martin jump with its suddenness, but it didn't frighten him. It was a horror movie, after all. He raised a hand to block the shimmering light from the projector and tried to spot Ted, the alcoholic projectionist, up there in the booth. Maybe the lush had arranged his own private screening.

Martin turned to see what was showing. It definitely wasn't either *Psycho* or *Halloween*. The picture was shot with a jerky handheld camera from a killer's point of view. No masks here, no coy cutting to Hershey's syrup swirling down the shower drain. Just a skinny, buck-naked teenage prostitute, pinned down in the back of a night-darkened SUV. Other than the few intelligible words Martin heard, her dialogue consisted of either pitiful yelps or guttural choking as the spidery male hand at her throat throttled her. Tears speckled the heavy eyeliner and blue eye shadow, overdone cosmetics that made the adolescent look like a kid who'd played with Mommy's makeup kit.

The camera showed little interest in her face, choosing instead to focus on the carbon-steel hunting knife that unzipped her bare belly. Martin gawked in dumb fascination as the lens plunged into the entrails bursting through the slit midriff, winced as if *he* were the one nuzzling his face in the slick innards as the dying girl squirmed at her body's violation. The theater's iron stench thickened around him.

Martin had never seen a movie like this—more like a snuff film than a teen screamfest. He wondered what it was. Had Sprague finally taken his advice and booked some torture porn for the Royale?

The screen remained a blurred smear of burgundy as the viewpoint protagonist wallowed in gore. It bothered Martin more than the other flicks he'd seen. The violence didn't have the jaunty, music-video editing or the exaggerated funhouse shock value of splatter. Instead, the ordeal dragged on, the girl dying by degrees, until her shrieks became grating white noise. And the longer it went on, the more Martin *felt* it, as if someone were nuzzling his own guts.

The shot grew so grindingly monotonous that Martin couldn't keep his eyes from wandering. And that's when he saw the silhouette outlined in the aisle seat, second row.

Good movie, Martin.

Martin flinched, for the voice hadn't come from the sound system's speakers but from inside his head. It played in his brain like a memory, echoing the brief conversation he'd had with Virgil Aldon Barnett. But its intonation was entirely new—sinuous and insinuating.

He stared at the back of the shadowy figure's head. There

couldn't be anyone else in the theater. He'd checked. There was nowhere Randy or Tom could have hidden from him.

I knew you'd appreciate my work, said the voice that he might have mistaken for his own thoughts. *You and me—we like* real *horror.*

It didn't occur to Martin until then that he should say something. "Y-you . . . you're not supposed to be here."

The voice ignored the interruption. *The others, they don't understand. My mom sure didn't.*

The scene onscreen abruptly cut to another location, with no attempt to bridge the transition with exposition or narrative logic. This time, the set was a tiny bedroom with pressboard paneling, the kind found in mobile homes. The camera looked down upon a nude female form on the bed, but this body belonged to a much older woman. The breasts and hips fleshy and rumpled, and the stomach bearing the stretch marks and C-section scars of multiple pregnancies. But something else was different: the body's skin remained livid when a hand swung into the camera's view and slapped the flabby tits, and the arms stayed as stiff and still as manikin limbs while the unseen cinematographer ground his pelvis against the prostrate woman.

The camera panned up the woman's torso, and Martin gagged. The neck ended in serrated tears of sawn skin, sinew, and spine, leaving only a gaping vacancy on the bloodstained pillow. But the lens focused on a bookshelf about a foot above the bed.

There, among thrift-shop knickknacks and ceramic figurines, rested the head of a trailer-park Medusa, her disheveled salt-and-pepper hair still partially rolled in pink plastic curlers, the color drained from her face along with the blood that oozed from the stump beneath her doubled chin. Her filmy, half-lidded eyes had rolled up toward the ceiling, unable to watch the spectacle even in death.

Doubled over by nausea, Martin braced himself against the seat nearest him and heaved, but couldn't seem to draw enough breath to vomit. He thought he'd seen everything—after all, he'd rented DVDs about guys like Edmund Kemper and Ed Gein, complete with buckets of corn-syrup gore. But he hadn't realized just how much of the reality the directors left out. Here he could almost feel the rubbery hardness of the lifeless breasts, the cold stiffening of the labia in the beginning stages of rigor mortis.

"Y-you've got to go," Martin stammered, trying to convince himself that this guy was only a bum looking for a place to flop for the night. "Or I'll call the cops."

He wished he had the wooden blocks back—any weapon, in fact—but doubted they would make any difference. His gaze again fixed on the figure in the second-row aisle seat. The head no longer lolled against the back of the chair but now tilted upward, peering avidly at the screen. Martin got the crazy impression that the celluloid images up there did not originate in the projection booth, but instead radiated out from the silhouette like an aura of atrocity.

Know why I killed myself, Martin? the echo in his skull asked. *Not from remorse, no matter what people would like to think. No, I couldn't stand the thought of spending the rest of my life in jail, never again to know the joy of torment, the ecstasy of annihilation . . .*

Martin spun around, the coruscating light from the projector dazzling him as he turned his back on the screen. He intended to run up the aisle and out of the theater, but the extremes of bright and dark disoriented him. The upward slope of the auditorium floor seemed to seesaw beneath him, tilting like the base of an upended cup, and when the blinding afterimages cleared from his eyes, Martin found himself skittering like a terrified insect *toward* the screen. He skidded to a halt mere feet from the second row aisle seat.

But the movie doesn't have to end. Now I can watch, and you can be the star.

The set onscreen morphed into a different location—a different bedroom—this one decorated in girly pinks and pastels and

Hello Kitty crap. Martin didn't need to see the bare body of the tween girl on the bed to know who it was.

"Rochelle," he croaked.

He had never seen nor ever wanted to see his kid sister naked. Now she was splayed out before him like any horror movie scream queen, arms lashed to the headboard with nylon rope. Except she was no Bijou Phillips or Linnea Quigley—this was a twelve-year-old whose preadolescent chest had barely begun to bud breasts. She thrashed on the mattress, bawling, her baby-fat face bunched in agony. Beneath her bony ribcage, her punctured belly button welled red over the bulge of her tummy.

So how about it, Martin? the whisperer goaded. *Are you a poser or a player?*

A sickening excitation stirred in Martin's crotch; it seemed he could feel his erection penetrate the wound, its shaft lubricated with blood. Although he would never have admitted it to anyone, Martin was still a virgin, and he'd always fantasized that his first time would be with a hot girl his own age—a green ticket— who'd welcome his touch with a sultry smile and deep tongue kisses. Not this—this fear, revulsion, and hatred. And certainly not with his *sister*. Sure, she irritated him but *this* . . .

"Go to hell! " Martin clapped his hands over his eyes, shouting defiantly at the shadow in front of him. "I won't watch any more! I'm not *like* you!"

The moment he said it, though, it occurred to Martin that he might be—probably was—imagining this whole thing. If so, his own mind had produced everything he saw on the screen . . . which meant he *was* like Virgil Aldon Barnett.

He'd shut his eyes, but the festival of depravities continued to unspool before his vision, as if his hands and eyelids had become transparent. Martin started to cry, and he let his legs fold up, expecting to sink to the floor. Instead, he found himself supported—comfortably cushioned for the next feature.

"I'm *not* like you!" His fingers clawed into the hollows beneath his brows, but he couldn't look away from the movie screen. *"I don't want to see!"*

The film rolled on . . .

***

Kids were already camped outside the Royale when Randy arrived at eleven in the morning to prep the theater for the first matinee. Evidently, neither school truancy laws nor the Fright Fest's "R" rating could stop the teens from trying to sneak into what the locals had dubbed the "Serial Killer Cinema."

Since the discovery of the killer's body, Charlene had flatly refused to enter the auditorium, which left Randy as the only other person on the day shift to unlock the theater exits and make sure that Martin the Slacker had actually cleaned up the place the previous night. As the sole staff member who'd actually seen the ear-to-ear gash gaping beneath the dead man's jaw, Randy didn't relish the thought of going in there again, but at least it was easier than having to deal with the hot dogs and popcorn at the concessions stand.

As he pushed open one of the double doors, the taint of blood in the air made Randy feel as if he was going to hurl again. He'd have to gas the place with Lysol. The queasy sense of *déjà vu* swelled when he saw a dark-haired figure seated in *that* chair—the one with the tattered black trash bag still draped over it. The fleeting notion that somehow Virgil Aldon Barnett's body had returned nearly sent Randy running from the theater.

But he quickly saw that the guy in the chair was not the dead serial killer. This figure rocked back and forth and made little mewling sounds as if weeping. And he wore the ill-fitting red vest of a Royale usher.

"Martin?" Randy moved down the center aisle toward him. "You spent the whole night here, buddy?"

His steps slowed when Martin didn't answer. He suddenly dreaded the thought of seeing Martin's face, particularly as the words Martin muttered grew more distinct.

"No more, please. I don't want to see any more . . ."

Martin's profile phased into view like a moon emerging from eclipse. He pressed his balled fists to his temples; trickles of blood and clear, viscous fluid ran from between the knuckles. Crimson drips trailed down his cheeks in lieu of tears.

The vacant gouges of the sockets gaped as if they still had eyes.

"Please stop. I don't want to see."

Randy reflexively glanced in the direction that Martin stared. He saw nothing but the Royale's blank white screen with its sagging rip. Randy backed away, his chest heaving, and ran up the aisle.

He nearly slammed into Ms. Sprague as he barreled out into the lobby.

"What is it?" The manager's expression darkened from quizzical to apprehensive. "Is something wrong?"

Randy was about to blurt what he'd seen, but he noticed that Charlene had already unlocked the front entrance and started to take tickets from the patrons who surged into the lobby. Two teen girls—the green tickets from earlier that week—had returned for an encore performance, giggling with excitement as they approached the double doors of the auditorium.

For the second time that week, Randy steadied his breath and bent to whisper in Ms. Sprague's ear. *"Mr. Casey is in the house."*

Transubstantiation

Marcus squeezed the ball in his hand until his fingernails dug into its rubber surface, as if to pump every drop of blood in his body into the little plastic bag connected to his arm. A white-coated Red Cross matron with flat-topped granny glasses hurried over to the cot where he lay.

"Whoa! That's enough!" She pulled the needle from his arm and placed a square of gauze padding over the hole in his arm. "If you could hold that for me a moment . . ."

He placed his left hand over the gauze and lifted his right forearm.

"Ah, I knew you were a pro at this!" She sealed and labeled the bag, which now bulged with burgundy fluid. "Sure filled that one fast." Nudging his fingers off the gauze, she taped the pad to his arm. "Now, you go ahead and lie here for a few minutes—"

Marcus sat up and swung his legs off the cot. "I'm okay."

"Are you sure?" She quickened her steps to keep up with him as he stalked toward the exit. "You know, you shouldn't drive until the dizziness passes."

He smiled at her. "I'm fine, really."

"Well, here." She bustled over to a table and dug some items out of an ice chest and a paper grocery bag. "At least take these along to fortify you." She handed him a half-pint carton of orange juice and a little package of chocolate-chip cookies.

The thought of drinking orange juice again nauseated him, but he accepted the gifts graciously. "Thanks."

Once outside the clinic, he dropped the juice and cookies in the nearest trash can, then ripped the tape and gauze off his arm and added them to the garbage. There wasn't even a scab left on his skin.

He checked his watch: half-past three. If traffic wasn't too bad on the Santa Monica, he could make it to the collection center downtown before they closed. That would make it seven pints today.

He used a different name, of course, but the routine was the same—the paperwork, the needle, the bag, the gauze. An hour later, Marcus found himself back on the street, chucking another helping of juice and cookies into a garbage can and thinking about dinner.

He'd developed a passion for corned-beef sandwiches recently, so he made his way to a little Jewish deli he'd discovered off Fairfax, stopping at a newsstand on the way to pick up the most recent papers. It amused Marcus to sit among the sandwich shop's older patrons and eavesdrop on their kaffeeklatsch, which they spiced with a sprinkling of Yiddish. He relished the irony, for most people thought he was a Jew. But he wasn't. He had never been a Jew.

Pausing occasionally to take a bite of his sandwich, he scanned the pertinent sections of each of the newspapers he'd bought, generally skimming past the major headlines to survey the smaller, marginalized articles: the *L. A. Times*, the *New York Times*, *USA Today*, the *Chicago Tribune*, the *National Enquirer*.

He liked to pick up the *London Times* or *Le Monde*, too, when he could find them, but so few vendors carried them here in the States.

Nothing in the newspapers caught his eye, and he grew despondent. His appetite gone, he abandoned his half-eaten sandwich, tossed a tip on the table beside the rumpled papers, and shuffled back out onto the street.

Gray in the day's twilight, the boulevard mirrored his melancholy. The streetlights hadn't come on yet, and shadows blurred the features of buildings and faces. Perhaps that is why the young woman strolling past on the opposite sidewalk looked so much like Julia.

Marcus had long ago become accustomed to these cases of mistaken identity. He'd met so many people in his life that nearly everyone he saw resembled someone from his past. After all these years, he believed himself immune to such self-deceptions, but the acute sense of defeat and desolation he felt that evening left him vulnerable to the comforting allure of a familiar face— particularly the face of his first wife.

Though his parked car was in the opposite direction, Marcus moved to follow the young woman as she and her female companion made their way up the street. Hastening his stride to keep her in sight, he gazed with longing at the ringlets of black hair tied up on the back of her head, at the hands that fluttered like doves when she spoke, at the full lips that parted in a carefree laugh as she conversed with her friend. Each facial detail, each gesture so much like Julia's that, for an instant, Marcus succumbed to the fantasy that this girl was his love reincarnated, her soul returned to him from the depths of Time's abyss.

Then her blonde companion leaned forward and whispered conspiratorially in her ear, glancing in Marcus's direction. Before Marcus could turn away, the dark-haired woman peered across the street at him, rolled her eyes, and put a hand over her mouth as she and her friend exchanged looks of mock horror and giggled. The reaction shattered Marcus's illusion. She was only a callow American girl, barely out of her teens, who took him for some pathetic, aging lecher.

His face hot with humiliation, he turned and marched back to his car, muttering inaudible curses in Latin. Wallowing in an unwelcome tide of nostalgia, he drove around for more than an hour, vainly searching for a wine shop or liquor store that carried Cecubo. He finally settled for one of the better Chiantis and returned to his hotel room to sulk.

With the muffled roar of the planes at LAX in his ears, Marcus consoled himself as he slouched in his room's sole chair and sucked wine from the bottle. Another day or two as productive as this one and he could move on. San Francisco next—he hadn't been there in months. Then on to Seattle, Detroit, Chicago, New York, London, Paris. With any luck, he'd circle the globe again within a year.

He lifted the bottle to eye-level and contemplated the dark dregs of the wine as they swirled inside the green glass. *For this is my blood of the new testament, which is shed for many for the remission of sins.* He'd memorized that bit—in eight different languages, no less. Sometimes he recited it to himself when he had trouble urinating in public restrooms.

That night he had the dream again, in its most awful incarnation yet.

The dying sun stretched from horizon to horizon in the sky above him, red and boiling in its final, furious glory. It had swallowed two of its children whole, and now it licked the earth with tongues of flame. The crimson glare was brighter than the blast of a billion hydrogen bombs, yet he did not go blind. A sea of molten glass that had once been a beach engulfed him, its searing, viscous fluid a grotesque parody of the evaporated ocean. He clawed toward the sky with his arm, and beads of glowing glass dripped from his immortal flesh.

Is this it? he wanted to scream. *Are you coming back now?* But no sound emerged from his scalded throat. The atmosphere had dissipated eons ago.

Marcus writhed in his sheets and awoke, whimpering.

Five billion years. Two millennia are like the flap of a hummingbird's wings compared to such a span.

Even then, it wouldn't end. The sun would shrink and shut down, leaving him on a frozen black rock to watch and wait for every star in the sky to wink out. Only human arrogance made people believe the universe would end with their fleeting existence. The true Apocalypse lay across a vast, vacant desert of Time.

Though it was barely three A.M., Marcus clambered out of bed and groped his way to the bathroom. Flicking on the fluorescent lights, he bent over the basin and ran cold water over his face, which still burned from the silicate lava in his dream. He glared at his pallid reflection in the mirror. Here was the ultimate indignity—to walk through eternity in a perpetual state of encroaching middle age. Kingdoms would crumble, galaxies would dim and disperse, but his balding crown and bloated paunch would remain the same forever.

As soon as he'd shaved and dressed, Marcus drove directly from the hotel to a newsstand to pick up the morning editions of the daily papers. With only the dome light of his rented Cadillac to read by, he passed the hours until dawn hungrily searching every sheet of newsprint for a sign. He found one on page three of the *Times*'s California section:

Shopkeeper, Shot Five Times, Survives
Medicine: Doctors call Ramon Torres's recovery remarkable.

By Maria Tanner, Times Staff Writer

Yesterday, he lay in a pool of his own blood with five bullets lodged in his torso. Today, he is sitting up in his hospital bed to receive a bouquet of flowers and a kiss from his wife Susan.

"Jesus pulled me through," affirms Ramon Torres of Gardena. Torres, 54, was shot five times in the chest during a gang-related hold-up at the downtown liquor store he owns and operates. The doctors who attended him upon his arrival at Memorial Hospital gave the critically wounded man little chance of survival.

Nevertheless, Torres's condition began to stabilize immediately following a four-hour operation, during which surgeons removed the slugs from his body, sutured wounds in his lungs and stomach, and replaced the massive quantities of blood he'd lost before medical assistance arrived at the crime scene . . .

Marcus removed the page containing the article, neatly folded it, and set it on the passenger seat beside him. The rest of the newspapers he stacked and carried to the nearest garbage can. With a renewed sense of purpose, he returned to his car and steered it toward the I-5 southbound.

By leaving early, he beat most of the rush-hour traffic and arrived at the UCI Medical Center in a little over an hour. If he
moved quickly, he could visit a dozen of Orange County's major
hospitals that day.

**

The donations began as a form of penance. *For this is my blood
of the new testament, which is shed for many for the remission of
sins*, the Jewish king had said. Marcus hoped that, if he shed
enough of his own blood to save the masses, perhaps he could ex-
piate the sin that had doomed him to become a deathless vagrant.

It had seemed a trivial offense at the time. The Nazarene was
nothing more than the leader of an obscure Jewish cult when they
brought him into the hall of the Praetorium. Marcus and his cen-
turions roared with laughter as they made sport of the impover-
ished prisoner's pretensions of being a king. The soldiers hung red
draperies on his emaciated shoulders for an imperial cloak and
shoved a reed in his right hand for a scepter.

"And no king should be without a crown," Marcus murmured,
carrying a circlet of thorns to where two guards had pushed the
prisoner to his knees. "Let this be your coronation, King of Jews!"

As he set the mock crown on the Nazarene's head, the con-
demned man's bony hand seized Marcus's wrist with disconcert-
ing strength and pressed the flesh of his palm onto the needle-
sharp spines.

Marcus recoiled in pain and surprise and stared in shock at his
hand, which had started to bleed. Rivulets of blood also dripped
down the brow of the Nazarene, who regarded him with a pitying
gaze. Enraged, Marcus raised his wounded hand and struck the
prisoner's impudent face.

A hush fell over the crowd in the Praetorium. "Take this king
away and crucify him," Marcus muttered to the guards.

Silent until then, the Nazarene suddenly spoke to him in perfect Latin. "I go now," he said, his voice grim, almost sad, "but you

shall be waiting for me when I return."

The guards led him away. Deaf to the jeers of the soldiers around him, Marcus looked down at his hand and saw the blood from the Nazarene's face mingle with his own—a heavier crimson suffusing the thinner, paler plasma. He watched the merged fluid retreat into the puncture wounds in his palm, which sealed themselves and vanished without a trace.

Like stigmata in reverse, he thought, several centuries later. It took several centuries for the concept of "stigmata" to evolve, for the cult of that obscure Nazarene to conquer the Empire. As the parade of history passed before him, Marcus witnessed the death of his family, his nation, his language, and his gods. And he began to have the dream.

Though the landscape of the dream changed from age to age, its essence remained the same. In one version, he shuffled through villages littered with corpses whose white skin bulged with red buboes. In another, he wandered through a blasted cityscape whose only residents were silhouettes of ash. Each vision portrayed the same fate: the human race had become extinct, leaving him to confront Eternity alone.

Alone.

He'd roamed the planet for nearly two thousand years, searching for some sort of reprieve from this ultimate desolation. He'd married a hundred wives, sired a thousand children, amassed enormous wealth, yet nothing offered him any promise of salvation.

When medical science revealed that a person could share his blood with his fellow humans, though, a new hope took shape in Marcus's mind. He considered how the Nazarene had recovered from a crucifixion in only three days, and recalled how his own hand had healed after his blood fused with that of the Jewish king.

What began as a form of penance soon became an obsession.

It was almost eight o'clock when Marcus returned to his hotel room that night. He notified the front desk that he intended to check out the following day, then called the airport and reserved a seat on an early flight to San Francisco.

Sighing as he hung up the phone, Marcus pulled the folded newspaper page from his coat pocket and reread the item he'd set aside that morning. He laid the article on the hotel room's desk, then opened his suitcase and took out a pair of scissors, a jar of rubber cement, and a large scrapbook.

Carefully clipping the piece from the surrounding copy, he pasted the article on the first blank page he came to in the scrapbook. With the latest addition to his collection secure in its place, he flipped back through the preceding pages and scanned the stories that covered them in a crazy-quilt patchwork of print. The headlines ranged in tenor from tepid to tabloid: "Girl's Leukemia in Sudden Remission"; "Car Crash Victim Emerges from Coma"; "Doctors Baffled by Hemophiliac's Vanishing HIV"; "142-Year-Old Man Alive and Well in Upstate New York."

Marcus stroked the articles' black-and-white photos with his fingertips, smiling wistfully at the faces of his future family. A family he could keep with him forever.

He would not face the end of times alone.

The Colorless People

Her arm glowed orange in the darkness as she reached for the doorknob, tiny white sparks jumping off the hairs that stood straight up along her skin. Lauren eased the door open and crept into the studio, listening again for the sound that had awakened her.

The room was awash in a dim blue phosphorescence, as if touched with St. Elmo's Fire, and here and there the luminescence stirred and swirled with currents of air. It flowed mist-like over and around the drawing table and easels, shrouding the room in sheets of pale light. Against the muted backdrop, the potted plants that hung from the rafters shimmered with green fire.

The door on the opposite side of the studio stood ajar. Lauren moved toward it, her bare feet leaving golden patches on the floor behind her.

A ball of yellow lightning wrapped around a dark center bounded through the open door toward her. Lauren gasped and stiffened, then relaxed as the shape of the Scotch terrier defined itself in the amber haze. "Angus!"

Smiling, she squatted to embrace the dog. Smears of pink played across his fur where she stroked him. "What have you been up to?"

Her smile faded as she felt the animal shiver, as she noticed the way the light around him sparked and flickered. She picked him up and stood, cupping him in her arms. The dog whimpered, and she glanced up to see a figure standing directly in front of her.

Outlined by a blue corona, the silhouette looked black and bottomless, for all light ended at the sharp edge of its event horizon. Lauren thought she must be having one of her nightmares until the silhouette reached out, put its dark hands on her shoulders, and pulled her toward it.

***

As far back as she could remember, Lauren had seen the colors. As a child, she welcomed the comforting amber gleam of her parents, the warm pink and gold of their touch when they cradled her or patted her belly. The street they lived on was a kaleidoscope of clashing hues, where the neon green of trees and shrubs mingled with the swirling turquoise of the air, where stoplight-red crows fought for trash scraps at the front curb and taxicab-yellow cats prowled the fences.

Lauren quickly learned to interpret the patterns of light around people as if they were facial expressions, though the patterns and the expressions did not always match. At first, it puzzled her how her father could sit crackling in red while her mother was wrapped in blue, yet they could still make quiet small talk to each other across the dinner table. She was only five years old then.

Still, it didn't surprise her when she found her mother in the kitchen one day furiously scouring a frying pan in the sink, patches of crimson and cobalt colliding and sparking around her. "What's wrong, Mommy?" Lauren asked.

Her mother sagged against the sink and began crying. Later she explained that she and Daddy didn't love each other anymore and were getting a divorce. "I thought so," Lauren replied.

It wasn't till the age of six that Lauren began to realize that other people didn't see the world the same way she did. For her, the colors were an ordinary part of vision, and she assumed everyone else could see them too.

That was before she saw the Colorless Man.

They were Christmas shopping at the mall. Her mother had stopped to look in a store window at a dress she couldn't afford, gripping Lauren's hand to keep her from wandering off into the holiday crowds. Lauren rocked back and forth on her heels and watched the parade of shoppers go by, bubbles of colored light drifting past.

The crowd parted for a moment, and Lauren caught sight of a bald-headed figure in a long black overcoat. She squinted at it and thought it must be another department-store dummy, for it didn't radiate the kind of glow a person would. Even the blue and violet of the air darkened around it.

A little boy in a plump down jacket waddled into view, head swiveling right and left as he searched for his missing parent. Orange blotches of fear and confusion skittered across the yellow cocoon of light surrounding him. The dark-coated figure moved unexpectedly, and Lauren realized it really was a man.

He knelt beside the boy and smiled. He said something, and the boy calmed down, even smiled back. The man still showed no luminescence and resembled a rock in a field of flowers. Yet when he leaned close to whisper in the boy's ear, he inhaled strands of the child's rich, honey-colored aura as if savoring the bouquet of a fine brandy. Tendrils of amber vapor curled into his nostrils and wafted over his teeth and tongue.

"Mommy," Lauren asked, "can someone be a ghost before they die?"

"What?" Her mother scowled at her. "What on earth are you talking about? Honestly, Laurie, I don't know where you get such ideas."

Lauren pursed her lips. Another large crowd of people got off the nearby escalator. By the time they'd walked past, the man and the little boy were gone.

She never saw the man again, though sometimes she thought she glimpsed his pale visage at the edge of her vision. As the years went by, however, she noticed other Colorless People: a homeless woman slumped in a doorway, muttering to no one; a teenage girl with gnawed fingernails, sitting alone in a coffee shop on a Saturday night; a blank-eyed businessman on a Metrolink train, hugging his briefcase to his chest. And in her dreams, dark, faceless figures pressed in upon her, smothered her, snuffed her.

Through her art, Lauren tried to show the world what she

saw. People must have sensed the underlying truth of her work, for her paintings became popular, even fashionable, and they sold well enough to make the payments on her small condo in Placentia. Most of them depicted the world as a glowing place, filled with people wrapped in the bands of rainbows. But a few showed outlines of human figures that contained nothing but black empty negative spaces, like the ash shadows left by a nuclear bomb blast. Those were the paintings she could never sell, the canvases most gallery viewers passed over with a hasty, nervous glance.

That was the first thing about David that attracted her. At one of her art openings, she saw him stand in front of "Isolation No. 4" for more than five minutes. He gazed almost without blinking at the central figure of the picture: a black silhouette of a man, crouched into a fetal ball and submerged in an organic red background suggestive of the inside of a womb. His lips parted as if he were about to say something, but only let out a sigh.

Lauren approached him. "You like this one?"

He looked at her, startled, and averted his gaze from the painting apologetically. "Hmm? Oh, uh, I don't know—not *like*, exactly, but . . . it's interesting." He glanced back at it and gave her a taut grin. "The artist must've been really depressed the day he did it, huh?"

"She," Lauren corrected and smiled back. "No, not really."

His mouth hung open. "Are you . . . ?"

"Lauren Maxwell. At your service."

He put a hand to his brow and shook his head. "I—oh, man, I'm sorry."

"Don't worry. Happens all the time."

"Well, it's comforting to know I'm not the only clueless one around." She chuckled, and he seemed to relax. "David Harper." He extended a hand, which she clasped. "Feel free to forget that. It would only be fair."

"And if I don't?"

"Don't say I didn't warn you." He turned back to the painting.

"I really love your work. You have a great eye ... well, two of them, actually." He snapped another rubber band grin. "Mind if I ask what inspires you?"

Lauren smiled enigmatically. She'd given up trying to explain her talent to others long ago, and instead told them the simple truth.

"I paint what I see," she said.

Lauren had to stay at the gallery for the wine-and-cheese reception, but she and David agreed to meet afterward at a coffee house down the street. She occasionally glimpsed him waiting on the fringe of the festivities, holding the same half-empty plastic cup of punch. He smiled when she made eye contact.

"So is this your first opening at the Webber?" David asked when they finally sat down in the cafe, lattes in hand.

"Yeah. Normally I show down in Laguna Beach, but I met Monica Webber at an reception in September and she offered me a spot."

David nodded. "I thought so. I work just down the promenade here and I like to drop in at the gallery and see what's new. I'm sure I would've remembered your stuff."

Lauren chuckled. "Thanks." She knew he was sincere, but she'd had so much treacle poured over her that evening, she felt as if she'd taken a bath in Karo Syrup. "Where did you say you worked?"

His gaze fell to the tabletop. "Oh, just the used bookstore up here on the left. My mom owns it. But I want to be a concert violinist."

"Really? That's great. When will you be playing? Maybe I could come see you."

David grimaced. "Yeah ... maybe." He shook back the stray strands of hair on his forehead and fingered the lip of his coffee cup. "You know what your paintings remind me of? You'll probably think this is really stupid—"

"No, what? Tell me."

"Well . . . have you ever heard of Kirlian photography?"

She frowned. "No."

"That's not surprising. It was a seventies New Age kind of thing. These psychic researchers would place someone's fingertip on a photographic plate, then run a small electric current through it. The exposed photo showed the fingerprint emanating a halo of colored light—supposedly the person's 'bio-energy.'"

"Yes." Lauren leaned forward. "And?"

"The halo changed in color and intensity depending upon the person's health or mood. That's what made me think of it. Your paintings look like Kirlian photos of whole people."

"Yeah. Kind of." She scanned the blobs of light around the other cafe patrons, as if noticing them for the first time. "But what about someone . . . dead? Do they still glow?"

David shrugged. "Beats me. I know they did experiments where they cut off part of a leaf and took a picture of it. Sometimes the photo would still show the energy pattern for the missing part of the leaf—a 'phantom leaf.'" Abruptly, as if it were a reflex, he looked at his watch. "Damn! Midnight. I gotta get home." He arose, agitated, and the yellow field enveloping him guttered like a breeze-struck candle.

"David, is something—?" Lauren began, but broke off when she saw the face hovering over his left shoulder. A dark oval mask with blank eyes and mouth, it floated by David's head like the negative afterimage that dances in front of one's vision after staring at a bright light source.

It looked like the Colorless Man.

"Listen," David said, patting his pockets in search of a pen, "I really enjoyed meeting you tonight and was wondering if . . . you know, sometime when you're not busy . . ."

She stared at the face that David couldn't see, now fading, and almost said no. Almost. Instead, she pulled a pen from her purse with quivering hands and wrote her phone number on a napkin.

That night, for the first time in almost a year, she had one of the nightmares again. Hungry, grasping ghosts reached for her, and she awoke to find herself covered in sweat and the orange fire of fear.

Lauren went out with David three times over the next two weeks, although she could hardly think of their evenings together as "dates" due to the lack of any romantic involvement. Indeed, she began to wonder whether he was even interested in her, for he always took her home promptly at eleven and left without so much as a goodnight kiss. He also refused to take her to his house and asked her not to visit him at the bookstore, presumably because he was embarrassed to be living with and working for his mother at age twenty-seven. Still, Lauren felt compelled to keep on seeing him, not so much for his charm and sensitivity, though he certainly had both, but because she sensed that he held the key to the mystery lodged deep within her ever since that day in the mall.

"Would you like to come in for awhile?" she offered when he dropped her off after their fourth night out.

David glanced from her face to where his car waited at the curb, then at his watch. "I don't know, it's kind of late . . ."

"Would you stop already? You're worse than the White Rabbit!" She tried to make it sound like a joke.

He laughed nervously. "Yeah, okay. Just for a few minutes."

An hour later, they were entwined together on the couch in her shoebox-sized living room. I guess he does like me, she thought, leaning back upon the sofa cushions as he kissed her, his tongue pressed against hers.

Then his cell phone rang.

David jerked to attention as if his name had been called.

"Leave it." Lauren pulled him close again. He relented, but squirmed with each successive ring.

A minute after the phone fell silent, David could no longer restrain himself. "I'm sorry," he muttered, and dug the cell out of his pocket to retrieve his voicemail. "Davey? Davey, are you there?" a sandpapery female voice slurred on speakerphone as he played the message.

David rubbed his forehead with his palms. "Christ! I should've known. I can't believe she did this."

"Davey? Pick up the phone, honey . . ."

"Who is it?" Lauren asked, perplexed and irritated.

"My mother." He rose and padded over to where they'd left their shoes by the front door, Asian-style.

"Davey honey? Are you—" David thumbed off the phone and shoved it in his pocket.

"What does she want?"

"I don't know! I don't know!" David jammed his feet into his sneakers and knotted the laces. He drew a breath and sighed. "I'm sorry. Ever since Dad left—" He paused by the door, one hand on the knob. "I'll make it up to you. I promise."

Then he left.

Lauren stared at the place where he'd stood, and again seemed to see the negative of a face lingering there. Her gaze dropped to the floor, and she saw that, instead of glimmering patches of color, David's stocking-feet had left craters of black in the haze of blue that drifted over the floor.

Angus jumped up to take David's place on the couch. Lauren took him in her lap and hugged him. She suddenly felt cold.

Lauren didn't hear from David for the rest of the week, and she wasn't sure she wanted to call him again. He saved her the trouble, however, by appearing on her doorstep Sunday morning, smiling and holding his arms behind his back.

"I believe I have a promise to keep." He proffered a small bouquet of red roses. "Mind if I come in?"

Lauren looked at the flowers she now held, then at her paint-spattered overalls. "Uh, I was kind of in the middle of something."

"Ah! But—" He pulled a scuffed violin case from behind his back with a flourish. "I'm a-gonna make you an offer you can't re-fuse!" he said, thrusting out his chin and doing his best Marlon Brando. Lauren shook her head and laughed. "Well? A command performance?" David waved the case in front of her. "You may never get another chance."

"All right, Paganini." She stood aside and motioned him forward. "Let's see what you can do with that thing."

He swept his hair back with comic flamboyance and strode past her. *"Grazie, signorina! Grazie!"*

Lauren settled on the sofa while David stood in the center of the living room and took his violin out of the case. He nestled it under his chin, and Lauren noticed that the violin's base meshed with a creased scar on the left side of his neck. She soon saw how he got the scar; he must have practiced incessantly to achieve such technical proficiency, and he played with a passion that bordered on violence.

He performed pieces that ranged from Mozart to Schoenberg to the *Godfather* theme, which he played with a wry grin. Little did he know that, for Lauren, the show was a visual as well as an aural one. He cascaded with sparks of flaring emotion, like a firework fountain on the Fourth of July.

When he finished, she jumped to her feet and applauded. "That was fantastic! You should be on a big concert tour."

David looked down at the bow dangling from his fingers. Already, the light around him had dimmed to its usual subdued level. "Yeah . . . someday. So how about Sunday brunch?"

They spent a wonderful, lazy day together, but David still insisted on leaving by ten o'clock that evening. She let him go with a kiss and a smile.

Returning to the painting she'd abandoned that morning, Lauren found that she'd lost interest in it. She set it aside and put a fresh canvas on her easel. She wanted to do something special for David, something to inspire him.

Lauren sketched a portrait of him in pencil, then began to apply swatches of thick oil paint with a pallet knife.

She meant to surround his face with radiant bands of primary colors to show him how dazzling he was when he played for her. However, as she painted, some innate artistic sense in her took over and the picture began to change. When she mixed the colors for David's face, they came out darker than she'd intended, and his image took on a dreary cast, as if shaded by a summer's cloud. The background boiled with the turbulence of dissipating energy, like the air rising from a sun-baked highway.

A sense of urgency seized Lauren, and she threw aside the pallet knife and instead pressed and rippled the oozing paint with her fingers. The canvas became a sort of Polaroid photograph, its image fading into view from blankness. Each smudge of her thumb added another detail to the final revelation. Lauren's throat tightened in anticipation.

Finally, at almost four in the morning, she stood back from the wet canvas, wiping her hands on a rag soaked with turpentine, her head aching. Only then did she see the anomalies in the upper left-hand corner of the picture, just over David's shoulder. Two smears that might be eyes, another that might be a mouth. Though marginalized, this suggested face seemed the focal point of the painting, the maelstrom of background hues all swirling toward it. Lauren stared at it, and wondered.

She went to bed exhausted and didn't get up again till after noon. When she rose at last, she set the painting in a far corner of the studio, facing it toward the wall. Another one that wouldn't sell, she thought.

Lauren resolved that day to help David shake the malaise she felt engulfing him—whether he liked it or not. The L.A. arts community was close-knit and, after calling some friends of friends, Lauren had made contacts at both the L.A. Philharmonic and the PSO. They assured her that, if David approached them, he could at least get an audition.

Excited, she hung up the phone after the last of her calls and glanced at her watch. Four o'clock. If she went down to the bookstore now, she thought, she could give David the good news and then go out to dinner with him when he got off work at five. Though he'd asked her not to come there, she couldn't see the harm in showing up just as the place closed.

The bookstore appeared deserted when she arrived, and for a moment Lauren wondered if she was too late. The door was unlocked, however, so she eased it open in order not to jangle the bells that hung on the inside knob.

She skulked past the front counter where the cash register sat untended and scanned the aisles between the looming bookcases. The air smelled of mildewed pulp and deadened every sound but the swish of the slow ceiling fan.

She found David at the rear of the store, where he stretched to put faded volumes on an upper shelf. Swathed in a feeble blue, he reminded Lauren of the pilot light in her furnace. She crept up behind him and slapped her hands on his shoulders. "Boo!"

He tensed and spun around to face her. His face turned white, while the pilot light around him darkened to violet. "What are you doing here?"

"Causing trouble." She grinned. "Besides, I've got some great news. I thought we could go—"

"Davey?" a voice rasped. "Davey, honey?" A spindly woman emerged from a doorway to Lauren's left. She wore a baggy housecoat that draped shapelessly over her gaunt frame and which she held closed at the neck, as if warding off a chill. Her gaze meandered over to David and Lauren, and she gave a crooked smile. Lauren drew a sharp breath.

No colors. The woman cast no colors.

"Davey, you didn't tell me we had a customer." She tottered toward them, bracing herself against the bookcase when she lurched to one side. Her drawn, sunken face and wispy hair swept back in chaotic tangles struck Lauren as somehow familiar.

David hastened to intercept her. "I thought you were taking a nap, Mom." He tried to steer her back the way she'd come. "C'mon, let's go take a nap."

She sidestepped away from him and approached Lauren. "I know! You must be Davey's girlfriend." She gave a laugh liquid with phlegm and reached to touch Lauren's cheek. "Oh, Davey, she's *pretty!*"

Lauren flinched from the cold, lightless fingertips. "Nice to meet you, Mrs. Harper."

David took hold of his mother's arm. "Okay, you've met Lauren. Now let's get you back to bed."

She leaned forward to murmur to Lauren confidentially, misting the air between them with a cloying alcohol scent. "Isn't he a dear? He takes such good care of me."

As she cast an affectionate glance at her son, her eyes and mouth drew swirls of violet vapor from the thinning field of luminescence surrounding him, and Lauren knew where she'd seen that face before. It was the afterimage that hovered over David's shoulder, the one she'd painted into his portrait.

"Uh, I guess I'll see you later?" David asked, herding his mother up the aisle to the shop's back room.

It took Lauren a moment to find her voice. "Yeah. Sure."

"Thanks."

Propped against her son, Mrs. Harper threw a final backward glance at Lauren before they disappeared around the corner. "Oh, Davey, she's so *pretty!*"

Lauren left the bookstore in a daze.

That night, she lay awake until well past midnight, seeing David's face in the shifting patterns of purple over her bed. When she finally slept, black fingers grasped at her glowing flesh as a voice wheezed *Pretty, pretty, pretty . . .*

Lauren's patience with David and his mother wore thin over the following week. Every night, David's mother would call, and he would always go to her.

"Why? Why do you baby her?" Lauren asked in exasperation as he started to leave Thursday night. "Can't you see you're just making it worse for both of you?"

"You don't understand." He pulled his car keys from his pocket before he even reached the front door. "Dad just walked out on her. Left her for some bimbo he met on a business trip to Florida. That's what made her the way she is." A flare of pink and saffron suffused his face as he looked at Lauren with watery eyes. "I can't abandon her that way."

Lauren sighed. I do understand, she thought. In spite of everything, she was his mother, and he loved her. Lauren let him go.

But when he came to her apartment Saturday night, she secretly switched off the cell phone in his pocket.

David had promised to come over and stay for at least two videos. Lauren planned for him to be there considerably longer than that. She chose the videos carefully—*Sleepless in Seattle* and *Say Anything*—and, as she hoped, they were into some serious cuddling before the beginning of the second feature. When she began to unbutton his shirt, he reflexively reached for the phone in his pocket.

Lauren caught hold of his hand. "Relax. She's fine."

"Yeah." The tension in his shoulders eased. "It's just . . . it's late . . ."

"No. It's early." She ran her hand down his bare chest and watched the shimmering pink fire where their skin made contact, the iridescent trail her fingertip left as she traced around his left nipple.

They embraced each other there on the living room floor, the aurora around them outshining the pale moonlight of the television screen.

David stayed the rest of that night. Lauren smiled beside him in bed the following morning, for he gleamed with a steady, placid gold that she'd never seen around him before. His eyes flicked open and gazed into hers for a long time.

"Did you sleep well?" she said at last.

"Yeah. Too well." He brushed his knuckles along her upper arm, goosepimpling the skin. "Thanks." They nudged toward each other for a kiss.

David cast a lazy glance at the clock on the nightstand and

shook his head. "I am in *big* trouble." He laughed, but made no move to get out of bed. "I suppose I should go now."

"You don't have to," Lauren said softly.

He looked at her and sighed. "I know." They nuzzled each other under the covers for another fifteen minutes, then got up and dressed. As David was about to leave, Lauren took his hand.

"Just in case." She smiled and placed a duplicate house key on his open palm.

He bit his lip and nodded.

The night with David left Lauren in such a good mood that, as soon as he was gone, she set to painting in her studio. She worked with such intensity that she forgot until that evening that she'd never turned David's cell phone back on.

Lauren gnawed at her thumbnail. Should she call him and apologize? He'd probably be ticked at her for the trick she'd played, especially after being chewed out by his mom. Still, when he remembered their night together . . .

She waited six rings before she heard a click on the other end of the line. No voice answered, however, and Lauren wondered if Mrs. Harper had picked up the phone instead.

"Hello? Is David there?"

"I am *now*." The voice was thin and edgy, but unmistakably David's.

Lauren fidgeted with the hem of her blouse. "Yeah. Look, I'm sorry if your mom's upset. I just wanted—"

"She's not upset." He gave a hollow, hiccuping laugh. "She's *dead*."

Lauren froze. "How . . . ?"

"She tried to drive. I wasn't there, and she tried to drive. Oh God . . . " Silence followed.

"David?"

A click, then a dial tone. She automatically redialed his number, but only got his voicemail. She tried six more times, but only left three messages. There were only so many ways to beg forgiveness.

David remained out of touch for the following week. The drapes were drawn at his house, and a "Closed" sign hung in the bookstore window. Knocking on the door of either received no response.

Lauren forced herself to keep working to stave off her own depression and guilt. How could she have known that his mom would go on a drunk-driving spree? she told herself, nearly slashing the canvas with her palette knife as she streaked paint on it in furious swipes. The woman was an accident waiting to happen—anyone could see that.

But Lauren couldn't quite suppress the thought that she had really wanted something like this to happen all along, that she was glad David's mother was finally gone. Dark, vengeful figures crowded her imagination and spilled out onto her canvases, engulfing the tiny glowing bodies at the paintings' edges.

Though her work exhausted her, Lauren found it impossible to sleep, and she grew more gaunt and drawn with each anxious night. Finally, after one particularly grueling evening at the easel, she went to bed and slipped into a fitful doze.

A few hours later, a small noise jarred her awake. As she padded from the bedroom into the studio to investigate, Lauren wondered if the soft shuffling sound she'd heard had merely been the ragged end of an interrupted dream. When she discovered Angus quivering in fright and looked up to find the black silhouette standing before her, she decided that she must still be dreaming. Relieved, she didn't even scream until the silhouette grasped her shoulders with cold, solid hands.

"Lauren! It's me."

Lauren mewled as she made out the inkblotted features of the face. "No, David, you can't be—"

"I'm sorry to come so late, but I had to see you." His hands squeezed her shoulders longingly. Angus leapt from her arms as David drew her closer. "I know what happened to Mom wasn't your fault. God, I've missed you."

His eyes lit up as funnels of electric yellow mist from Lauren twisted into his obsidian pupils. He touched her cheek, and she recoiled, gasping as if choked with asthma.

"Please, Lauren. I need you." He enfolded her in a constricting hug. "You're all I have left."

The strength ran out of her knees, and she sagged against him. She hugged him back and wept as his consuming loneliness washed over her.

Sealing her mouth with a kiss, he eased her slack form to the floor and lifted the oversized T-shirt she wore as a nightgown. Maybe it would be okay after all, Lauren thought. She could help him, share with him, reignite the spark within him. Surely she had more than enough love within herself to give.

She shivered as he lapped at the luminescence of her breast, blue sparks arcing from the areola to the tip of his black tongue. "You're so beautiful," he whispered, "so . . ." . . . *pretty*, Lauren thought as she stared at the dark mask of his face.

She started and glanced down at her glowing body. It dimmed like a cooling heater coil beneath his touch. In her mind, she saw it fade to black.

With a shriek, she writhed out from under him, kicking back at his grasping hands as she scrambled across the floor toward the door to her bedroom.

"Wait! Lauren, I'm sorry. Please!"

She charged through the door and slammed it behind her, bracing herself against it.

"I love you. I want to care for you, to make you happy," he vowed from the other side, his voice shrill, insistent.

Hungry.

"Don't," she whimpered. "I can't see you anymore. Please go."

"But I need you." His fingernails scraped against the door, and five threads of ocher steam trailed from her temple to disappear into the wood. "Don't abandon me like this."

Her heart clenched. What if he wouldn't leave?

Then *she* would have to go, she told herself—climb out the bedroom window, run next door, call the police. After that, she could have the locks changed, get an unlisted number, even move away. But she had to end it now.

"I'm sorry, David," she breathed, quicksilver tears streaking her cheeks. "I can't save you."

He clawed at the door, pleading. Lauren steeled herself against his cries and looked down at the trembling hands she cupped in front of her. Though the orange flame around them flickered as if in a high wind, it refused to go out.

The Silent Majority

And so tonight, to you—the great, silent majority of my fellow Americans—I ask for your support.
                              —Richard M. Nixon, November 3, 1969

On the morning of the day the Apocalypse was due to commence, Richard Milhous Nixon, thirty-seventh president and late commander-in-chief of the United States of America, clawed his way out of his grave in the quaint formal gardens behind the memorial library that bore his name.

Although the darkness was absolute inside his casket, Nixon knew where he was, *what* he was, and what he had to do. He rammed his flattened palms against the coffin's satin-embossed roof—not from panic at the stifling confinement, which he had no reason to fear, but from a sense of urgent purpose, of a sacred duty he must perform.

Divine authority must have coursed through his embalmed flesh, for the hinged cover began to give, allowing dust to whisper into the upholstered interior. At the time of his death at age eighty-one, he could hardly have budged the casket's wooden lid, much less the hundreds of pounds of earth heaped upon it. Would the others be as strong when they returned? he wondered. If so, his mission was that much more crucial.

Clumps of sod tumbled in beside him as he forced the gap wider, until the trickle of soil became a flood. Nixon let it swamp him; he was counting on the dirt to prop the lid open enough for him to worm his way out of the coffin. The ground had settled and become hard-packed during the nearly three decades since his interment, and he had to rend and plow the loam with the hooks of his arthritic fingers as he swam upward through the solid earth. Dirt filled the flared nostrils of his pointed nose, smothering him with an odor of mold and earthworms, and he spluttered in disgust. If he'd been like Mao or Lenin, placed on public display for reverent hordes to file past, he could simply have cast aside the glass case that enclosed him and stood up, immaculately preserved and attired and ready for business.

Never in his life had Dick Nixon so wished he'd been a Communist.

At last, he thrust a hand through a final foot of cold sod and felt warm, open air. Pulling himself up, he broke through a mat of grass and found himself blinded by the almost unbearable brightness of a Southern California springtime.

Almost as soon as he shut his eyes, however, he opened them again, savoring the wonder of vision. His eyes should have shriveled like raisins long ago, yet somehow they had been restored to him. He glanced down at his hands. They were gnarled with age, as they had been, the skin pallid and filthy, but they were neither desiccated nor skeletal. Though all the laws of Nature dictated the impossibility of the miracle, he had sight, he had strength, he had mind. Would the others—those who came after him—be as fortunate?

A phrase—a verse—returned to him from his Quaker childhood, one read to him by his sainted mother: *Behold, I shew you a mystery: we shall not all sleep, but we shall all be changed, in a moment, in the twinkling of an eye, at the last trump: for the trumpet shall sound, and the dead shall be raised incorruptible, and we shall be changed.*

Incorruptible. Nixon wanted to laugh that such a word could apply to him, a man whose name had become synonymous with the Committee to Re-Elect the President and its dirty tricks, with enemies lists and wiretapping, and ever and always, Watergate.

Yet he'd been granted a second chance to prove himself and he needed to make the most of it. If only his voice worked as well as the rest of him . . .

Nixon snorted dirt from his nose and surveyed the garden around him, redolent with the pleasant aroma of freshly mown grass. Somewhere, a war raged—there *had* to be a war involved, of that he was sure—and attendance at the Richard M. Nixon Library and Birthplace was sparse. Nevertheless, here in his hometown of Yorba Linda, in Orange County, the moribund heart of Republican conservatism, the disgraced president still counted some admirers, and at least one of them had come to pay her respects. A plump, silver-haired matron in a floral blouse and peacock-colored hat and skirt had propped herself on a walker outside the rectangle of foxgloves, roses, and shrubbery that bordered the burial plot. She'd frozen, aghast, as the lawn at her feet heaved and unfolded.

Still sunk up to his chest in soil, Nixon extended an arm toward her. Ripping open the threads that sewed his mouth shut, he spat grit and cleared his throat. "'Scuse me, ma'am, but would you mind giving me a hand here?"

The woman paled, the excess of rouge on her cheeks making her look if she'd been slapped. She shrieked and waddled away, practically vaulting over the walker in her haste.

Nixon grunted. If you wanted anything done right . . .

He dragged himself, hand-over-hand, free from the grave, stood, and brushed dust from his suit. Although he remembered this spot as well as if it were the Oval Office itself, he still took a moment to imbibe the memories it evoked. To his left, just over the low hedge of blooming flowers, was the refurbished white farmhouse where he'd been born, the equivalent of Abe Lincoln's log cabin in the personal mythology he'd constructed for himself. Around him blossomed the fastidiously manicured flora of the First Lady's Garden, named for his darling Pat.

Finally, his gaze fell upon her grave marker, the one next to his. He did not know if his new eyes were capable of tears, but his throat tightened as he read the inscription, the way it had the last time he'd seen it, on the day of her funeral: EVEN WHEN PEOPLE CAN'T SPEAK YOUR LANGUAGE, THEY CAN TELL IF YOU HAVE LOVE IN YOUR HEART.

How he wanted to wait right there, until she, too, sprouted from the ground like the finest flower! He trembled as he imagined how he would drop to his knees in front of her to beg forgiveness for everything he'd put her through, to offer his unworthy thanks for loving him anyway.

But Pat, like the others that followed him, might not be . . . intact. Dick couldn't bear the thought of seeing her that way, and the image it conjured prodded him to get on with his mission. He had to get out of this place before its nostalgia buried him more completely than six feet of soil ever could.

Straightening his stained tie, Dick Nixon lurched away from the burial plot without daring to read his own headstone. For if there were one thing the thirty-seventh president feared even after death, it was how humanity had labeled him.

Climbing over the hedge, he stalked in the direction that the old lady with the walker had fled screaming: past the beds of roses, along the reflecting pool lined with palm trees, and into the library's main gallery with its peaked roof of red tile. His wobbling gait improved as his stiff limbs got used to walking again, and he paused to regard his reflection in the glass door. He wanted to enter with some dignity, so he picked a few lumps of mud from his hair, smoothed his lapels, and stepped inside with his head held high.

The woman with the walker had plopped down on a padded bench in the lobby, where a bespectacled female docent attempted to calm her.

"I tell you, I know what I saw!" the old matron insisted.

"I'm sure you do," the docent said in soothing tones, "and I promise you, we'll investigate." She indicated the diminutive, baby-faced guard beside her, one of those short men with the pugilistic posture of a bantam rooster.

Nixon cut in. "Pardon me, ladies, but—"

The matron gaped at him and pointed, hyperventilating. "*That's him!* That's the man from the garden!"

She snatched up the walker again and made a break for the exit, leaving the startled docent to wonder whether to stop her or flee with her.

The guard whipped the pistol out of his side holster with a Dirty Harry flourish. "Hold it right there!"

Nixon brushed aside the command and advanced. "For God's sake, son, put that thing away! I need to see the president on a matter of national security, and I need you to take me to him."

"You mean *her*."

Nixon glowered at the docent, who slapped hands over her mouth to keep herself from speaking again.

Dick was a bit flummoxed. Things had changed more than he'd realized in his absence. "Yeah, well . . . whatever. The president. *Her*."

"You're not going anywhere." The guard still brandished his gun, but the brass had gone out of his words. "Stop or I'll shoot!"

"Watch it, young man. Can't you see who you're talking to?" Nixon's ill-fitting jacket bunched around his shoulders as he raised both arms to indicate the plethora of pictures that plastered the walls around them, photos from every phase of his storied career.

The guard's eyes flicked from Dick's face to the pictures and back again. Same widow's peak, same scowling brows, same bulldog jowls. Yet he refused to lower his weapon.

"I'm warning you! I'm not afraid to use this." His hand trembled as he said it, however, and Dick suspected that the gun subsequently went off by accident.

The shot slammed into Nixon's chest right above the heart, rocking him backward and nearly toppling him. *That's gonna leave a mark*, he thought.

The bullet did make a small hole in his dress shirt, but no blood came out. Fortunately, the guard hadn't had the presence of mind to shoot Dick in the head. He yelped as Nixon shrugged off the wound and kept coming.

"That's no way to treat a former chief executive!" Nixon closed the gap between them. The guard screeched and dropped the pistol as Dick grabbed his shirt.

"Now, listen to me, you little [expletive deleted]. You're going to take me to the [expletive deleted] president or I'm gonna kick your [expletive deleted] ass out of *my* library!" Dick released the whimpering guard with a shove and looked down at his feet, which were shod only in a pair of bedraggled black dress socks. "And, for Christ's sake," he roared at the dumbstruck docent, "get me some [expletive deleted] SHOES!"

***

Dick ultimately had to submit to a DNA test before anyone in Washington would entertain the idea that he was anything more than a hoax. The delay cost him precious hours, but at least it gave him time to procure a new navy-blue suit and a decent pair of Florsheims. He also washed his face and hands, although removing the grime only brought out the ghastly lividity of his complexion. There was still dirt under his fingernails, but that felt good to him, as if he'd done honest work.

A private jet flew him from Orange County to D.C., John Wayne to Ronald Reagan. A West Coast C.I.A. operative briefed him during the flight. There was, indeed, a war going on. As in the Yom Kippur War during Nixon's own administration, the Middle East had erupted into violence and ethnic hatred. As he had done, the present commander-in-chief had thrown U.S. support behind Israel, funneling American arms into the hands of Israeli troops to help repel Islamic forces from outside the country while purging Palestinian terrorists within. Tens of thousands of people— Muslims and Jews, military and civilians—had perished over the course of the three-year conflict. As Israel appeared to falter, the president had committed U.S. troops to the country's defense, leading to even heavier casualties.

And then, within the past five hours, an unknown party had

detonated an atomic bomb in New York City, killing an estimated seven million American citizens.

The last trump had sounded.

Washington was in a state of siege, with Army and National Guard checkpoints hastily erected throughout the city and traffic into the Mall restricted to approved vehicles. As perversity would have it, they'd closed off the Arlington Memorial Bridge, so the black Lincoln limousine that conveyed Nixon to the White House had to detour via I-66 and the E Street Expressway, past the Kennedy Center.

The chauffeur glanced back at Nixon through the open window of the privacy partition. "Well, there it is!" he said with a big, dopey grin, as if Dick needed to be told.

"Yep. There it is." Nixon found his gaze drawn irresistibly toward the tiered, U-shaped building that glowed in the evening twilight outside the car's left-hand windows: the southern structure of the Watergate complex.

In the years since his resignation, he'd avoided coming anywhere near the place and had vainly hoped it might be demolished in the name of urban renewal. But it remained, decade upon decade, a monument to his failure, as damnably eternal as the Pyramids or nuclear waste.

Dick had only been playing politics the way he'd been taught: gloves off, bare-knuckled and brutal. If you couldn't take it, you had no business in the ring. Had he demanded impeachment hearings when Daley's goddamn Chicago machine threw the '60 election to that bastard Kennedy? No, he'd conceded defeat rather than put the country through a contested election—but he wasn't going to let it happen again.

In retrospect, Dick realized that he needn't have bothered with dirty tricks in the '72 campaign. George McGovern was an idiot lib who'd have hanged himself if Nixon had simply played out enough rope for him. Instead, Dick had entrusted his career to morons like Hunt and Liddy, who hired even bigger imbeciles to bug the Democratic headquarters at the Watergate. He then compounded his error by covering up their incompetence instead of sending them all to the wall as he should have.

Yet was that mistake so horrible that it outweighed everything else he'd ever done—the opening of China, détente with the Soviets, the Clean Air Act, the Consumer Product Safety Commission, the Environmental Protection Agency—all of it? Nixon couldn't bear the thought that, to most people, he was nothing more than an easy punch line for stand-up comedians.

There was still time to change that, he told himself. Someone—some *thing*—knew that he was capable of more than that. A higher power had chosen him, made him whole again, for a reason. He dared not disappoint its faith in him.

When the limo arrived at the White House, Nixon let the sight of that glorious pediment with its Greco-Roman columns blot out all thoughts of the Watergate complex. As the chauffeur let him out of the car, the years since he'd flown away in that last helicopter ride following the resignation seemed to evaporate.

He was home.

The Oval Office had changed, of course. For one thing, a huge plasma-screen teleconferencing monitor curved along one wall, upon which a dozen displays broadcast news reports from around the world about the tense international situation in the wake of the nuclear attack. For another, a woman with iron-gray hair sat in the leather chair behind the desk, conferring with the cluster of dour-faced advisors that surrounded her. As soon as the Secret Service bodyguards led Nixon into the room, the muttered conversation ceased, and the woman got to her feet.

"My God . . . it really *is* you," she said.

He made a stiff bow. "Madame President."

Attired in a gray tweed suit, she seemed to be in her early seventies, which would have made her a teenager back in his administration. Dick prayed that he could reason with a hippie.

"How did you come back?" she asked.

He lifted an accusing finger. "*You* brought me back. If you retaliate to this terrorist act, it'll be the beginning of Armageddon." He quoted Revelation 20:13. "'*And the sea gave up the dead which were in it; and death and hell delivered up the dead which were in them.*' I'm only the first, but there will be billions more—more than all the people now alive. You *must* hold off the attack."

One of the advisors, an impudent whelp with slick black hair, shook his head. "I can't believe you're even listening to this guy. He's obviously a fraud sent here by the enemy. If we allow the New York atrocity to go unpunished, there's no telling which of our cities they'll obliterate next."

The president's expression hardened. "He's right. The people are screaming for blood. You of all people should know how that works: 'Death before dishonor,' and so on. They want me to nuke something, and right now it's not a matter of *if*, it's a choice of which target."

"But you don't even know who was responsible!" Nixon protested.

"And we may never know. Hezbollah, Hamas, al Qaeda—does it really matter? A full investigation could take months, but the U.S. must demonstrate its force now."

"Even if it means doom for the whole human race?" Dick tried to stride across the floor's plush presidential seal to confront her face-to-face, but the Secret Service agents caught hold of him. Although he could have flung them across the room like a couple of rag dolls, he relented.

"*Look* at me!" he beseeched the president. "You know who I am. Don't make the same mistake I did and let pride lead you into carrying on a war you can't win."

She stared at him, and Dick could tell that she needed no DNA test to prove his identity.

Then, with soul-deep weariness, she lowered herself back into her chair.

"Back in '71, I put flowers in my hair and marched in the streets of D.C. chanting 'Make Love, Not War' because you wouldn't get out of 'Nam. Now the kids are protesting *me*." She pleaded to Nixon with her eyes, the bags beneath them heavier than his own. "What should I do?"

"Negotiate."

The mousse-haired advisor exhaled disgust. "We don't negotiate with terrorists."

"Not with the terrorists, you jackass," Nixon said. "With the Israelis and the Muslims. *Use* this crisis to fashion a lasting peace."

The president raised her hands in exasperation. "But if Armageddon has already begun, what's the point?"

"It's not Armageddon until you make it Armageddon." Nixon shook off the grip of the bodyguards, who seemed inclined to let him go, and approached her desk. "Don't you see? The human race chooses the hour of its own destruction. Pull back from the brink before it's too late."

"Maybe it's already too late." The announcement came from a Hispanic female who would later introduce herself as the White House press secretary. During the debate, her attention had been drawn to the video monitors. "Madame President, I think you should see this."

Even before he looked, Nixon knew what he what he would find on the screen. There was only one story that could possibly distract the world's news media from coverage of the recent nuclear holocaust.

In footage from CNN, thousands of charred corpses from the ruin of New York—those that had not been vaporized by the initial blast—staggered out of the rubble to rip the limbs off relief workers in white radiation suits. On Fox News, a shaky cell phone camera showed somnambulating bodies from a hospital morgue overwhelming a nurse, gouging strips of flesh from the victim with their hands and teeth. Similar scenes played out on channels from around the world as text crawls in Japanese, Arabic, and Russian scrolled superfluous explanations across the screens.

Dick saw his worst-case scenario confirmed. Unlike himself, these dead seemed to have lost all trace of humanity as they tore into the living with a blind wrath propelled by envy and vengeance. They had returned to scourge the world that had sent them to their graves.

Nixon imagined Pat reduced to a ravening, rotting animal, pictured her ravaging Tricia and Julie, the grandchildren and great-grandchildren. No . . . no, she would never—there had to be some way of reaching her, of reaching all of them . . .

"That's it, isn't it?" The president sounded more lifeless than the walking cadavers on the monitor. "We're finished."

"No." Nixon leaned toward her, clenched his fist in sudden resolve. "This is precisely the motivating force you need to bring the Arabs and Israelis to the bargaining table. Nothing unites foes like a common enemy."

He flailed a hand toward one of the displays on the monitor, in which a hyperventilating Al Jazeera anchorman babbled beside shots of a burned-out Lebanese suburb where bombing victims walked side-by-side with dead G.I.s to mob the survivors of a recent battle.

"The Middle East will be overrun with corpses from the recent war. Offer both Israel and the Muslim countries U.S. military aid against the dead in exchange for concessions on a Palestinian homeland and official recognition of the Jewish state."

"Spoken like a true Machiavellian." The president's mouth twisted, as if she were washing the proposal over her tongue to see how it tasted. "But tell me, Dick . . . may I call you Dick?"

Nixon grimaced. "Everyone does."

"How am I supposed to offer military aid when I'm going to need every available soldier and weapon to defend *us*?"

"Let me talk to them."

"Who? The Arabs?"

"No. The dead."

The president darted a glance toward the mute malevolence

of the massed corpses onscreen. "Can you *do* that?"

Nixon chuckled, a deep baritone gurgle. "Can't be any worse than dealing with Mao or Brezhnev."

The slick-haired advisor shook his head. "Madame President, you can't be serious—"

"Shut up." She didn't take her eyes off Nixon. "Tell me what you need," she said.

* * *

In truth, flying to China for the first time was easy compared to the task Nixon faced now. To make a rapprochement with any adversary, one had to meet him on his own turf. Therefore, as a gesture of good faith, Dick would have to go to the only place in the world he dreaded more: the Watergate complex.

The Vietnam Veterans Memorial was situated on the Mall between the Lincoln Memorial and the Washington Monument, less than a mile from the White House, but the walk there seemed as long to Nixon as the road to Damascus. Although Dick had lived for more than a decade after the monument's completion in 1982, he had never dared to visit it. When he finally stood at the crux of that broad V of polished black stone, he could feel the weight of accusation that he'd avoided all those years. More than two hundred feet long and over ten feet high at its tallest point, the sheer wall of ebony granite appeared almost white with the density of text etched upon it.

Names. Thousands upon thousands of names. The monolith was a mammoth tombstone for an entire generation of American soldiers. At its base, the faithful had laid photos, flowers, Purple Hearts, and other offerings to show the dead that they had not been forgotten.

Dick gazed up at the columns of names that rose more than a yard above his head. So many. How much longer and higher had he made this wall by refusing to admit defeat until it became inevitable? He put out one quavering hand toward the reflective surface of the stone but couldn't bring himself to touch it.

"They're coming," the president announced from behind him, as if reading his mind. "Are you ready?"

Nixon nodded and turned to face out toward the moonlit reflecting pool of the Mall. He squinted at the painfully bright floodlights the satellite television crews had set up to illuminate the Memorial for the imminent broadcast. His speech would be transmitted live on all channels, on every radio station, and through every public address system in the nation. Special trucks equipped with loudspeakers would drive through every major city blaring his words.

In front of Nixon stood a single microphone on a stand. The solicitous White House press secretary asked him if he wanted a teleprompter or prepared speech, but Nixon refused. Tonight, he would be speaking from his heart, even if it wasn't beating.

Barely visible beyond the bright lights and cameras were a squad of National Guard soldiers armed with M-16s and grenade launchers—the last line of defense should anything go wrong. Secret Service bodyguards in flak helmets and bulletproof vests flocked around the president herself, who had insisted on remaining at Nixon's side over the vehement objections of her advisors. Together they stood, shoulder-to-shoulder, and waited for the others to arrive.

Across the Potomac, in the Arlington National Cemetery, row upon row of cement slabs, identical but for the names and dates chiseled upon them, shone stark white in the light of the gibbous moon overhead. In the darkness, the lush grass swelled like waves in a black sea. Miniature American flags left over from Memorial Day wobbled and fell over as the turf beneath them blistered, burst open. Even the Tomb of the Unknowns cracked and disgorged its anonymous remains. The creatures who shambled forth from the desecrated ground had become nearly as identical as their headstones, distinguishable only by the tatters of the dress uniforms that still clung to them. Their faces had withered to the bone, reduced to the death's-head that underlies every human visage. They represented every conflict since the Civil War—both World Wars, Korea, Desert Storm, Iraq, and, of course, Vietnam—but they now ranked themselves into a united force, speechlessly advancing, a legion of the silent yet unquiet dead.

Three hundred thousand strong, they marched in chaotic, stumbling cadence from their scattered graves to cluster at the two-lane entrance of the abandoned Arlington Memorial Bridge. Although security forces across the country had discovered that one could incapacitate the animate corpses with a direct hit to the head, the troops that blockaded the bridge earlier that day had long since withdrawn to defend the White House and the Vietnam Memorial. Unimpeded, the undead flowed en masse across the bridge to spill out onto the Mall, drawn onward by some sense more certain than the sight endowed to their eyeless sockets.

Nixon saw them swarm around the Lincoln Memorial, a black tide of silhouettes that surged forward as sinuously as a plague of rats. A few of the Guardsmen cast a contemptuous glance at the deceased commander-in-chief and raised their weapons, aimed into the onslaught.

Nixon raised a hand. "Hold your fire!"

When he failed to begin his speech, even the current president grew nervous.

"Dick?" She gaped at the coming horde. "You're *on.*"

He stepped up to the microphone but waited a moment more, until that undifferentiated mass drew close enough for him to pick out individuals in the crowd, however decomposed and unrecognizable, to whom he could address his remarks.

"My fellow Americans." Nixon spread his arms as if to embrace them all. "For you *are* still Americans—every last one of you."

Loudspeakers echoed his words across the Mall; television and radio carried them across the continent. Yet they did nothing to slow the ghoulish army's advance. The National Guard soldiers fidgeted, fingers restive on triggers, but any resistance now would be token at best.

"Many of you have already made the ultimate sacrifice for this country we love. Tonight, I must ask you to make that sacrifice *again*."

Dick noted that one corpse missing a leg was able to hop forward by curling an arm around the shoulders of one of its comrades. If they could demonstrate that kind of altruism toward one another, he thought, perhaps they could still be made to care about the loved ones they left behind. It was his only chance.

"I know that many of you may feel that you died in vain, before your time, for a cause and a war you didn't believe in." He gestured to the wall of names behind him with one hand, spread the other on his chest. "Some of you are out there because I helped put you there. But *I* let you down—not your country."

Mere yards from the barricade the Guard unit had erected in front of the Memorial, the shuffling multitude halted, staring at Nixon with inscrutable impassivity. Had a flicker of comprehension flitted over their expressionless faces?

"Tonight, your country—your America—has resolved to leave behind its mistakes and misbegotten wars of the past." He indicated the president, who stepped free of her entourage to be recognized. "It has tried and failed to do so many times in its history and it may do so again.

"Does it deserve another chance? No, it does not, just as I did not. No one *deserves* another chance. Mercy cannot be earned; it is an act of grace.

"Therefore, I ask you all, across this great nation of ours—those who died in battle and those who did not—to pardon whatever injustice you may have suffered; abandon your wrath, however righteous it may be; and return to your rest. Don't do it for me. Don't even do it for your country. Do it for those who still revere your memory." He swept a hand toward the Memorial with its heaped bouquets and mementos of bereavement. "Be the heroes—the Americans—you were and *are*."

His arm dropped to his side, and his final words were so soft that they were barely audible even when amplified. "Be *better* than I was."

Nixon still didn't know whether his new eyes were capable of tears, but they felt as if they were about to melt inside his skull and run down his nose. He closed them and bowed his head.

When the throng of dead soldiers did not storm over the barricade to maul the humans huddled in front of the Memorial, the president cautiously approached the edge of the monument's foundation and peered out at the spectral assembly before her. They hadn't moved since Nixon fell silent, merely gazed upon the scene with judicial gravity. They had been charged with the task of ending the human race and the decision was now theirs.

And one by one, they turned and walked away, until the last of them disappeared into the early morning mist that drifted in from the Potomac.

The president watched them depart, her mouth hanging open in wonder, until the press secretary waved to get her attention. "Ma'am! We're getting reports from across the country." The Latina cupped a hand over her ear-bud cell phone to hear better. "There're a few holdouts that security forces are cleaning up. But most are retreating voluntarily."

The president beamed. "You did it, Dick! You did it!"

But when the president wheeled around to flash a "V for Victory" sign at the elder statesman, she found only a mummified cadaver collapsed beside her, too withered to fill the new navy-blue suit that sagged around it. Of the familiar widow's peak on the scalp, only a few scraggly white hairs remained. The jowls had shrunk into starched, lumpy furrows, and the membranes of the eyelids now stretched like yellowed foolscap over vacant sockets. She could see that this was the same face, however, yet it had changed in a more profound way than the mere superficial disfigurement of decay. It bore a new expression of tranquility that death and time could not mar, of a sleep too restful to disturb.

Whatever power had brought Richard Nixon back to aid his nation evidently understood that his work was done.

***

Despite the hectic schedule of diplomatic negotiations she arranged in the days that followed, the president traveled to Southern California for the re-interment. She made sure that Richard Milhous Nixon, her predecessor and mentor, received a state burial befitting a former chief executive, complete with honor guard and twenty-one-gun salute. As he was lowered back into the small, flower-bordered plot situated between his Birthplace and his Library, she read the epitaph on Nixon's grave marker. It seemed more appropriate than ever:

THE GREATEST HONOR HISTORY CAN BESTOW IS THE TITLE OF PEACEMAKER.

Serial Killers

The driver turned up the volume on the radio, and the newsreader's deadpan voice swelled inside the bus. Janet didn't want to hear it but listened anyway, as did everyone around her.

"... local residents discovered another victim of the so-called 'Sunday Slasher' early this morning in the Dumpster of an apartment building on Rosemont Boulevard. Like the previous victims, the body of Mrs. E. L. Lester, an elderly widow, had been ritualistically mutilated. Police still have no clue to the identity of the murderer, who has claimed the lives of at least five men and seven women in the city during the past three months. In other news . . ."

His curiosity satisfied, the bus driver turned the radio down. The passengers relaxed into contented detachment again, their hunger for headlines sated. Like vultures, Janet thought cynically.

No, not vultures, she decided. Like people in a doctor's office, waiting for their names to be called. Not morbid. Expectant.

The bus turned, jostling her against a middle-aged man in a business suit. He coughed and turned away. She renewed her grip on the overhead handrail and scanned the faces of the passengers around her. The old man with the quavering jaw. The young housewife absorbed in her paperback romance. The gum-chewing teenager slouching in evident boredom. Strangers.

The all avoided even the most casual interaction. In the dim light of the bus's interior, Janet fancied she could almost see the cold auras that isolated each of them from the others. It was hard to believe one of them might be a murderer . . . or even a victim.

As Janet looked around, she inadvertently met the gaze of a handsome but morose-looking young man in the rear of the bus. His eyes were watery and red-rimmed, as if he had cried recently.

Janet flashed a brief but cheerful smile at him, then quickly focused her attention on her feet. She shifted her weight to try to relieve the dull ache in her left arch, and wished again that her boss would understand that waitressing required functional footwear. She shut her eyes and wondered what to do with her evening. Maybe she would call David.

The bus jarred her eyes open again, and she realized that the next stop was hers. She pulled on the wire above her to notify the driver. A bell rang. It rang again, though she had only pulled once. The bus drove past two more intersections and swung over to the curb beside a weather-faded bench and a bright blue sign. Janet nudged her way through the crowd and stepped out into the night.

A small group of passengers disembarked at the stop, then drifted apart. With her tired feet, Janet didn't want to walk all the way around the block to get to her apartment, so she cut across the parking lot of the supermarket on the corner and turned down the alley that ran behind her building. She felt exhausted; maybe she wouldn't call David after all.

A shadow suddenly blocked her way. She looked up from the ground, and her brow furrowed as she tried to distinguish the figure before her. "Oh . . . hello," she said hesitantly, recognizing the young man from the bus. Those eyes. "Live around here?"

The man merely stared at her, trembling, on the verge of tears. *"Please,"* he rasped. And with a flick the blade sprung, glittering, from his fist.

Janet screamed and bolted back the way she had come. But the man was quick. He caught her around the waist, knocking the wind out of her, then threw her up against one of the Dumpsters that lined the alley.

"Please," he repeated, desperation in his voice. He held the knife up for her inspection.

Squirming violently from his grasp, she thrust her knee in his groin. He doubled over, and she took off down the alley, stumbling as she kicked off her high heels to run faster.

With seemingly superhuman effort, the man lunged and caught her in a running tackle. They dropped heavily onto the asphalt, his weight grating Janet against the rough pavement, skinning her arms, her legs, her cheek.

He turned her over on her back and sat on her, straddling her waist. Sobbing, she saw his pained face through the strands of her tousled hair. *"No!"* she yelled, and struggled to free herself.

"Please," he begged, and pressed the cold steel of the knife's handle into her palm.

Her sobs quieted as she saw the knife in her grasp. She looked into the yawning blackness of his pleading eyes, plumbing the depth of the despair. She recognized it now, had seen it in the eyes of everyone on the bus, everyone on the street. It ran like a polluted river through their lives, sweeping their consuming loneliness and accumulated misery along on its ebony tide. Her eyes dilated to receive the rush.

Her fingers closed around the knife's handle.

The man showed her how to make the incisions.

***

Hours later, Janet languidly rose from her bed and went to her apartment's sole window. Black stains spotted the pillow where her mascara had run, and telltale streaks had dried on her face. Other stains covered her dress. She felt hollow, worthless, saturated with grief. But most of all, she felt alone.

And the only consolation she had as she scanned the blinking black nothing of the city was that, somewhere in the darkness, she, too, would find her savior.

In the City of Sharp Edges

"So the dream is always the same?" Dr. Ingalls asked. Paper rustled, pen-point scratched.

"It always *starts* the same," Alan amended. "In the same place."

"Do you recognize this place? Have you ever been there before?"

Alan grimaced. "I don't think anyone has been there before."

"Why do you say that?"

"Because it makes no sense. Doorways that end in stone walls, hallways that seem to go on forever and lead nowhere, vast rooms with no floor."

"And you are the only one there?"

Alan shifted in his chair, grateful that Ingalls let him sit upright. He'd never been to a psychiatrist before and had feared the indignity of having to lie on a couch.

"No other people are there," he said. "But I'm not alone. Another . . . being is with me."

"Have you seen—" Ingalls paused to rephrase the question. "Can you describe this being?"

"It changes. Sometimes it's so cold, it burns, like dry ice. Sometimes it crackles and sparks, hot and stinging, like the static on clothes fresh from the dryer. Sometimes it has skin; sometimes, scales."

"Then how do you know it's the same being?"

"Its smell." Alan's nose twitched. The overly masculine musk of the psychiatrist's cologne nettled his nasal membrane. "I've never encountered anything like it."

"Hmm." Ingalls's tone was noncommittal, even uninterested. "And you feel this being is pursuing you?"

"Yes."

"Is anything troubling you at the moment? Work? Family? Depression?"

"No."

"How about issues from your past? Any childhood trauma?"

With his index finger, Alan absently rubbed the lower lid of his right eye beneath his glasses. "There was some bullying, as you might imagine. But that ended ages ago."

"Granted. But sometimes these suppressed conflicts can manifest themselves years after the fact. If you continue to have the dream, perhaps you should try confronting the beast rather than fleeing from it. You might find out what it truly represents."

Alan swallowed, hoping saliva would moisten his parched throat, but his mouth was also dry. "Wouldn't that make the dreams worse?"

"Only until you wake up. And, contrary to old wives' tales, a dream can't kill you."

"How do you know that if all the people who've died from dreams never wake up?"

Dr. Ingalls chuckled but did not answer the question. More scribbling, followed by rustling and tearing. A chair creaked, and the psychiatrist placed a scrap of paper in Alan's hand. "I'm prescribing a mild sedative. With any luck, it'll knock you out all night, and if you have any dreams, you won't even remember them in the morning. If you do dream, however, try taking control of the dream, as I suggested. At the very least, it will give us more to talk about the next time you come."

"Thanks," Alan said, although he wasn't sure what he had to be grateful for. He placed the scrap of paper in his wallet, then took the folded cane from the pocket of his tweed jacket and, with a single shake, snapped it to full-length. He had been told the cane was white, just as he had been told that his glasses were black. The names of these colors meant nothing to him, but they signaled his condition to those with vision. Indeed, he wore the glasses strictly for the benefit of others, for his eyes were as opaque as the lenses that hid them.

He tapped his way out of Ingalls's office to the elevator, pushed the appropriate Braille-marked button, and descended to the building's foyer. As he exited, the street greeted him with the bracing aroma of exhaust, the air brisk with the first nip of autumn.

On his way home, Alan dutifully had the cab driver stop at a pharmacy so he could submit the paper Ingalls had given him to collect his prescription. When at last the taxi dropped him at his apartment, Alan pulled a bird and a dog—a twenty and a ten—from his wallet and handed them to the cabbie.

"Keep the change," he said with a grin. There were other ways of distinguishing one denomination from the other—the engraved ridges on Andrew Jackson's portrait differed from those of Alexander Hamilton's, for example—but the whimsy of the folded origami amused him.

When Alan at last entered his second-floor walk-up, he sighed with relief and collapsed his cane. Here he could maneuver by memory alone, for everything was in the exact place where he'd put it. Five paces forward and two to the right would take him to his desk, upon which rested a computer with a Braille display instead of a monitor. Nine paces straight ahead sat his workbench with its rack of apothecary flasks. The living room had no lamps, and although the apartment management insisted that the overhead lighting fixture have functional bulbs in case of emergencies, Alan never turned them on. Darkness was the medium in which he lived, and he thought no more about it than a fish noticed the water in which it swam.

He shoved the folded cane in his jacket pocket, then shed the coat and hung it on a rack beside the door. Six paces to the left took him into the apartment's kitchenette, the soft tread of carpet beneath his feet giving way to the squeaky slickness of linoleum. Lightly pawing the air before him until his fingertips contacted the metallic monolith of the refrigerator, he gathered ingredients for his supper with impulsive haste. It was early for dinner, but he felt a need to drown his senses in stimulation: the grassy tang of fresh basil pesto, the whir of the food processor that sliced mushrooms into pliable, earth-scented cross-sections, the burble of garlic and sun-dried tomatoes sautéed in olive oil.

He turned on his stereo and listened to Vivaldi as he listlessly dined alone. It was no use: the memory of the dream-sensations seeped into his consciousness like leaking gas, smothering the humble comforts with which he tried to distract himself. A crackling shriek as shrill as feedback warped the harmony of strings that emanated from the speakers, and the food went sour in his mouth. And the smell—indefinable yet noxious, just the thought of it rankled his nose.

Alan retrieved the plastic vial of sedatives from the pocket of his coat, twisted off the childproof cap, and shook two of the slick capsules onto his palm. He popped them onto his tongue, but before he could wash them down with water he reconsidered. What if the medication didn't prevent the dreams, but merely prolonged them by keeping him asleep? Captive in that hive of senseless halls, unable to wake . . .

He spat out the pills, then dumped them into the kitchen garbage basket with the uneaten remains of his dinner. Maybe Ingalls was right. He ought to grapple with the dream-demon and overcome it or else he would never be rid of it.

It was early still, and Alan did not feel the least bit sleepy. He tried reading a book, but his finger skidded over the pinpricks on the page without interpreting them. Having resolved to endure the nightmare, he became impatient to get on with it.

Without light to demarcate the division of day and night, Alan often suffered the plague of insomnia, which he attempted to combat by adhering to a strict schedule of rising and retiring. Tonight, however, he reclined on his bed in his pajamas and tried to drift off, even though the position of the exposed hands on his old-fashioned electric alarm clock told him it was barely past eight o'clock. Thoughts of the nightmare so preoccupied him as he lay there that he believed he must already be dreaming, but the scent and feel of laundered sheets affirmed that he was still awake.

At some uncertain point in the night, he slid into oblivion in a seamless transition of unvarying darkness.

Alan gradually became aware that his body had changed position. He felt himself to be standing upright, his arms hanging at his sides, though he had no memory of having risen from his bed. He had been stripped of the linen cocoon of pajamas and bed sheets, and clammy air stippled his naked skin with gooseflesh. Textured stone abraded the soles of his bare feet, confirming to Alan that he had arrived in the dream city.

With no cane to tap, he put out his arms to full length in front of him, then swung them in a semicircular arc to the left and right. His fingers contacted nothing.

"*Hello!*" he called, not expecting a response. Rather, he gauged the echo of his voice; it reverberated back to him from either side, but rolled away distantly in front of him. He deduced that he must be in a narrow corridor.

Alan pivoted to the right and toed the floor with his right foot. Gingerly, he planted the foot and ventured forward, pawing the space before him to sense any hazards. Although he realized that he was merely dreaming, his childhood fear of falling made each step feel as if he were teetering on a precipice.

His fingertips touched hard stone. A wall. Fashioned from the same material as the floor, it felt like chiseled glass, with the smooth whorls and sharp ridges of an obsidian arrowhead.

Relieved to have the wall to guide him, Alan sidled along the rough plane as if clinging to the ledge of a skyscraper. As he felt the way ahead of him, his right hand reached a sudden, jagged end to the rock. He folded his fingers around the corner, and the razor keenness of the stone slashed his palm.

Chuffing breath at the sudden pain, Alan jerked his hand

back. Liquid trickled down his wrist. He licked his palm and tasted the salt and iron of blood.

From somewhere far down one of the branching tunnels came a screech that made the glassy walls ring like fine crystal. Alan slapped his hands over his ears, yet the sound hummed in his molars, throbbed in his skull. He wanted to run, but didn't know where to flee. It was difficult to tell from which hallway the cry emanated, for the bizarre architecture of the place seemed to share the deceptive acoustics of a cathedral dome's whispering gallery, causing the shriek to come at him from every direction at once.

A humid draft bellowed through the passageway—in and out, to and fro, as if the entire cavern were respiring. Its warm breath carried that fetor that Alan had come to know so well yet still could not identify: not animal, nor vegetable, nor mineral, but with hints of all three, as of a stalagmite encrusted with guano and fungus.

The odor inspired an irrational revulsion in him, and he groped his way back to the tunnel that branched off to his right, cutting his hand again as he stumbled around the serrated wedge of the stone wall to enter the adjacent passage. The shrill and the smell swelled in intensity until they fused into a revolting synesthesia—an odor that grated, a sound that stank.

Alan shuffled faster, the soles of his bare feet chafing against the rough-hewn rock.

Then the wall abruptly ended. His right hand fluttered, seeking solidity. In his haste to relocate the spearhead of rock where the wall branched off, Alan became careless in choosing his steps. Only when he felt his toes curling in empty air did he realize that he teetered on the shard-sharp brink of some unknown precipice.

The shock of the discovery unbalanced him, and he pinwheeled his arms to keep from pitching forward into the abyss. He overcompensated and fell heavily onto the floor behind him. His whole body throbbed with the smack of hard stone.

The humidity thickened around him like gelatin, congealing

the ineffable stink into a tactile putrescence on his skin. The thin treble shriek slid down a register to a deep-bass howl, yet the sound grew louder—nearer—as if the Doppler shift of a passing train whistle were played in reverse.

It was closing in on him.

Alan rolled over and frantically fingered the edge of the pit, seeking a way around it, but the ledge extended from one wall of the tunnel to the other. He extended his right arm down into the depression to gauge its depth and could not feel the bottom.

With no way forward, Alan considered back-tracking to the junction of the previous hallway. For all he knew, the thing was already there, or would overtake him as soon as he re-entered its path.

This is nothing but a dream, he reminded himself. At worst, falling into a chasm or being devoured by a bogeyman would only wake him up, and he desperately wanted to wake up.

Alan decided to take his chances with the pit. Perhaps, he thought, it was not as deep as he feared, and he could jump down and continue fleeing on foot.

Belly-down, he snaked his body until his feet stuck out past the ledge. Gripping every hand-hold he could find on the chiseled floor, Alan gradually lowered himself until his chest and waist pressed against the sheer face of the ledge. His toes brushed the cliff without finding purchase. He inched downward until only his forearms clung to the ledge, yet his feet still hadn't touched anything solid.

The tunnel above him belched a hot, gaseous roar like dragon's breath.

None of this is real, Alan told himself again, and let go of the ledge.

Nothing happened. Rather than falling, he remained impossibly pasted to the wall of the cliff.

Alan stretched an arm up to the ledge again to make sure it was still within reach. Yes, it was there—he hadn't moved at all.

The space around him seemed to tilt, inverting the directions of up and down, and he had the dizzying impression that the stone plane he lay against was now the floor of a tunnel, and that the ledge he touched was the edge of a pit below him. Had he somehow imagined lowering himself into the hole? But the sound—and the smell—continued to emanate from the opening, so it *had* to be the passageway he'd just left.

Skittish about moving, he pushed himself onto his knees, then got to his feet with coltish uncertainty. If he was correct, he now stood at right angles to where he'd been a minute before.

He had no time to marvel at this miracle. The reek flooded this new passageway, a fetor of commingled species, like a pet store full of unclean cages. Alan staggered to the right until he contacted another stone wall. He spun around and fled in the opposite direction, his left hand tracing the wall, his right pawing the air in front of him.

He'd barely waddled fifty paces forward when he ran into another wall in front of him. Alan moved along it, feeling for another opening, but only came to another corner on the right. A dead end.

He turned to retrace his steps, but the onrush of air in his face stopped him. If the thing was right behind him, it now blocked his retreat.

Intuitively, Alan pressed up against the wall at the end of the passage and strove to convince himself that it was now the floor. Then he scrabbled forward, gecko-like, up the plane of graven rock.

Again, the bizarre dream-gravity of the place rotated. The fluid in Alan's inner ears shifted and settled like the bubble in a carpenter's level, adjusting to the new frame of reference. He soon lost all internal sense of direction, for it felt as if he were crawling in place while the universe revolved around him.

When he reached the cut corner where the wall joined the roof, something brushed the bare skin of his left leg: a membrane as soft and slippery as the underbelly of a fish. It squeezed his calf—the liquid lap of a giant tongue—and he recoiled so violently that he pushed himself onto the ceiling of the corridor. He now lay upside-down, provided that such a relative position had any meaning in this directionless abyss.

Although it no longer touched him, he could sense the beast seething beneath him. Its unimaginable bulk filled the tunnel until it deadened the echo of the stone, and every ripple of its form shivered the thin current of air that separated it from Alan. Yet it made no move to capture or consume him.

"What are you?" Alan shouted. *"What do you want?"*

In response, the creature emitted a nerve-shredding vibrato, a dog-whistle amplified to excruciation. But that was not what made Alan grab his head and convulse in apoplectic agony. Clashing sense-memories inundated his brain, as if it were an antenna receiving interfering broadcasts from a thousand different transmitters. He guessed that some of the impressions were visual images, such as sighted people had attempted to describe to him throughout his life, but the other perceptions were of senses that he was certain no human possessed: frequencies and wavelengths of energies beyond the receptivity of eyes and ears, chemical syntheses too rarefied for nose or tongue, tactile stimulation that would lacerate mere skin.

The creature was trying to answer him—to tell him what it was and whence it came.

Alan howled. Unable to process the onslaught of alien perception, his mind imploded, collapsed into the catatonia of the insensate.

The transition out of nightmare remained ill-defined. As consciousness returned, only the presence of the familiar—sheets and pajamas damp with sour-smelling sweat—reassured Alan that he had awakened at last. Reflexively, he touched the fingers of his left hand to the palm of his right, but did not feel any gash nor any dried blood on his wrist. It still stung, though, as if sliced by finely-honed rock.

For hours, Alan lay in bed in a state of anxious enervation, too fretful to sleep, too exhausted to rise. He had no idea what time it was and did not care enough to touch the exposed hands of his alarm clock to find out. Finally, the fear of accidentally dozing off prodded him to get up and get on with his day, if only to keep his mind from relentlessly turning over the imponderable images from the dream.

He dressed, shaved, picked at a meal he couldn't bring himself to finish, vainly trying to submerge himself in the world of the tangible and mundane. Seating himself at the table in his living room with its rack of small vials, Alan strove to embroil himself in his work. Ordinarily, he savored the olfactory challenge of blending scents, a skill that had enabled him to operate a success-ful aromatherapy business. Today, however, every aroma he un-corked—sage, vanilla, jasmine, cardamom, lavender, patchouli, lemongrass—all struck him as dulled and flat, as though he'd con-tracted a head cold. He waved an open bottle of fragrant oil be-neath his nose, but his thoughts wandered to that other smell, that mutable odor that evoked so many terrestrial scents yet transcended them all.

Alan stoppered the flask, stood, and shuffled from the work-bench to his desk. If he couldn't think of anything but the cursed dream, then he might as well do something about it.

Seating himself at his computer, he aligned his fingers with the Braille-marked keys of the keyboard. In front of the keyboard sat the long but narrow rectangular box of the Braille display. Alan typed in the Web address of his usual search engine, which his "screen reader" software repeated in a mechanical yet pleasant artificial voice that emanated from the speakers on either side of the desk. He then entered his search terms.

"Blind," the screen reader said calmly. "Dreams. Nightmare."

It listed a variety of pertinent articles for him. He selected the first and moved his right hand to the Braille display. He could read the text faster and more accurately than the screen reader could drone it. At first smooth, the row of touchpads on the display sprouted tiny pinhead-sized bumps to form the Braille letters of the first line of text. Alan ran his right index finger across the display, then pushed a button to scroll to the next line. The domino-patterned dots of Braille danced beneath his touch. As he worked his way through the article, his finger began to twitch so badly that it became difficult to read, yet he steadied his hand and finished the article.

Several hours and dozens of articles later, Alan sank back in his chair, his index finger rubbed raw. Absurd, half-formed theories battered the inside of his skull, clamoring for release. Having spent the better part of the day convincing himself of the impossible, he now wanted someone to tell him it was all nonsense.

Alan took out his voice-activated cell phone, but before he could speak Dr. Ingalls's name, he paused. No . . . Ingalls would never understand. Alan needed to speak to someone who shared *his* world.

He only hoped she still had the same number.

"Call . . . Stacy," he enunciated, and the phone dialed.

                             * * *

The following afternoon, Alan sat at a wrought-iron table on the patio of his favorite cafe, trying to think of nothing but the autumnal sun on his face. He had to be careful about such exposure: as a boy, ignorant of the sun and its power, he'd once gotten so sunburned his skin blistered. Though he now wore a broad-brimmed Panama hat to shade his brow, he could not resist reclining his head every so often to bask his cheeks and forehead. The warmth enveloped him in comforting nullity, numbing body and mind like ether . . .

Alan shook himself and hunched forward, swilling the cold dregs of his fourth triple-espresso from the cup in his hands. He hadn't allowed himself to sleep since the night before last and had drunk so much coffee to stay alert that its acid burned his throat in a backwash of bile.

Then, at last, he sensed her presence. Perhaps it was the light ticking of the tip of her cane, the distinctive clop of her low-heeled, leather-soled shoes, but he recognized her even before he heard her say "Thank you" to the hostess who'd led her to his table.

"Alan?"

He stood. Her hand squeezed his upper arm, and he wrapped her in an embrace. "I'm sorry to drag you out like this."

"No, it's fine," she insisted, the voice a soft balm to his ear. Everything about her was just as he remembered from their days as kids at the Institute: the tender roundness of her cheek, the faint citrus of her perfume, the frizzy ringlets of hair at her temple that tickled his nose. She may have been a bit thicker at the waist than when they'd last hugged, but so was he.

"I must admit, you scared the crap out of me, calling when you did." She pulled away and he reluctantly released her. The scrape of the chair opposite him cued him to retake his own seat.

"Yeah, sorry about that. I didn't realize how late it was." He cleared his throat. "So how have you been?"

"You didn't bring me all the way across town for the first time in four years just to catch up," she chided. "What's wrong?"

His face warmed and not from the sun. Alan had always hated admitting that he needed anyone—it smacked of dependency, which he despised. It was the primary reason he had allowed Stacey to drift away from him once they'd finished school. But he needed her now.

"You ever have dreams, Stace?" he asked.

"Sure. Doesn't everyone?"

"Bad ones?"

"Yeah. So?" Her tone of annoyance indicated that she thought he was still making small talk, dodging the real issue.

"Can you describe them? The bad ones, I mean."

"I don't know . . . I'm usually in an unfamiliar place and I'm lost."

"Are you alone?"

She hesitated. "There aren't any other *people* around, but there are all these weird sounds . . ."

"And a smell?"

Her sudden silence answered his question. "I don't get what this has to do—"

"Did you know that congenitally blind people have nearly four times as many nightmares as sighted people or those who became blind later in life?"

Stacey sighed. "And why are we talking about this?"

Her dismissive tone made it even harder for him to begin. "Tell me if any of this sounds familiar," he said at last, and recounted his repeated sojourns in the strange stone labyrinth.

Stacey did not respond immediately when he'd finished, and Alan fretted that he sounded crazy. When she finally spoke, however, it was with a more thoughtful voice.

"It's not really like my nightmare place. Mine is a vast, dusty plain. There's nothing to hold on to, so I always have to crawl on my hands and knees. There are plants with prickers sharp as pins. And every so often I feel indentations in the dirt, like the footprints of—" She either couldn't or wouldn't describe what made the tracks. "But isn't all that just an expression of our anxieties? We have a lot more dangers to deal with than sighted people."

"*Is* that all the dreams mean?" Alan asked.

"What else would it be? Have you talked to a psychiatrist about them?"

He recalled the consultation with Ingalls. "Yes, and he's useless."

"So what do *you* think they mean?"

He tried to moisten his lips, but the excess of coffee had left his mouth dry. "You know the old saw that being blind sharpens your other senses?"

"Yeah. Which is kinda true."

"Well, maybe it sharpens senses most people don't even know

exist. Maybe we can perceive worlds beyond the physical one we live in, particularly when our conscious mind isn't interfering. Maybe we even project ourselves to these places in astral form."

Before Stacey could reply, a male voice intruded. "Hi! Can I get you folks anything?"

Alan was chagrined to think the waiter might have overheard his delusional theory.

Flustered, Stacey ordered a latte. "You think they're real?" she whispered when they were alone again. "Those things . . ."

"If I can convince myself they're all in my head, maybe the dreams will stop. Until then, they're real to me."

"What are you going to do?" Stacey asked softly.

"I'm going to find out as much as I can about this place I go to, and everything in it. Real or imaginary, I'll figure out how to escape it."

The waiter delivered Stacey's coffee, but Alan did not hear her lift the cup from its saucer. "Do you want me to stay?" she offered.

He considered the invitation. For once, it was not pride that made him decline her. Rather, he did not want to expose Stacey to possible contagion from whatever unearthly perceptions he'd been receiving. She had her own nightmare world to cope with.

"No." Alan slid his right hand along the surface of the wrought-iron patio table until it found where Stacey's hand lightly rested on the porcelain of her latte cup. "Just sit with me a while."

She let him take her thin, soft fingers in his grasp, and they sat that way until the clink of china around them dwindled and the waning radiance of the sun let the world go cold.

***

That night, the atmosphere in the tunnel felt frigid and stagnant.

Alan pawed the chiseled floor with his bare toes, ran his hand over the glassy, rough-hewn wall to his right, verifying that he had returned to the same dream-labyrinth. This time, he would not wait for the beast to find him.

"Where are you?" His cry echoed away into hollow vacancy. "Come and get me!"

He waddled forward, bolder than before now that he knew he would not plunge to his death if he walked into one of those gravity-defying pits. *"Do you hear me?"*

Nothing answered but his own reverberating voice. Alan did not expect the creature to understand his words, but he thought the sound alone would draw it out. Was it gone?

Tracing the wall with his right hand to guide him, he advanced to what seemed to be another intersection of passageways. The edge of another cliff nicked his toes, and when he let out a yell the sound rebounded to him from a half-dozen different directions.

From above, Alan heard a faint, yawning roar, as of a dragon awaking in its lair. This time, the draft that misted his face was cold, redolent of mold, chalk dust, and offal yet not entirely any one of those scents.

Alan pressed himself against the wall closest to him until he felt his bearings shift to reorient the world around him. Then he scrabbled upward toward the source of the roar.

When he crawled into the passage that had once been directly above him, the roar had scaled up to a bat-like chittering, and Alan wondered if the thing were using echolocation to find him just as he was trying to find it. The headwind of its odor blew stronger now; it was closing the distance between them.

Alan pushed himself to his feet again, flailed his hands to search for a wall to guide him. Although he expected more of the flinty ridges and whorls, his hand glided over a surface as smooth as polished granite. Only a series of perfectly rounded indentations, some circular, others oblong, pocked the stone. Their irregular yet deliberate domino patterns were so teasingly similar to Braille that Alan traced the lines of incomprehensible dots and furrows as though he could interpret the inscriptions. They reminded him of when his mother had let him touch the grave marker after his father's funeral. Who had written this unfathomable text? Did the petroglyphs tell what this place was . . . and what inhabited it? If only he could read them . . .

A fusillade of percussive popping noises, like a million suction cups being peeled loose in sequence, accelerated toward him from the corridor to the right. Clinging to the wall, Alan instinctively staggered a few steps in the opposite direction before deciding to stand his ground. He'd intended to face the thing, after all. Why not here?

The popping sounds ceased, and the beast emitted a saurian bellow whose force knocked Alan back against the wall. He pushed himself upright, turned, and put out his hand. His fingers brushed over a thicket of wriggling, chitinous spines, as if the legs of a millipede had been magnified to the size of cattails.

The creature screeched as he touched it, and Alan nearly collapsed as another onslaught of incomprehensible sense-images infiltrated his brain. Still, it made no move to capture or consume him; rather, it seemed to await some action from him.

Alan sidled along the wall and into the passageway on his left. He heard a squishing and slurping as the thing trailed him; the air at his back seethed with its presence. When he paused, it stopped. When he advanced, it followed.

For the first time, Alan suspected the being might be imprisoned here just as he was. Maybe it was blind in its own way and dogged him in hopes he could lead it out of the labyrinth. Perhaps, if he freed it, the dreams would end.

But how could he release it when the maze seemed to have no physical exit? The only way Alan himself escaped each night was to wake up.

That might be the key, he realized. If the prison was a mental one, then maybe the only exit was psychic as well. For whatever reason, the trapped creature could not "wake up" on its own as he did. If he could establish a connection with it, then maybe he could pull it out of the labyrinth with him.

Alan halted and reached toward the thing again. Where the spines had quivered a minute before, his hand now sank to the wrist in a mass as viscid as aspic and as frigid as liquid nitrogen. Like water in a vacuum, the flesh felt as if it existed at the triple-point—solid, liquid, and gas, freezing and boiling simultaneously.

Alan yowled in agony, yet did not pull his hand away. He fought to concentrate as the being, in attempting to communicate, again barraged him with fragmentary impressions of impossible shapes and places.

With their minds thus conjoined, Alan focused his mental energy on a single aim.

Wake up!

The compressed enclosure of the tunnel seemed to dissolve. Sound no longer echoed but instead drifted away to infinity. The floor beneath Alan's bare feet fell away, leaving him tumbling in a bottomless maw. Where the creature went, he could not tell, for this pit seemed to have no gravity at all, nor walls to fall upon. Alan flailed in a vacuum, deprived of touch, taste, smell, and sound.

Then he heard himself gasp and gulp air, and felt the trampoline bounce of his bed's box-spring beneath him as he flopped about on the mattress like a tuna on the deck of a fishing trawler.

Alan sagged into stillness, trying to process the nightmare. He'd bonded with the dream-creature in a deeper way, sensed that he was close to understanding it fully, yet now that he tried to reconcile his impressions of it, he could not assemble the parts into a whole. He was like the blind men in the parable, unable to conjure the mental image of a complete elephant from the feel of tusk and tail and leathery skin. Insectile spines, membranous flesh, vocalizations that ran from a rumble to a squeak. And that unclassifiable reek . . .

Alan's nose squirmed. Just recalling the scent made it feel as if the odor still clung to him. He wanted to shower to cleanse himself of the imagined miasma.

Before he could rise, the smell thickened around him. Alan grabbed at the sheets beneath him, afraid he might still be dreaming. But no—he was in his bed, swathed in the comforting reality of its cotton and sweat.

Then a dank draft billowed over him, and something permeated the thin material of his pajamas to brush the bare skin beneath. The touch was coarse and hairy—gelatinous and clammy—prickly and caustic, all at once.

Only then did it occur to Alan that the cryptic inscription he'd discovered in the dream-city might have been a warning.

Like a stray pet, the thing had followed Alan out of its nightmare prison and into the freedom of his waking world.

Alan's rarefied senses grew even more acute, and an Eye opened in his mind, endowing him with a new and terrible Vision that had nothing to do with light.

As the creature enfolded him, Alan at last saw it in its true totality, and screamed for blindness.

The Olverung

"Four hundred sovereigns." Shivering as he stood among the cemetery's moss-encrusted headstones, Lord Atherton held up his guttering candle and squinted at me, trying to discern some chink of humanity amidst the blackness of my hat and mask and cloak. "A hundred now, and three when I get the Olverung."

I merely looked down at him with my mask of black silk, which shrouded my visage like a headsman's hood. I've found such silence more conducive to my negotiations than a lot of senseless dickering.

"Well?" Pearls of perspiration began to roll from underneath the old man's wig as he grew unnerved with the stillness of my figure and the melancholy of the moonlit churchyard that I had selected for our rendezvous. By design, I limited his Lordship's light to the solitary candle, which he clutched in his hand like a rosary. "Five hundred, then! Or six! For God's sake, name your price!"

"How do you know the king even possesses this mythical bird?" I leaned toward him till my veiled face loomed inches from his own. "How do I know you're not merely enticing me to put my neck in His Majesty's noose?"

"Because I've seen it." His face took on a desperate, defeated look. "Because I've *heard* it. The king—he displays it for the diversion of the nobles, holds parties and forces it to perform like some ha'penny minstrel! Squandering its beauty . . . " He shut his eyes, sealed in a rapture of sorrow. I knew then that he spoke the truth.

"I accept your commission," I announced, "for a thousand sovereigns. Leave half the gold in the hollow tree outside the gate. I shall collect the rest in person when I deliver your prize."

I extinguished the candle's flame with my gloved fingers. The old man cried out at the sudden darkness as I ran through the cemetery in the moonlight. I climbed over the churchyard's low stone wall and onto Obsidian, my steed, and rode off at a trot. Glancing over my shoulder, I could see the bobbing lantern of Atherton's coachman, who sought his master among the graves.

***

The Olverung is an ugly bird. Its bulbous head juts from the spout of a scrawny neck, and warts dot the bridge of its fat beak. When it struts upon the ground, its pot-bellied body waddles with the ludicrous gait of a town drunkard. Its plumage has the black iridescence of a fly's abdomen and is too coarse even for pillow stuffing. Yet the fowl possesses one singular attribute that princes and popes have coveted for centuries, and it was for this sole virtue that Lord Atherton entreated me to steal the creature from the king.

Atherton knew me strictly by reputation, of course, when he sought my services. Intrigued with the novelty of the theft, I arranged the meeting with his Lordship through my informants. The following morning, I collected my bounty from the hollow oak, once I assured myself that none of His Majesty's musketeers were watching. In truth, the money meant little to me; I would have accepted Atherton's challenge for a farthing. Ennui has always been my personal curse, you see, constantly goading me into performing ever-greater acts of mischief to satisfy my insatiable longing for sensation.

I conceived a plan for the crime, and two days later I journeyed to London to seek a man I had not seen—and had not wished to see—since I was a lad of nine.

I found one of his apprentices in the market at Newgate. A small, dirty-faced boy in shabby clothes, he stood amidst a small circle of housemaids with their shopping baskets and produced a seemingly endless string of colored handkerchiefs from his tiny, closed fist. The women giggled at the trick and tossed a few coppers in the upturned cap that lay at the boy's feet. He bowed and thanked them, and I remembered how I had once performed the same trick, the same bow, hour after hour, day after day.

"You're quite the conjurer," I told the boy as I approached him. He bowed again. "Thank you, sir!"

Squatting until we were eye-level, I produced a silver half-crown and held it up before his widening eyes. "I might have need of a talented magician such as yourself . . ."

"I'll take that!" A gnarled hand with long, yellowing nails plucked the coin from my fingers. I glanced up to see my former mentor, wizened by the years and now completely bald. "I'm the boy's father," the man claimed.

"Then I must be his mother," I retorted, drawing myself up to my full height. "I guessed that you would be somewhere nearby, Adolphus."

His eyes narrowed. "Pardon me, sir . . . have we met before?"

I smiled coldly. "Don't tell me you've forgotten your favorite protégé."

He scrutinized my features, and his lips stretched into a wicked grin. "Ha-ha! My wayward fowl finally comes home to roost!" A gust of gin-sodden breath blew from his mouth as he cackled.

"Hardly." I waved the offensive air away from my nose. "I do, however, have a business proposition to discuss with you."

"And what would you be needing me for? Seems like you've done quite well for yourself." He eyed the richness of my coat.

"I don't need you. I need the Seven White Ladies."

"Always one for the Ladies!" He gave another rasping laugh. "Come on, then. And have your purse ready."

As I turned to follow him, I placed one of Atherton's gold sovereigns in my open hand and held it behind my back, out of Adolphus's view. Small fingers scraped my palm, and the coin disappeared. I heard the young apprentice scamper away into the crowd, and hoped he had the good sense not to come back.

Adolphus led me through a labyrinth of narrow, putrid streets to the dismal residence of brick where he dwelled, its façade still blackened with soot from the Great Fire. "I see that you haven't lost your taste for luxury," I commented, as we entered his Spartan room. A rat trundled across the floorboards in front of us.

"Better than the common room at the lodging house." He kicked at the rat, which squealed and scurried under the chamber's sole bed.

The room might have been the twin of the one I'd once shared with him. In one corner lay a rolled-up mat and a wooden bowl—most likely the same items that served me when I was his apprentice. On one side of the bed sat a half-filled chamber-pot; on the other side, a rack with a row of pegs had been mounted to the wall. A threadbare surcoat and a pair of knee-breeches hung from the first two pegs, while a willow switch dangled from the third. I grimaced, for the old scars on my shoulders still stung with the memory of that switch.

That's not it! The willow stick stropped my back. *A blind man would have seen you palm that coin! Now do it again!* Another lash. *Again!*

I glared at Adolphus. "You still find that orphans make the best magicians?"

"They make the best money." He moved among the room's only other furnishings, an assortment of dust-shrouded magical apparatus, including a cabinet shaped like a coffin, a box pierced by crossed swords, and impressive reproductions of a headsman's block and axe. "As I recall, you wanted my Seven White Ladies. Sadly, all the damsels are deceased. Allow me to introduce the Seven Gray Gentlemen." He shoved an oblong wicker chest toward me, from which emanated the sound of cooing and fluttering.

"Doves?"

"Pigeons. Bloody stupid birds. But they'll do as I've taught 'em. Now then . . ." He patted the chest and smiled. "What are they worth to you?"

After haggling at length, we finally settled the matter for twenty pounds, for which I purchased several of his other tricks as well. Though I would have paid five times what I offered, I feigned reluctance at agreeing to such a price. If Adolphus got wind of how valuable his birds were to me, he would have demanded a share of the spoils from my scheme. Even as he counted out the gold I gave him, he regarded me with suspicion. "I'm surprised you still have an interest in the Art. Tell me, how do you intend to use my Gentlemen?"

"For my own amusement," I answered truthfully, lifting the lid of the wicker chest to peer inside. One of the Gentlemen flapped from the cooing congregation of his kinsmen and perched on my outstretched hand, inspecting me with eyes of ebony.

Given time, I could have trained my own birds and saved myself the expense and irritation of dealing with Adolphus. Atherton informed me, however, that the king intended to show the Olverung at a party within a matter of days, which left me little opportunity to educate a flock of fowls in the Art of Illusion. The Seven Gray Gentlemen would have to do.

Even with the aid of these feathery accomplices, I barely had time to prepare myself for the festivities at the palace. I had not practiced magic in many years and needed to rehearse the tricks for my performance. Fortunately, deception and knavery are skills common to both magicians and thieves. Small wonder, then, that Adolphus's training had served me so well in my later career.

Early on the morning of His Majesty's party, I loaded a horse-cart with my props and illusions and hitched a swift gelding from my stables to the wagon, then set out on the road to London.

When I reached the outskirts of the capital, I paused briefly to don my costume for the evening's performance—a peaked cap, white silk stockings and dark breeches, and a surcoat of motley colors. The coat could be turned wrong side out to display a more somber hue, should I wish to change my demeanor later in the evening. I then powdered my face with flour, blackened my eyebrows with charcoal, and rouged my lips and cheeks.

The sun hung low in the west as I finally arrived at Whitehall

Palace, where I joined a line of wagons bearing food and wine for the gathering. One of the king's Life Guards grinned at me as he approached my cart. "Well, aren't you the pretty Fool?" He called over to a fellow member of his regiment. "'Ere, Tom! We've got Master 'Arlequin 'imself as a guest tonight."

"Don't remember anyone saying anything 'bout a clown," his jowly comrade replied.

"Nor do I. What would be your business with 'is Majesty, Master 'Arlequin?"

"The name's Monsieur Renard, magician extraordinaire." I quickly made one, then two, then three balls appear between the fingers of my right hand. "I come to entertain the king, courtesy of Lady Castlemaine." From one of my informants, I'd heard that His Majesty's favorite mistress had gone to take the waters in Bath and would not be in attendance that evening.

After a brief consultation between themselves, the two guards bid me wait while they sent a lackey to fetch the steward of the king's household. The messenger returned with a small, stooped man, who berated both the lackey and the guards for wasting his time with such trivialities.

"You there!" The steward tilted his nose up to glare at me through his spectacles. "We didn't ask for any clowns. Be on your way!"

"As you wish, sir." I doffed my cap. "I've been paid, either way. But her ladyship will be terribly disappointed that you turned away her gift to His Majesty."

I moved as if to maneuver the cart back toward the lane, but the steward called for me to stop. "Oh, very well!" he muttered. "I suppose you can do your tricks after Moll Davis sings . . ."

"How very gracious of you, sir!" I smiled and tipped my cap to him again as I steered the cart into the Tilt Yard across from the palace.

The evening's festivities were due to take place in the Banqueting House, a grand hall two stories high lined with two tiers of Greek demi-columns. A long-faced footman named Bell helped me tote my magical apparatus into the enormous chamber, where servants were already lighting the candles on the chandeliers and arranging the tables and chairs for the feast. On the ceiling above us, sumptuous paintings by Rubens depicted the glory of the Stuart monarchs, with Heaven itself welcoming King James into its airy dominion—this in the same room where Charles I spent his final hours before stepping onto Cromwell's scaffold. Rich tapestries hung the length of the rectangular hall, blocking the view from the downstairs windows.

"I understand the king has some special entertainment planned for this evening," I remarked to Bell as we carried a folding wooden screen into the hall.

"Could be," the footman said, his face expressionless.

"I've heard it's something of a prodigy."

"Could be."

"Would it be possible for a curious soul to have a closer look at it?"

Bell's eyes shifted to meet mine. "Could be."

Further questioning revealed that it "could be" possible for twelve guineas.

A group of musicians sat at one end of the hall, readying their instruments, and I arranged my apparatus, including a perch for my birds, beside them. Bell and I unfolded the wooden screen to serve as a curtain for my entrance and exit. Disguised by the arcane runes painted on the screen's wooden panels, a pair of eyeholes gave me a reasonable view of the chamber at large. I set Adolphus's wicker chest behind the screen and sat on it, eating some bread and cheese I'd brought with me and drinking a small mug of ale that Bell brought from the kitchen. My meal finished, I opened the chest and gently placed each of the Gray Gentlemen in one of the seven drawstring bags concealed in my costume.

Before long, a pair of servants opened the doors at the upper end of the chamber and stood aside to allow a procession of nobles to file in by twos and threes, the men dressed in embroidered vests and tunics, the women in satin gowns. Lord Atherton, I noticed, entered alone, silent and pensive. I watched the parade of aristocrats with indifference—until I saw the Lady Barbara Castlemaine, sometime lover of the king and the woman I'd falsely claimed as my patroness, step into the room.

Even without its layer of flour, my face would have blanched at that instant. She wouldn't dare to speak to the king at such a public function, not with the queen in attendance, I told myself. Nevertheless, my eyes instinctively scanned the room for avenues of escape. I also vowed that I would soon have words with Toby Tulliver, the reprobate who'd earned five crowns by telling me her ladyship had gone to Bath.

The assembled company took their places at table, yet remained standing as a herald announced the arrival of the king and queen. The monarchs ascended to an elevated table at the head of the room, Charles smiling and at ease, Catherine somber and stiff. The tall heels of the king's shoes elevated him in stature above his wife, and his wig seemed longer, darker, and curlier than that of any other man in the room, its coal color matching his neatly trimmed black mustache. The monarchs seated themselves in adjacent thrones as the guests cheered their appearance. His Majesty acknowledged their applause and bade them sit down, and servants in satin livery filed in bearing lavish foods on plate of gold.

For some time, the company dined on fricassee of rabbits, boiled mutton, haunch of venison, and other such extravagances, but His Majesty insisted that all dining cease as Mary Davis stepped up to perform. Commonly called "Moll" Davis for her reputation as a libertine, the actress had caught the king's eye with her rendition of "My lodging is on the cold ground" in *The Rivals*, a ballad she now sang with the accompaniment of the musicians seated beside me. The queen, a plain, swarthy Portuguese, frowned at the attention His Majesty paid to the pale, buxom singer.

The nobles in the audience, of course, all knew of Moll Davis's liaisons with the king, and they responded to her pleasant ditties with polite applause. As soon as she had finished her recital, the servants brought in a selection of pies, cakes, and puddings, and refilled the company's goblets with spiced wines and beers.

It was then, in the midst of this clamor of clattering plates and cups, that the irascible steward introduced me to the audience. "My lords and ladies," he brusquely announced, "as a token of friendship, one of His Majesty's many ... *admirers* has sent us a splendid magician for our amusement this evening. I give you— Monsieur Renard!"

I exhaled my pent-up breath, and silently thanked the good steward for his discretion in withholding Lady Castlemaine's name. Before he could leave the floor, I bounded out from behind the screen and shook his hand with comic vigor. This gesture won the first chuckle from my audience of nobility.

I peered at the steward as if perplexed. "Did you have squab for dinner tonight, sir?"

The little man grew flustered. "What on— No, I did not have squab!"

"Then what, pray tell, is this?" I reached under the flap of his surcoat and produced the first of the Seven Gray Gentlemen. With a gentle nudge from my hand, the pigeon flew up and alighted on the steward's head. The audience roared with laughter as he frantically shooed the bird off his scalp and hurried off the floor.

"Evidently, squab does not agree with our friend. A pity, because I have enough here for a feast!" Striding out into the crowd of seated nobles, I made the other pigeons appear in rapid succession, producing them from under handkerchiefs, from behind earls' heads, and from under women's skirts. I released each bird in turn, and it flew across the chamber to roost with its companions on the perch I had prepared for them.

At last, all the birds sat cooing in a row. "My lords and ladies, may I present my mentors in magic—the Seven Gray Gentlemen!" I said with a grand sweep of my arm, and bowed as the audience applauded.

I proceeded to regale them with parlor tricks and patter. I even placed Adolphus's rune-covered box on the head of the Duke of Albemarle, and then made it appear that I pierced his skull with crossed swords. "Fear not, good people!" I assured his fellow peers. "The noble duke has no brains to damage."

The assembly roared again and applauded. "What a perfect rogue the fellow is!" the king murmured, little suspecting he spoke the truth.

While the chamber of nobles cheered, I gave a final, deep bow and carried the perch bearing the Seven Gray Gentlemen behind the screen with me as I made my exit. I put six of the pigeons back in the wicker chest and placed one in a drawstring bag beneath my surcoat. Peering through the screen's hidden eyeholes, I could see the sullen steward sheepishly step forward.

"My lords and ladies," he implored, "we beseech your patience as we prepare for the evening's final performance."

The audience quieted as servants carried in an upholstered bench and a marble-topped table and arranged them at the near end of the room. On the table, they set a red velvet pillow from which dangled several white ribbons. A moment later, a white-gloved footman entered with a brass stand surmounted by a domed cage. As the footman set the stand beside the table, a hidden fluttering stirred the embroidered linen draped over the cage.

The steward cleared his throat. "Signor Salveri, if you would be so kind . . ."

A corpulent man with lowering brows rose from the ensemble of musicians beside me and stepped forward, a black valise in his hands. He bowed to the king, the queen, and the court, acknowledging their applause. The buttons of his waistcoat strained at their bonds as he seated himself on the bench before the table with the velvet cushion. He nodded to the waiting footman, then opened his valise.

Inside the case, two rows of silver thimbles nestled in contoured crevices of velvet. A long thin spine of metal extended from the head of each thimble, and the point of each spine ended in some form of hook, needle, or razor. Signor Salveri held up his hands, and servants placed the implements on the tips of his fingers and thumbs.

Meanwhile, the footman folded back the linen shroud on the cage and reached inside to grasp the unseen captive. The servant's hands girdling its squat body, the bird swiveled its ungainly head in panic as it emerged, its iridescent black wings flapping impotently.

The Olverung was every bit as ill-formed as its legend had promised.

With some difficulty, the footman turned the bird on its back and held it fast to the pillow, its wings splayed, while his fellow servants bound the animal with the white ribbons.

Signor Salveri set to work on its belly with his instruments, and the first notes of the Olverung's song burst forth.

A wavering, ethereal vibration rose from the creature's throat, such as the sound made when one rubs the rim of a fine crystal goblet with wet fingers. It swelled in volume until the very windows of the Banqueting House hummed in sympathy. Salveri plucked at the animal's flesh as though playing a harp, artfully increasing the creature's pain to elicit a crescendo of poignancy from its cries. Such is the bird's nature: a dull, chittering fowl when content, it only unleashes the mystical beauty of its voice in the throes of agony.

The melody trembled between major and minor keys, angelic and anguished all at once. First ringing one's head with dizzying ecstasy, then clamping it in the vise of unbearable grief. It promised delight beyond measure, yet, an instant later, dashed all hope of happiness.

It was the sound of Love.

Men and women alike sobbed openly. The queen let out a strangled cry and buried her face in her hands. The king dabbed daintily at his eyes with a handkerchief. Some wept for joy, some wept for sorrow, but all wept for Love.

Even I was not immune. I, who have known neither a mother's tenderness nor a friend's loyalty in my wretched existence. I, who have never wooed a woman for more than a night's dalliance. A stranger to Love, I recognized its voice as surely as if seeing my own twin for the first time: terrible and glorious, beautiful and cruel, eternal yet fleeting.

My ice-bound heart shivered to the point of shattering, and tears turned the flour on my cheeks into trails of paste.

Signor Salveri concluded his concerto, and the Olverung's final notes faded in its throat. A reverent hush hung over the room for several moments, punctuated only by small cries. Scattered clapping soon swelled into a rousing ovation as Salveri stood and bowed to the court, while the white-gloved footman untied the Olverung and placed the unconscious bird back in its cage. The footman carried the cage out of the hall as his fellow servants entered with more wine for the nobles, who jabbered among themselves.

Seated behind the screen, I barely had time to blot the moisture from my cheeks before I felt a tap on my shoulder. I turned to find Bell regarding me with the same emotionless expression he'd worn that afternoon. He nodded toward a door on our right, and I followed him out of the banqueting house into a passageway that connected the hall to the royal apartments. Carrying a pair of mounted candles to light our way, he led me down the corridor and up a flight of stairs.

When we reached the second-floor landing, he motioned for me to stop, then leaned around a corner to peer down another hallway. After a moment, he waved me forward and handed me one of his candles. "Third door on the right. What you do there is your own affair."

I nodded and placed a bag of guineas in his upturned palm.

Bell hurried off down the stairs as I advanced to the indicated door and entered the king's private library. Although I encountered no one in the darkened hallway, I knew that the king's party might disperse at any moment, allowing the servants and guards to return to their stations throughout the household.

The library was a rectangular room so large that my candle's meager flame could not illuminate the far end of the chamber. Cabinets burdened with leather-bound tomes ran the length of one wall, while a long window in the opposing wall offered a view of the moonlit waters of the Thames. As I moved about the room, the circle of light from my candle swept over furnishings of polished walnut and mahogany, a brass telescope, a globe of the heavens. Finally, I found the brass stand with its linen-draped cage in a far corner of the chamber.

Setting my candle on a nearby table, I lifted the linen veil and opened the cage door. The Olverung lay on the floor of the cage with its eyes shut, exhausted by the attentions of Signor Salveri. I gingerly scooped the dormant bird into my hand and slid it into one of my drawstring bags. Somewhat larger than a pigeon, it made for a tight fit.

I then replaced the rare fowl with the Gray Gent I carried. With any luck, the flutter of wings beneath the cage's cover would prevent the theft from being discovered for hours to come.

The Olverung snug in the bag beneath my surcoat, I hastened back to the Banqueting House. The western face of the palace bordered the Thames, and, as I did not have a boat waiting for me at the river, I would have to exit Whitehall on the eastern side, the way I'd come in.

No sooner had I rejoined the soirée in the great hall than the officious steward bustled up to me, shaking his finger. "There you are! Come with me: His Majesty wishes to speak with you."

My heart quickened, and the weight of the bag beneath my coat seemed heavier than before. Resisting the urge to flee, I gave an ingratiating smile. "It would be an honor."

The steward guided me up to the head of the room, where the King stood conversing with the Duke of Albemarle, the Earl of Southampton . . . and the Lady Barbara Castlemaine. The queen had evidently retired early that evening.

His Majesty grinned as I approached. "Ah! Here is the knave himself! Delightful show, my good fellow."

I bowed. "Your Highness is too kind."

The king gestured magnanimously with his hand. "Pray, sirrah, favor us with more of your splendid tricks."

A tremor of apprehension ran through me. Out of the corners of my eyes, I could see the guards who stood in vigilance a few yards to either side of us.

"I am a *sorcerer!*" I objected with mock indignation. "I would never dare to *trick* Your Highness. Tricks are for scoundrels. Take this fellow here—" I stepped up to the Earl of Southampton and pretended to pull a sovereign from his ear. "He has obviously been plundering Your Majesty's treasury!"

The king, the earl, and the duke burst into laughter, while Lady Castlemaine tittered demurely with one gloved hand held over her mouth. My anxiety eased.

As it turned out, my own cleverness proved my undoing: each trifle I performed only served to whet the king's appetite for more. "Another! Another!" he urged after each illusion, obliging me to continue my improvisations.

Beneath my coat, I felt the Olverung stir within its drawstring bag.

Sweat matted the flour on my forehead as I made the earl's snuffbox vanish from my hand, then produced it from a pocket on the duke's waistcoat. "I thank you, my lords." I bowed again as they applauded. "Sadly, I must now take my leave—"

"Surely not!" the king insisted with boyish petulance. "One more, please."

The drawstring bag throbbed as though it were an egg about to hatch. I bowed once more and disguised my impatience with false modesty. "Your Highness taxes my humble skills—"

"Nonsense! Another, please."

"Your Majesty," a familiar voice interrupted from behind me, "shouldn't we take this opportunity to discuss the Dutch situation?"

The king sighed. "Honestly, Atherton, do you think about nothing but business?"

I smiled inwardly. His lordship must have deduced my identity and stepped forward to aid my escape. Although Atherton and I avoided looking one another in the eye, I could have kissed his sour old face right then.

"I leave for Paris on the morrow, Your Highness," he said sternly. "King Louis will want to know our position."

"Yes, but can it not wait another half of an hour?" the king muttered.

"With all due respect, Your Majesty, I am an old man with a long journey ahead of me. I must to bed."

The king sighed and turned to me. "Monsieur Renard, it seems we have some duties to attend to. However, we insist that you return to entertain us again."

"Of course, Your Majesty," I lied. "At your pleasure." As court etiquette dictated, I genuflected and moved to leave, cautious not to turn my back on the king until I was a discreet distance away.

"What a charming clown!" I heard Lady Castlemaine purr. "Wherever did you find him?"

The steward, who remained standing in attendance at the king's elbow, cleared his throat. "M'lady, the magician claims that *you* employed him this evening."

She laughed. "Surely another of his jests! I've never seen him before in my life."

I did not wait for the steward's reply. Quickening my steps, I returned to the other end of the hall. To avoid arousing further suspicion, I resolved to carry the wicker chest as I made my exit, even though I no longer needed it. Once I had the chest outside, I could secretly replace the remaining Gray Gentlemen with the Olverung, thereby removing the twitching bird from my person.

In my haste, alas, I lifted the chest with such force that it crushed the hidden drawstring bag against my side.

Roused by the pain, the Olverung began to sing.

Within moments, everyone in the Banqueting House, from the king down to the lowliest servant, fell silent in astonishment. Muffled yet unmistakable, the plaintive melody grew louder in the chamber's sudden stillness. For an instant the company remained perplexed, unable to comprehend what they heard.

Then the steward's eyes gaped with the realization. "He has the Olverung! Guards!"

Answering the call, two guards rushed toward me from the door to my right. "The bird! Get the bird!" the steward shrieked at them.

Both soldiers aimed their muskets at me. "Very well," I said. "You may have the bird."

I dropped the wicker chest on the floor, jerking the lid open as I did so. The six remaining Gray Gentlemen flapped out into the Banqueting House.

Afraid that the bird he was supposed to retrieve was about to fly away, one of the guards threw down his gun and attempted to snatch the Gentlemen as they fluttered around him. The other still pointed his musket at me, but before he could pull the trigger, his bird-chasing comrade stumbled in front of him.

I drew a sword from Adolphus's rune-covered box illusion and dashed toward one of the hanging tapestries on my left. Guards from every quarter of the hall converged on me, their progress slowed by the crowd of murmuring aristocrats, all of whom were too stunned or fearful to move. A few of the soldiers stopped and raised the barrels of their guns.

The steward raised his hands in protest. "Don't shoot, you fools! You might damage the fowl!"

As the guards hesitated, I thrust aside one corner of the tapestry and climbed onto the deep ledge of the window behind the arras. Just before he disappeared from my view, I thought I saw the king laugh.

I had given His Majesty one final trick after all.

Once hidden behind the tapestry, I turned the window latch and thrust open one of the casements, then leapt out onto the cobblestone pathway that threaded between the Banqueting House and the palace's bakery and scalding-house.

Shouts of alarm rose over the palace grounds as I ran to the tilt yard, where my horse and cart sat waiting at the far end of a long line of coaches and sedan chairs belonging to the king's guests. Lanterns drifted through the darkness as stable boys and coachmen moved among the carriages, tending the horses. Startled by my appearance, they did not stop me as I clambered onto the cart and used Adolphus's sword to slash the harness that tethered the gelding to the wagon. With the Olverung still keening its ethereal elegy, I cast aside the sword, leapt onto the gelding's back, and charged out of the yard at a gallop.

Before I'd even reached Charing Cross, I could hear hoofbeats clattering up on me from behind. Casting off my peaked cap, I spurred my horse on to Haymarket, haphazardly turning right and left among nearly deserted streets of darkened shops. When I'd lost my pursuers for the nonce, I reared the gelding to a halt, swung myself off the animal, then swatted its flank to send it on up the avenue.

As the riderless horse galloped away, I hastily turned my surcoat wrong side out, exchanging the motley colors for a black that matched the night around me. Striding toward the darkness of an adjacent alley, I opened the top of the drawstring bag just enough to allow the Olverung to stick its misshapen head into the chill evening air. At any other time, I would have sold my soul to hear the melody that continued to pour from its throat; at that moment, however, I only wanted the bird to shut its wart-spotted beak.

"Hush . . . hush," I whispered, and stroked its bristling feathers as tenderly as I could. "I won't let them have you."

The melody dwindled to a wistful whistling. As the Olverung calmed beneath my touch, it began to coo quietly.

Wiping the remaining flour off my face with my sleeve, I cradled the bird close to my chest as I crouched in the cover of the alley's shadows. Not more than a minute later, I saw two of the king's guards ride past on horseback, vainly hunting a fugitive Harlequin.

**

I rode home the following morning on a mare I purchased from the tavern keeper at the king's house in Drury Lane. He charged me twice what the animal was worth, but I paid him without complaint. Lord Atherton had delayed his departure for Paris to speak with me, and I did not want to keep him waiting.

As appointed, we met that night in the cemetery of our first encounter. His single candle flickered among the headstones like a forgotten wish.

"You have it, do you not?" He trembled with desire as he gaped up at my silken hood. "I've brought the rest of your gold."

"No doubt you have." I lifted a sack of five hundred sovereigns from beneath my cloak and threw it at his feet.

The old man looked at the bag and shook his head. "What's this?"

"Your original commission. You shall not have the bird."

Rage and fear rippled through the flesh of his face. "If this is a charade to increase your bounty—"

"No. It is not." I walked away.

"Two thousand! Three!" When I failed to turn around, he hobbled after me. "We had an agreement!"

His shouts became sobs as I neared the churchyard wall. "You don't understand! My late wife . . . she *speaks* to me through the bird's song . . ."

I climbed onto Obsidian's saddle.

"I'll find you!" Atherton screamed at my back as I rode away.

"Do you hear me? I'll see your neck stretched before the fortnight is out!"

In truth, I pitied him. But no amount of gold would make me part with the Olverung.

When I returned to my modest country house that night, I stripped off my mask and stalked through the richly furnished but vacant rooms of my home until I reached my Vault of Treasures, the small study where I hoard the finest prizes of my career. I ran my fingers over each of the trophies. Here sat the Eye of Oram, an emerald the size of an apple, which I took from a heretical cult in Barchester. There hung the ceremonial sword of the family Anwick, which I pulled from the bleeding body of the Earl himself. And here rested the gilded skull of the Vicomte de Vernier, his hollow eyes filled with fire opals, his teeth replaced by shards of violet amethyst.

I pored over these and dozens of other mementos, the spoils of a life spent pillaging the fortunes of the rich and wicked. None of them stirred even the slightest sentiment in me. Whatever thrill I experienced in stealing them had dissipated as surely as the intoxication of a fine brandy, and now they were nothing more to me than the dusty relics of empty victories.

I moved on to the bronze cage in the far corner of the room, in which the Olverung sat placidly preening its feathers. How much it must have suffered through the centuries! I mused in awe as I opened the cage door and cupped my hands around the quivering bird.

The Olverung fluttered in my arms and nestled against my chest as I gently stroked its back. It seemed to take comfort in the touch of the man who had liberated it from Whitehall. My fingers trembled at the memory of its agony.

And I twisted its wing until it sang a song of such overwhelming beauty that the frozen sea within me cracked and melted.

I know that, of all my sins, this is the one that will surely damn me. Sometimes I resist the temptation. Inevitably, though, the gray parade of insipid days leads me back to the solace of the bird's music.

I possess neither the tools nor the talent of Signor Salveri, but what I lack in training I make up in invention, the novelty of my torments. I sit here alone, the Olverung in my lap, and compose a breathtaking serenade of suffering—a private melody of misery made all the more heartbreaking for the fact that the only one who hears it is the one who will never let it end. I play, and the Olverung sings, and I weep and weep and weep.

www.ingramcontent.com/pod-product-compliance
Lightning Source LLC
Chambersburg PA
CBHW070446030726

47503CB00004B/916